MURDER'S IMMORTAL MASK

MURDER'S IMMORTAL MASK

PAUL DOHERTY

ISIS
LARGE PRINT
Oxford

First published in Great Britain 2008
by
Headline Publishing Group

Published in Large Print 2009 by ISIS Publishing Ltd.,
7 Centremead, Osney Mead, Oxford OX2 0ES
by arrangement with
Headline Publishing Group
an Hachette Livre UK Company

British Library Cataloguing in Publication Data
Doherty, P. C.
    Murder's immortal mask. – Large print ed.
    1. Helena, Saint, ca. 255–ca. 330 – Fiction
    2. Claudia (Fictitious character: Doherty) – Fiction
    3. Women spies – Rome – Fiction
    4. Rome – History – Constantine I, the Great,
    306–337 – Fiction
    5. Detective and mystery stories
    6. Large type books
    I. Title
    823.9'14 [F]

ISBN 978–0–7531–8240–6 (hb)
ISBN 978–0–7531–8241–3 (pb)

Printed and bound in Great Britain by
T. J. International Ltd., Padstow, Cornwall

To my wonderful children
Ashley, Ben and Stephanie
with all my love, Dad

(Mr Filer)

ulvers

PRINCIPAL CHARACTERS

THE EMPERORS

Diocletian:	the old Emperor
Maxentius:	formerly Emperor of the West, defeated and killed by Constantine at the Milvian Bridge
Constantine:	new Emperor of the West
Helena:	Constantine's mother, Empress and Augusta
Licinius:	Emperor in the East

IMPERIAL OFFICIALS

Anastasius:	Christian priest and scribe, secretary to Helena
Burrus:	German mercenary, captain of Helena's bodyguard
Chrysis:	chamberlain

THE VILLA HORTENSIS

Attius Enobarbus:	*scrutor*; Emperor Maxentius' henchman
Drusilla:	Attius' concubine
Frontinus:	Attius' freedman

THE PALATINE PALACE

Macrinus:	tribune, former commander of the *vigiles* in the Caelian quarter
Julius Philippus Lucretius Narses Gemellus Severus Petilus Gavinus }	*scrutores mortuorum*; Emperor Maxentius' henchmen; colleagues of Attius Enobarbus

CHRISTIAN CHURCH

Militiades:	Pope, Bishop of Rome
Sylvester:	Militiades' assistant, principal priest in the Christian community in Rome

AT THE SHE-ASSES

Polybius:	the owner
Poppaoe:	his common-law wife
Oceanus:	former gladiator
Januaria:	serving maid
Claudia:	Polybius' niece
Murranus:	a gladiator
Simon:	the Stoic
Petronius:	the Pimp
Sallust:	the Searcher
Sorry:	tavern boy
Caligula:	tavern cat

Torquatus: the Tonsor
Narcissus the Neat: former embalmer
Mercury the Messenger: tavern herald
Bellato: dog-handler, owner of Pugna
Titus Labienus: manager of the acting troupe
                             "the Satyricons"
Celades: tavern cook

CAELIAN QUARTER

Ulpius: a banker
Achilleos }   *vigiles*
Nereos   }

THE HOUSE OF ISIS

The Domina Agrippina: owner
Silvana: a maid
Livia: one of the recruits from the
                             Tullianum prison

THE CIRCUS MAXIMUS

Scorpus   }   champion charioteers
Pausanias   }

THE SUBURRA

Lord Charon:	self-styled ruler of Rome's underworld
Cerebus:	Charon's lieutenant
Hecate:	Charon's witch
Decius:	one of Charon's followers

Introduction

During the trial of Christ, Pilate, according to the gospels, wanted to free the prisoner. He was stopped by a cry that if he did so, he would be no friend of Caesar's. According to commentators, Pilate recognised the threat. Every Roman governor and official was closely scrutinised by secret agents of the Emperor, "the *agentes in rebus*", literally "the doers of things"! The Roman Empire had a police force, both military and civil, though these differed from region to region, but it would be inaccurate to claim there was anything akin to detectives or our own CID. Instead, the Emperor and his leading politicians paid vast sums to informers and spies. These were often difficult to control; as Walsingham, Elizabeth I's master spy, once wryly remarked, "He wasn't too sure who his own men were working for, himself or the opposition."

The *agentes in rebus* were a class apart amongst this horde of gossip-collectors, tale-bearers and, sometimes, very dangerous informers. The emperors used them, and their testimony could mean the end of a promising career. This certainly applied to the bloody and Byzantine period at the beginning of the fourth century AD.

The Emperor Diocletian had divided the Empire into East and West. Each division had its own emperor, and a lieutenant, who took the title of Caesar. The Empire was facing economic problems and barbarian incursions. Its state religion was threatened by the thriving Christian Church, which was making its presence felt in all provinces at every level of society.

In AD 312 a young general, Constantine, supported by his mother Helena, a British-born woman, who was already flirting with the Christian Church, decided to make his bid for the Empire of the West. He marched down Italy and met his rival Maxentius at the Milvian Bridge. According to Eusebius, Constantine's biographer, the would-be Emperor saw a vision of the cross underneath the words "*In hoc signo vinces*" ("In this sign you will conquer"). Constantine, the story goes, told his troops to adopt the Christian symbol and won an outstanding victory. He defeated and killed Maxentius and marched into Rome. Constantine was now Emperor of the West, his only rival Licinius, who ruled the Eastern Empire.

Heavily influenced by his mother, Constantine grasped the reins of government and began to negotiate with the Christian Church to end centuries of persecution. Helena favoured the Church but soon realised that intrigue, robbery and murder were no respecters of emperor or priest. The Christian Church emerged from the catacombs, that labyrinth of tunnels and secret passageways dug beneath the roads leading out of Rome. The new religion brought its own problems and unresolved issues whilst the dark runnels of the catacombs still held secrets and mysteries waiting to be brought into the light of day. There was unfinished business in Rome, and the *agentes in rebus* had their hands full . . .

The quotations before each chapter are from the *Life of Constantine* by Eusebius, who was a contemporary of Helena and her son. The author's note at the end gives the historical context for the plot of this novel.

Prologue

*The cruel and senseless immolation
of human victims.*

The man who liked to call himself the Iudex — the Judge — slouched on the throne-like chair and sipped at his goblet of chilled white Falernian. He smacked his lips appreciatively and, once again, stared at the skeleton crucified to the thick wooden beams embedded in the red-brick wall of the cellar. The Iudex toasted the skull and the gaping jaw as he studied the now yellowing bones. Really, he reflected, he had done a skilled job with the crucifixion, the nails hammered expertly between the bones of each wrist, through those little gaps so conveniently provided for such a ritual. After all, a nail through the palm of the hand was futile; the victim simply struggled and the nail would plough through the soft flesh and break loose. One well-sharpened iron nail in each wrist would hold him fast, and the same for the feet. True, the Iudex reflected, that had been harder. He had fastened a small wooden rest to the beam before hammering the larger spike through the gap between the bones in the ankles. It had all been done before the drugged *posca* had worn off and the victim had regained consciousness. Oh, that had been good! The shock, the surprise, the agony, the screams and the curses, the pleading and the wheedling! The Iudex had listened to that for days, watching his victim slowly die, blood bubbling out from the wounds in wrists and ankles; the effort to breathe, to pull away from the nails, thrusting up on throbbing ankles to free the ribcage and gasp a breath of the hot air of that cellar. The Iudex picked up a second red-stone goblet and sipped at the *mulsum*, the honey-sweetened wine, as he pondered the meal he'd be served later that evening in his favourite cookshop. Yes, he'd choose the lamb this time, and perhaps the baby dormice or the suckling pig roasted to crispness. He stared again at that skeleton fastened to the wood.

"I've made enquiries," the Iudex murmured, as if talking to an old friend. "How to preserve your bones: a kind of lacquer, though that will prove expensive. I mean, I do want to keep visiting you and recall old memories." He sucked on his teeth and stared at the crude drawing on the wall to the right of the crucifixion. Etched in black charcoal, the picture displayed two gladiators fighting each other whilst behind them a woman, tied to a stake, was being menaced by a monstrous black-maned lion. The artist had written the word *Christiana* — Christian — near the woman, and the Iudex wondered who had drawn it. Someone who had hidden here? He could follow the story clearly enough; one of the gladiators had to kill the other before going to defend the woman against the lion. The Iudex idly speculated whether both gladiators had loved her. Would one offer to die quickly? Or would only one of them save her, and had to fight desperately realising two lives depended on his skill? Were they really Christians? the Iudex wondered. Was it a true story some artist had scrolled on the wall? A legacy from a few years ago when the Emperors Diocletian and Maxentius had savagely persecuted the new faith?

"Ah well," the Iudex whispered to the crucified skeleton, "how the wheel turns, heh? Our new Emperor," he continued, "and his bossy mother Helena now favour the faith of slaves and commoners." The Iudex realised how his voice was echoing, so he put the cup down and reflected, fingers to his lips. The Christians had emerged from the catacombs and other hiding places to be respected and favoured by the Great Ones of Rome. They had even been given some of the temples and lands of the old gods, whilst their Pontifex, Militiades, and his shadow, Presbyter Sylvester, were now regular visitors to the imperial palaces on the Palatine.

"Ah, yes." The Iudex cradled his cup and winked at the skeleton. "Everything has changed since our day, but will it change again?" he asked airily. "Emperor Constantine rules the West, Licinius the East. No." The Iudex stirred in his chair. "They will have to go to war soon enough to decide who will be *imperator totius mundi*: emperor of the whole world."

The Iudex toasted the skeleton with his goblet. It was growing increasingly difficult to realise that those pathetic remains had once been a human being, full of blood and passion. He glanced at the paltry possessions piled beneath the nailed feet: combs of boxwood, ivory and tortoiseshell, white and purple fillets for the hair, a bronze hand mirror, silver earrings and a cornelian bracelet from Thebes in Egypt. The Iudex smiled even as the tears came. He remembered buying her that. He rose and went across the underground cellar, lighted only by close-set iron grilles high in the wall, stopping before the long casket of polished cedarwood carved intricately and carefully as he had instructed. He ran his hand along the side and felt the hieroglyphs which concealed the secret prayers to send the soul, the ka, of the beautiful young woman inside across the far horizon into the eternal west. He stroked the polished surface of the lid and peered at the lotuses and lilies carved there. He closed his eyes and leaned against the casket, then opened them and stared at the four canopic jars on the inbuilt shelf above it. He lifted the casket lid, gently tilted it back, pulled away the gold linen sheets and gazed on she whom he called his Nefertiti, the great and splendid love of his life. He stared at the beautiful cheeks, the straight nose, the full red lips and those eyelids resting like butterflies so gently on the skin which looked as if it been brushed by gold dust. The Iudex closed his eyes. He'd hired the best embalmer in Rome. He wanted her to remain as he had always known her: eternally beautiful, all agony removed, an immortal mask which would conceal the horror of her death.

Sometimes the Iudex thought he was going insane. Life had changed so much! He'd found such happiness, until . . . He turned savagely and walked back to the crucified skeleton, draining his goblet and throwing the dregs at the grisly spectacle he so often visited. He turned away, but then came back and peered at those empty eye sockets which had once glared fierce and malevolent at him.

"They say it's begun again, but," he hissed, "how could that be . . . ?"

Fausta the whore was pleased with herself. She had been invited to a dinner party thrown by the banker Ulpius. She'd fed her young, plump body most royally on three helpings of boar's neck, four of pork loin and the hip bones and shoulder blades of tender rabbit. In the large napkin she'd stolen, she now carried some roast thrush, oysters, mouthfuls of cake, a few grapes and apples, sticky figs, mushrooms and slices of grilled turtle dove. She held all these tightly beneath her tawdry grey cloak. Ulpius, Fausta reflected as she tripped to the jingle of her cheap jewellery down the alleyway, had been a most generous host. He had served rich, dark Opimian wine as well as platters stacked with ribs of pig, meadow birds, half a mullet, an entire pike, strips of moray eel and chicken legs in a spicy sauce. All Fausta had been required to do was tend to an old merchant, let him fumble with her breasts and then accept his invitation to join him on his more comfortable couch for even more sensitive fumbling. Fausta had complied reluctantly, but in the end she'd certainly eaten well and drunk just as deeply.

She paused and leaned against the wall to straighten her sandal, one smooth, well-oiled knee peeping out from beneath the folds of the cloak, her ringleted hair falling down to hide her face. The merchant had liked that; he'd praised her coiffure as he fed his face with dormice sprinkled with honey and poppy seed followed by pastry thrushes stuffed with nuts and raisins. Once the evening was over, Ulpius had dismissed her. Fausta was determined to reach the She-Asses tavern in the Caelian quarter before darkness truly fell. Soon all the denizens of Rome's underworld, the raptors and the *latrones*, would come crawling out of their hiding places in the rotting, fetid cellars of the great *insulae*, the towering houses divided by speculators into a myriad of small lodgings, narrow passageways and gloomy corners. Fausta half listened to the noises of the night: screams and cries, the jingling of a tambourine, the click of castanets, the faint words of a song, a dog barking at the dark, the screech of mice. She wished she had left earlier. She recalled the graffiti scrawled on the walls of her own *insula*: "You are a fool to go out to dinner without making a will." Only the rich in their scarlet cloaks, their host of retainers carrying torches and brass lamps, journeyed safe. Only the gods could help those who had to be escorted by the moon or the feeble light of a candle with its preciously guarded wick.

Fausta walked on but paused at the corner of the alleyway. The slime-covered wall glittered in the light of the smoking cresset torch fixed in its niche beside the entrance to a long tunnel leading down to a noisy *taverna*. She was tempted to visit it but then recalled the She-Asses and the travelling company of actors camped near there, as well as the promise of Polybius, the taverner, that he'd be serving milk-fed snails fried in oil. Despite the food Fausta had both eaten and stolen, her mouth watered. She passed by the tunnel entrance with its grotesquely enlarged penis carved above the doorway. Graffiti on the ill-lit wall caught her eye: "All the drunks of this tavern love Fructus"; "Wine dictates their drink"; then one done in blue paint held her gaze: "Beware the Abomination!" Fausta's throat went dry, her heart fluttered and she immediately ducked into a narrow recess in the wall, trying to control her panic. She wished she had left with an escort. Perhaps she could have persuaded Ulpius to provide one. Now she had to confront her fears. This area was dangerous enough, but now the Abomination — Nefandus — the name given to the killer who used to wander these dark, needle-thin streets some two to three years ago, had returned. A man who liked killing whores, prostitutes like herself.

Fausta recalled Calpurnia, the old whore who always acted as the harbinger of bad news. She had certainly terrified Fausta and the other Daughters of Isis as they gathered in the murky light of the Net Man, a tavern on the street leading down to the Colosseum, frequented by whores of both genders; former gladiators, raptors and all the other lowlife who infested the sewers and narrow, smelly lanes of the Suburra, the slums of imperial Rome. Calpurnia had been full of tales of the Nefandus, the hideous character who, during the reign of the old Emperor . . . who was it? Ah yes, Maxentius, defeated at the Milvian Bridge by the present Emperor, Constantine. Fausta picked at the quick of her fingernail. She'd learnt these names by consorting with soldiers from the city garrison. A dog abruptly yipped. Startled, Fausta stared up at the sky. A hunter's moon, that's what they called it. She suddenly felt exhausted, tired of being frightened, of hiding like some terrified creature in this alleyway reeking of urine and all kinds of foul smells. She heard a sound, caught her breath and peered out. Nothing! Yet the terror still swept through her. She'd heard rumours how the Nefandus had reappeared. One of her sisters from the House of Isis had been cut and killed in a most barbaric way.

A voice shouted. Fausta, all anxious again, peered out, but it was only Achilleos and Nereos, the *vigiles* of the quarter, strolling up the alleyway laughing and talking to each other. Had they glimpsed her? Fausta prepared to step out and greet them until she recalled their brash, surly manner, the rough way they would tease her and the other girls. She changed her mind. Instead, she drew deeper into the recess, opened a bag, a small pouch attached to the cord around her waist, shook out drops of faint perfume and patted them on her face. The Domina constantly maintained that women had one weapon and they should always be prepared to use it. Fausta was determined that, before she reached the She-Asses, she would seek some custom, earn a few coins. In the meantime, she'd let these two policemen pass. She crouched deeper into the shadows. Achilleos and Nereos were still laughing about something. At first Fausta thought they were going to pause and peer into the narrow alleyway, but they passed on.

12

The street fell silent. Fausta realised she only had a moment before other figures would appear. She stepped out and, sandals tripping, ran down the alleyway and turned a corner. At the far end echoed some bustle and noise; lights from a tavern winked through the murk. She'd go there. She reached a corner and was about to run across when a sound made her turn.

"Are you seeking custom?" The man emerged out of the shadows. He was dressed in a scarlet cloak like an officer, a gleaming helmet on his head; because of the broad cheek guards Fausta couldn't make out his face, but her simpering smile was answered with a clink of coins. Fausta relaxed. She'd found some custom! She approached the officer, who turned and walked down the street, then turned up an alleyway. Fausta closed her eyes and groaned. She'd feel the sharp stones of a wall against her back before she was finished. Nevertheless, she followed her customer into the dark.

The man turned and stepped closer. Fausta peered up. She opened her mouth to scream at the hideous mask over his face, but a knife pricked her belly as a rough hand seized her arm . . .

In the Villa Hortensis, which lay in its own grounds just beyond the Aurelian Gate leading on to the Via Appia, Drusilla, bed-companion and maid to the architect Attius Enobarbus, stared despairingly at the great oaken door locked firmly from the inside. Her knuckles were red from knocking and she was beginning to panic. She stared at Attius' freedman, Frontinus.

"What can we do?" she wailed. "I've knocked and I've knocked!" She crouched down and peered through the keyhole. "It's locked from the inside; the key's still there, isn't it?"

Frontinus also inspected the lock.

"Yes," he breathed, "no doubt about it. The key is still in the lock!"

"I know the master has recently returned to Rome," Drusilla wailed. "He is tired, but . . ."

Frontinus, thick-set and heavy-faced, his little eyes almost hidden by rolls of fat, shook his bald head and wiped the sweat from his shaven cheeks.

"I don't know why the master hides down here," he said. "Ever since his return, he's sheltered here. He barely goes out. Now this." Frontinus turned away, swearing under his breath.

Drusilla heard him go up the passageway and climb the steps into the courtyard. A short while later he returned bringing every able-bodied slave, groom, servant and cook boy. Four of them carried a heavy bench; under Frontinus' direction they began to pound the chamber door. Drusilla hoped this would at least rouse her master, but the battering continued and no sound was heard. Her heart skipped a beat. She'd been so pleased to see Attius return; a good enough master, even though he had strange customs and practices in bed. Nevertheless, she had kept him happy, yet he'd become so withdrawn, insisting he live here in this fortified room beneath the villa. There was no other entrance; just a grille in the wall to allow in light and air.

14

The battering continued. Servants, sweating and cursing, swung the bench backwards and forwards. Neither door nor bench showed signs of giving. Frontinus shouted to use more force. The sweat-lathered men tried even harder, the crashing echoing along the stone-flagged passageway like a discordant roll of drums. More servants and slaves were gathering at the far end near the steps. Lanterns, lamps and torches glowed. Drusilla coughed at the wisps of black smoke which came trailing down. She realised that her first panic had not been some wild hysteria. Attius always locked that door to keep himself and what he called his precious Icthus casket safe.

Heart beating fast, the palms of her hands wet with sweat, Drusilla tried to recall what Attius had muttered to her. He had returned from his travels through the Empire wary and absorbed, ranting how the old ways were dying, quietly mouthing curses against the Emperor and his august mother Helena. Drusilla had become truly frightened. Imperial spies flourished everywhere, as thick as fleas on a dirty tavern blanket. Drusilla did not understand what was happening. She just wanted Attius to remain safe and retain the favour of the court. However, he'd become a recluse, staying in the villa, locking himself in this room. At night he would have his main meal, always by himself, and drink too much uncut wine. On occasion he would summon Drusilla to help him in bed, but it was always the same: he would just lie there, absorbed in other matters, not really thinking of her. How long had he been back here? Drusilla closed her eyes. Two weeks? Attius had kept to himself. Messengers had arrived from the imperial palace summoning him to this meeting or that; Attius would always feign sickness. And now this! Drusilla's throat went dry. Attius always prided himself on being of the old school, revering the memory of ancient republicans like Cato. Had he taken the Roman way out? He'd once threatened to open his veins after dousing his senses with goblets of wine.

Drusilla startled as the door buckled, the stout pivots beginning to snap. The wood around the heavy lock had already splintered. Frontinus was shouting at the servants: "Harder! Harder!" The men now had the rhythm. The bench, chafing their hands, swung backwards and forwards into the door. An ear-splitting crack and the door broke free of one of its pivots. Again the battering ram was used; the door snapped completely off and fell back with a crash. Frontinus immediately ordered everyone to step back, but Drusilla didn't care. She answered to Attius, not to his freedman. She went ahead of him into the darkened room. The lamps had burnt low; most were extinguished. Only one on the great oaken table glowed eerily. There was no sight of Attius. Drusilla peered through the darkness to the far corner where Attius had his bed. Frontinus, having inspected the lock, was already striding across telling Drusilla to search for the Icthus chest on the desk. She did so. From the darkness she heard Frontinus groan.

"Too late!" he murmured. "Drusilla!"

She hurried across. At first she could make out nothing wrong. Attius lay on the bed, his face turned to the wall. Then she noticed his right eye was open. She hurried back, picked up the lamp and brought it over, then stared in horror. Attius lay sprawled on the bed. The long-bladed dagger thrust deep into his back had snuffed out his life.

CHAPTER
ONE

Constantine said about midday he saw with his own eyes, the symbol of the cross of light in the heavens, above the sun, bearing the instruction: Conquer by this!

"He has it! He has it! Scorpus, we love you!"

The shout echoed like a crash of thunder, rising between the two ancient hills of the Palatine and the Aventine which housed the Circus Maximus in their cradle. Nature seemed to have created this deliberately for the wildly dangerous four-horse chariot race about to begin. On the south side of the circus rose the *cavea*, the stalls built into the hillside for spectators. The lower tier was of marble for the senators and *equites*; the second was of wood; the third tier were tufa seats hacked out of the hillside for the crowd of 150,000 who'd swarmed through the marble-arcaded entrances. Across the circus, on the north side, ranged seats for the Lords of Rome, the purple-draped, gold-embossed imperial enclosure, or *pulvina*, which housed Constantine, Beloved of God, Emperor of the West, and Helena, his mother, the *Gloria Purperae Atque Gaudium Mundi* — "The Glory of the Purple and the Joy of the World". However, the Beloved of God and the Joy of the World were not too happy. They slouched in their silver-encrusted, scarlet-draped throne-like chairs staring blankly down at the chariots streaking along the bed of sand, which sparkled as the mineral grain mingled in it caught the sunlight.

Both the Emperor and his mother seemed totally oblivious to the four chariots which had emerged from the *carceres*, the caverns on the western side of the Circus which housed the stables and quarters of the chariot teams and their staff. The Imperial pair stared blank-eyed at the Spina, the great embankment which cut the arena. The chariots would race around this turning at the *metae*, the gilded bronze posts which marked the end of the Spina and the beginning of the next lap. In the centre of the Spina rose the obelisk of Rameses II, Pharaoh of Egypt, looted from Heliopolis, a stark reminder how the glory of empire could soon fade and how the spoils of one dynasty could easily become the plunder of another. Indeed, Emperor and mother had seemed self-absorbed from the moment the *quadrigae*, the four-horse chariots, splendid in their bejewelled electrum, emerged from the *carceres* and lined up behind a rope which stretched between the two Hermes marking the start. Each of the four chariots represented a faction in the city: Whites, Blues, Greens and Reds, all eager for the race. The horses, garlands on their heads, pawed the ground, their tails held high in the air by knots tied beneath them, their manes decorated with cloth of pearl, the blood-red breast-plates studded with sacred emblems and scarabs, the reins decked with the coloured ribbons of their faction. In each chariot stood the driver, his short tunic the colour of his party, his thighs covered in similarly coloured swathing bands; his bare feet, the toes ringed, gripped the sanded floor of his carriage. On the head of each charioteer was an ornate helmet decorated with a nodding plume. The reins of their horses were bound around their waist, while strapped to their left arm was a dagger to cut them loose in the event of an accident.

The race had hardly begun when such an accident occurred. Glaucus from the Greens, impatient to get his four-horse chariot round the *metae* of the Spina, had desperately tried to manoeuvre his outside horses, stallions not harnessed to the shaft but only to the leather traces, into a tight turn. He miscalculated and crashed into the *metae*, and, as the poet declared "ended his race with Death's dark dusty steeds". Now Scorpus of the Blues headed for the second lap, chariot bouncing, wheels whirling, his four black horses, lathered in sweat, eager to reach the turn as the crowd erupted into another hymn of praise.

Constantine, however, just stared, mouth half open, eyes glazed, whilst Helena, the "Glory of the Purple", studied her son closely. She did not care which colour won. She was involved in a different race and believed she was well trained and skilled to win it. Helena sat enthroned like some Vestal Virgin in pure white, a purple stole around her shoulders. No jewellery flashed at ear, neck or finger. Nothing to distract attention from her long, pale, unadorned face with those large expressive eyes which had so captivated Constantine's father when, according to rumour, he'd been an ambitious army officer and she the daughter of some tavern-keeper. Of course, no one dared say that now. Helena was Augusta, much loved, who exercised complete power over her son, a relationship she was determined to continue. She drew herself up as Scorpus, now in the lead, cleared the *metae* for the third lap around the Spina. The seven grey bronze eggs on their stand, carved in the shape of a fish and used to number the laps, were now down to four. Scorpus, Rome's darling, coloured helmet gleaming in the sun, braced himself against the jolting of the chariot, skilfully managing the reins, keeping his four sleek blacks close to the Spina. The champion was determined to blind his opponents and keep them on the outside, confused by the billowing dust.

Constantine was certainly confused, Helena reflected: too much wine, roast pork and bouncing young courtesans! It was time her son went back to training. She turned and smiled dazzlingly at him, and he glared back, his slightly bulbous eyes all red-rimmed. Helena noticed the unshaven cheeks, the slightly slobbery lips. Constantine went to pick up his goblet of Falernian. Helena snapped open her fan and wafted herself vigorously. She touched her black ringlets and glared at Constantine over the top of the fan. The Emperor sighed noisily, his hand fell away and he slouched like a petulant schoolboy, lower lip jutting out. Helena wafted the fan again. Yes, Constantine was fat! Well, September was always free of festivals and official occasions; he could go down to exercise with Murranus, that great former gladiator, and lover — Helena pulled a face —

21

perhaps, of her "little mouse" Claudia. Helena narrowed her eyes, breathing in deeply, impervious to the rattle of the chariots, the drumming hooves, the screams and yells of the mob, the constant glint of the sun on bronze, gold and silver. She shut out all such distractions, even the screeching laughter from Rufinus the banker's stupid, empty-headed wife, who sat just behind her, and became more deeply absorbed in her own thoughts.

Constantine glanced quickly to his right. Good, he thought, his mother was diverted with her own elaborate schemes and secret plans. The Emperor picked up the wine goblet and relished the warm fragrance of Campania, such a welcome relief from the ever-pervasive stench of garum, that fishy sauce so beloved of his subjects, as they sat with their platters of steaming food purchased from the makeshift cookshops in the arcades of the Circus. Constantine drank deeply. He needed that! He also needed to think and reflect, to plot on what his mother called the *res secretissima* — the most secret business; and, as always, there was Licinius! Constantine ground his teeth and slurped again from the goblet. Two years had passed since he had defeated his rival Maxentius at the Milvian Bridge, seized Rome and made himself Emperor of the West, dividing the world with his rival Licinius, now lurking in Nicomedia across the straits of Byzantium. Constantine was determined to end that. Later this year, when the harvest was in and the weather cooled, his legions would tramp east, his war galleys probe Licinius' maritime and coastal defences. He would

22

annihilate Licinius, as Licinius had so recently tried to destroy him.

Constantine half closed his eyes, recalling the imperial villa at Baiae, the sun setting, the breeze blowing cool. He clearly remembered that fateful evening. He'd been enjoying a light meal of hot wine and savoury lentil soup, laughing at the travelling troupe of clowns. One had had his wig blown off, whilst the other two had put theirs on the wrong way round. Constantine had watched the mummery, half listening to the gardeners sharpening stakes for the vines or weaving new beehives. Suddenly the laughter had stopped. Two jugglers had sped towards him. No game or revelry! Each was armed with a curved dagger. Constantine, not as drunk as he so often pretended, kicked a stool at one of the assassins and rose to meet the other, smashing into him like any wrestler in the arena. He had reacted even faster than his guards. The conspirators were seized, three men and a woman. Constantine himself questioned the men, staking them out in the garden, placing boiling hot plates on their chests then lifting these off to pluck away skin and flesh, leaving the open wounds raw for the fiery charcoal and urine his torturers immediately poured on. All three confessed to being assassins dispatched by Licinius. They had inveigled themselves in with false letters of introduction to the Master of Revels. Constantine ordered that hapless official to be dragged at the tail of a horse from Baiae to Rome. By the time the mounted Sarmatian mercenaries reached the outskirts of the city, only a leg remained. The three male assassins had been crucified, their woman accomplice sent to the Flavian amphitheatre. She'd been strapped, hands tied behind her, on the back of a wild bull, to be knocked, bruised and finally gored. A public reply to Licinius that his plot had failed!

Constantine gnawed on his knuckles and glared round the imperial box. Conspiracy, threats, blackmail! Whom could he trust? The standard-bearers, his personal guard in their white and purple tunics and gleaming cuirasses, the pelts of bear, wolf and panther decorating their heads and shoulders? Yet all these men had fought for him at the Milvian Bridge. Rufinus the banker, with his wide-eyed, noisy wife? Yet he'd attached his estate and life, house and fortune to Constantine's star; if the Emperor fell, Rufinus would certainly follow. Chrysis, the bald-headed chamberlain, with his prim-purse mouth and little beady eyes? A strange one, Chrysis! He dabbled, so it was gossiped, in the black arts. Tales were rife about how he listened to the black frogs croaking in the Styx. A man who hid behind a mask of flesh and mirth and yet, if the story was true, also sacrificed a black she-lamb during the night of the full moon, a votive offering amongst the cypress trees of the imperial gardens; a sacrifice from which a screaming spirit flew out trailing flames as it went to meet Hecate the Ancient One. Or was that just malicious gossip? Chrysis had made many enemies. He was a self-professed poet and wit. A powerful courtier had once asked him why he had not sent him one of his poems to read?

24

"Lest you send me one of yours!" the chamberlain had retorted.

No, Chrysis had too many enemies to change sides. What about the others? Burrus, the glory of Germany, standing on the other side of Helena, hand on the hilt of his sword, dressed in thick leggings and a shaggy bearskin despite the autumn heat? Constantine laughed quietly to himself. Burrus, with his straggling hair and beard, looked like a beast from one of his own dark forests. He and his group of ruffians had only one god, one allegiance, one loyalty and life: Helena! And those others, sitting behind him? Constantine stole a quick glance over his shoulder. The courtiers, flunkeys and officials were all intent on the race, clutching their bets in one hand, their lucky talismans in the other. Time-servers, Constantine reflected, except for the group sitting further to his left, among them Sylvester, the shaven-faced Christian priest, the powerful adviser to Militiades, the Bishop of Rome, who claimed spiritual authority over all Christians in the Empire as well as beyond its frontiers. Constantine shifted uneasily. He was wary of Christianity, the faith of slaves, who believed a crucified Jew was God Incarnate. Yet Helena believed in it and, of course, there were those visions he himself had experienced before the Milvian Bridge. What was their true cause? The falling sickness, the result of fatigue, of uncut Falernian? Yet the vision, or dream, or whatever else it was, had promised victory to Constantine if he adopted the cross and the chi-rho symbol of the Christian faith. He had, and he'd won!

Constantine had granted the Christians toleration, and they'd emerged from the sewers and catacombs of Rome and elsewhere. He had been truly astonished at how many senators and *equites* secretly adhered to this new faith, which stretched like a tangled root through all levels of imperial society and beyond. Helena regarded Christianity as the basis of a new empire. The Emperor straightened in his chair. And a new city? He glanced quickly at his mother still absorbed in her own thoughts, then startled at a fresh roar from the crowds. He looked quickly over his shoulder again and caught the gaze of Claudia, Helena's "little mouse". Why had his mother invited her here? Attius' death? The blackmail threats? But surely that was all too sensitive? Constantine blinked and stared down. Across the Spina, Scorpus, in a thunder of electrum, wood, steel, bronze and swirling dust, was holding his own against the Greek Pausanias who, in silver helmet and scarlet cloak, thundered behind with his magnificent bays. Constantine sipped from his goblet and wondered yet again why his mother had invited Claudia. He glanced quickly out of the corner of his eye. Good, Helena was still locked in the secret chambers of her own soul. Perhaps he should have another goblet of wine.

Helena did not object to Constantine's drinking. She would nag him later and persuade him to go down to the exercise yard. Nor was she concerned about Licinius and his plotting in Nicomedia. Her son was a better general, and support for Licinius was crumbling both within his own provinces and elsewhere. Helena had seen to that. The Christian Church had tentacles which stretched direct into the heart of Licinius' most secret councils. Helena smiled. Licinius would soon discover that, but by then it would be too late. She was more concerned about what would happen afterwards: a new Rome, a new empire, a new faith, one religion, one God, one creed, one code. The Christian faith could achieve that, be the binding force of a new empire. True, Helena mused, people might become a little confused over who was Emperor and who was Pontifex Maximus; Constantine or the Bishop of Rome? Helena chewed her lip. Could Constantine also be Bishop of Rome? An interesting thought. She must ask Anastasius, her deaf-mute secretary, now busy in the secret writing office of the Palatine Palace behind her, preparing everything for the meeting that would take place afterwards.

Helena sighed. That brought her to her little mouse, Claudia, with her sweet round face under a mop of black hair; a mere chit of a woman, comely, neat and unpretentious, except for those eyes, black and keen, and that teeming mind behind its innocent mask: a perfect *agentes in rebus*! Indeed, one of the best. Claudia observed people and lulled them into security as she critically observed, questioned and reflected. Helena needed her. She had to drag Claudia away from that colourful rabble which haunted Uncle Polybius' tavern near the Flavian Gate. She glanced up and stared across the race track, oblivious to the roars and cheers as another great bronze egg was taken down. Only two more courses to run. She surveyed the sea of faces. Somewhere along the top tiers, clutching their bone-shard tickets, would be Polybius and his gaggle of customers from the She-Asses.

Helena turned as if to talk to her son, then changed her mind as she remembered the Nefandus, that sordid killer stalking the filthy streets and alleyways of the Caelian quarter. She wondered if Claudia knew anything about that. There, however, a more pressing matter: the truly mysterious murder of Attius Enobarbus. Was his death a threat to Helena's vision of a new Rome? An obstacle to the *res secretissima*, the most secret business? Helena stared down at the Spina. Were those stories true? she wondered. Had Peter the Galilean, the bosom friend of the risen Christ, the first Bishop of Rome, been crucified in a place like this, upside down on a cross? And was his corpse secretly buried beneath the place of execution? A sudden roar startled Helena from her reverie. She stared down. Scorpus had turned too close to the *metae* and the left wheel of his chariot must have struck the post, for it was now wobbling. Pausanias had swung out, rushing past him, thundering towards the finishing line. Helena leaned over and shook Constantine by the shoulder.

"I know, Mother," he declared without turning. "Expect the unexpected!"

"No, dearest son," Helena hissed. "Watch for the sudden mistake which can lose everything." She looked over and caught Claudia's sharp, unblinking stare. Yes, she reflected, nodding at her little mouse: it wasn't the malice of her enemies she feared, but the mistakes of her friends. Helena was about to walk a long and dangerous path. Prudence and vigilance were her sure defence against bloody murder and intrigue. She glanced back again. Oh yes, and Claudia . . .

Claudia cleared her throat and stared round the Chamber of Hercules in the Palatine Palace. The race had finished, the crowds cheering or booing according to whether they had won or lost. Many cries were raised that the race had been fixed. Claudia didn't really care. She'd been preparing to leave when Burrus, captain of Helena's German mercenaries, had made it abundantly clear why she had been invited to share the imperial box. The Augusta wanted to see her.

"I know that," Claudia had hissed back at the German's grinning bearded face, reeking of wine, meat and perfume. Now they were here, sitting leisurely as if attending some intimate symposium, yet the real reason for their presence must be that some crisis brewed. Claudia sat before the "Most August of Mothers". Constantine, on Helena's right, slouched red-faced and half asleep; a mask, Claudia reflected. Constantine was lazy but very able, capricious yet ruthless. In many ways a born actor, he'd make a good addition to Labienus' troupe "the Satyricons", now quartered near the She-Asses. On Helena's left sat the enigmatic Sylvester in his simple tunic and cloak. He was a placid-looking man but another actor, Claudia reflected, a man just as dangerous as Constantine and Helena with his visions of this world and beyond. Behind the Augusta was the ever-vigilant Burrus, a killer to the bone, and next to him, Anastasius the deaf-mute, talking to Claudia with his eyes, warning her to be careful. Murranus lounged on a stool beside Claudia, muscular legs slightly apart. The former gladiator was becoming accustomed to such meetings, even more so now he was employed as bodyguard to Sylvester. Claudia took great comfort from that; anything rather than the arena!

She stared at the mural behind the Augusta glorifying the exploits of the man-god Hercules stealing the red cattle of the monstrous winged Geryon whilst forcing other giants back into the fiery vaults of an underground hell, then sighed and shifted her gaze to the polished table of rare African citrus adorned with ochre-coloured terracotta ornaments.

"Attius Enobarbus," Helena's voice shattered the silence, "former centurion in the XXth Victrix Legion and, until recently, engineer and architect. You've heard of him?"

Claudia shook her head.

"Macrinus, formerly Tribune of Vigiles in the Caelian quarter near the Flavian Gate?"

"Before my time, your Excellency; perhaps my uncle . . ."

"Frontinus," Helena continued harshly, "freedman of the said Attius?"

Claudia decided to remain quiet.

"Julius Philippus, Lucretius Narses, Gemellus Severus, Petilius Gavinus, decurions in the same XXth Legion, all engineers, architects and draughtsmen?"

"The XXth Victrix?" Claudia stammered. "Surely that was one of Maxentius' legions in the civil war against —"

30

"Against me, their legitimate Emperor," Constantine drawled. "The XXth was the backbone of the opposition." He yawned and rubbed his face. "If I'd had my way I would have crucified the lot!"

Claudia nodded understandingly.

"You disbanded the legion, your Excellency?" Murranus stammered.

Constantine grinned lazily and waved at his mother to carry on.

"The XXth was disbanded," Helena continued evenly. "Anastasius here, clever boy, has assembled all the information."

Claudia smiled up at the deaf-mute, even though she suspected she was *not* being given all the information. Something about this meeting fascinated her. Sylvester was very quiet, whilst Helena was speaking far too harshly, as if she wished to rush matters.

"As I said, the XXth was disbanded," Helena continued, "but Attius Enobarbus and his comrades were excepted from any punishment." She glanced quickly at Sylvester, who was sitting as if carved out of marble. "You see, Maxentius used these as *scrutores mortuorum*."

"Searchers of the dead?"

"Of the Christian dead, to be more precise." Sylvester spoke up at a sign from Helena. "Diocletian and his successor Maxentius instigated the most ferocious persecution of our Church; you know that. They wanted to destroy us root and branch. They raided the catacombs, smashed our altars, violated our sanctuaries and —"

31

"But the *scrutores*?" Claudia demanded.

"Our Church . . ." Sylvester's heavy-lidded eyes held a hint of sarcasm, which was reflected in his voice. He was deliberately drawing a line between himself and Claudia; her parents had been Christian, she was not.

"Your Church?" Claudia queried.

"Lays great store on its martyrs and saints, its rich heritage."

Claudia nodded even as she groaned to herself. Helena's obsession with relics of the Christian tradition was well known. Even Uncle Polybius had sold her some!

"Or should I say," Sylvester chose his words carefully, "on certain ones. During the reign of Nero, some two hundred and fifty years ago, our first apostle, the Galilean Peter, was crucified upside down in the Emperor's circus on the Vatican Hill. He was later buried close to the execution site. Peter was the founder of the Church of Rome. His tomb is very precious to us. It holds the remains of a man who walked with Christ. Such a tomb underwrites the power of our Pontiff, the Bishop of Rome." Sylvester's face had become slightly flushed. He was staring fixedly at Claudia, who held his gaze. Power! Claudia knew exactly where the presbyter was leading. One day, perhaps sooner rather than later, Sylvester might be the new Pontifex. Claudia had worked secretly with him, a link between the presbyter and Helena. She and Sylvester knew each other's minds, even if Claudia did not share his vision.

"Peter's tomb was kept as a *magnum secretum*, a great secret," Sylvester continued. "It had to be hidden away from the likes of Aurelian, Severus, Decius, Diocletian and those other emperors who strove to destroy our faith. The precise location was known to the descendants of the family who first buried Peter's remains. Some others may have been told," he shrugged, "but only when the persecutions ceased would such a secret location be revealed. In our days," Sylvester coughed nervously, "the Mystery of the Blessed Peter was held by one of our deacons, Valentinian. However, some eight years ago he disappeared, either fled or killed during the great persecution. No one knows."

Claudia was about to question him on this, but she caught Sylvester's sharp glance. He was telling her to remain silent, at least for the moment.

"Attius and his colleagues," Helena took up the story, "were appointed by Diocletian and Maxentius to search Rome, to ransack the city for the shrines and relics of Christian martyrs, Peter's in particular. Being engineers and architects, they could plumb the mysteries of the underground passageways, grottoes and tunnels. They found several tombs and destroyed them."

"But the Galilean's?"

Sylvester blinked at Claudia's use of the common title.

"Never!"

"But they pursued Valentinian?"

"Yet apparently never found him."

"So why did you spare these *scrutores*? After all, they were Maxentius' minions."

"Because they knew what had been done; perhaps they knew more than they confessed."

"And what did they confess to?"

"Oh, they admitted they had searched for Peter's tomb but never found it," Sylvester replied. "It remained a mystery. They also knew nothing about Valentinian, which was strange. Valentinian was a high-ranking Christian; if he'd been arrested and killed, some record would have remained, but we searched for this and found no trace."

"True," Helena spread her hands, "Valentinian could have died from natural causes, fled, been spirited away, or killed in secret."

"So," Claudia declared, "the *scrutores* admitted they knew nothing but they were still pardoned and restored in full."

"Clasped to our bosom," Constantine slurred as if half asleep. "Like errant lambs. We truly believed they had much to tell us, at least until Attius was murdered three nights ago."

"We decided to use them." Helena spoke so quickly, Claudia wondered what she was trying to hide in her rush of words.

The Augusta wetted her lips before continuing.

"Attius and his company were dispatched to the Hellespont to plan the rebuilding of the fortress town of Byzantium, which controls the straits. They returned two weeks ago, and were lodged here at the palace to write their reports and answer any questions we had.

We wanted them kept together. They were looked after by Macrinus; he was a sort of military expert, their guardian. On their return, Attius' conduct became strange. He feigned sickness, stayed at home and did not join the rest at the palace. He never went out. For most of the time he locked himself in a secure chamber in the basement of his villa. If this had gone on much longer, we would have intervened. Anyway, three evenings ago, Attius' mistress Drusilla tried to rouse him. The door to his chamber was locked from the inside. When she received no reply, Drusilla summoned Frontinus, Attius' freedman. The door was eventually forced and Attius was found murdered, a dagger thrust into his back. No other sign of violence could be detected, except the Icthus casket was missing."

"Icthus?"

Helena pulled a face.

"We did not know of its importance until now. Apparently it held precious papers, possibly something about the mystery of Peter the Galilean's tomb."

"Why do you think that?"

"Yesterday evening . . ." Helena paused. "Well, you know the Pillar of Secrets?"

Claudia nodded. Who didn't? A great iron casket placed at the foot of the Palatine Hill just within the palace enclosure, it bore the face of a wolf, its jaws opened to receive anonymous information from any citizen who wished to betray the secrets of another, a system which kept the *agentes in rebus* and the *secretissimi*, the eyes and ears of the Emperor, very busy.

Helena raised a hand, snapping her fingers. Anastasius passed across a small scroll which Helena gave to Claudia. The parchment was of good quality, the writing neat and well formed. The letter simply informed the August Ones that, following the mysterious death of Attius Enobarbus, the secret whereabouts of Peter the Galilean's tomb could be theirs for three million in gold solidi from whatever mint. The arrangements for the sale would be given once the August Ones had signalled their assent and that of Presbyter Sylvester, in a *billa* posted in Caesar's forum, that they wished to purchase *aliqua sacra* — certain sacred items. The letter was signed with a flourish, "Charon, Lord of the Underworld".

Claudia smiled to herself. She had certainly heard the name of this "Imperator and Rex" of the *inferni* and raptors, the murky underbelly of Rome. Lord Charon was the leader of the gangs of robbers, murderers, assassins, thieves and conjurors who swarmed along the dark, stinking alleyways of the city.

"So," she declared, "Attius had the secret all the time."

"As we suspected."

"Anyone else?"

"Perhaps the other *scrutores*, but we don't want to frighten them yet; that is why we have summoned you. You must investigate." Helena leaned forward, one foot tapping the purpled paving stone. "Discover the truth about Attius' death." She moved uncomfortably on the *cathedra*, a chair with a sloping back, its ends adorned with the damascened copper heads of cherubs. "You'll move amongst panthers, Claudia." She paused, choosing her words carefully. "Attius and the other *scrutores* were members of the Schola Lunae, the School of the Moon; they worshipped Diana the huntress and wore the *signum purpereae calicis*, the sign of the purple chalice, on their arms."

Claudia felt her face drain of colour. Her stomach pitched and her mouth grew dry even as she extended her hand to quieten Murranus' agitation. Years ago Meleager, a gladiator with a similar emblem on his arm, had raped Claudia and killed Felix, her simple-minded but beautiful brother, trapping them along a lonely part of the Tiber . . .

"Claudia, Claudia," Helena whispered. "Murranus killed Meleager."

Claudia just stared at the Empress. Helena's eyes were soft and gentle. A mask? She glanced quickly at the others. Constantine was scratching a spot between his eyes, peering at her through his fingers. Sylvester was examining the ring on his left hand emblazoned with the chi-rho symbol. The others had caught the tension. No one moved. The silence was broken only by the buzz of a bee hovering over a bowl of sweetened sandalwood.

"We have no proof against the others," Helena continued, "but Attius was suspected of being the Nefandus."

Claudia gasped and broke from her own ghastly memories.

"The killings amongst the prostitutes ended just before my son's glorious victory at the Milvian Bridge."

Helena breathed in deeply. "Attius could certainly be violent with prostitutes. He was known and feared by their guild, the Daughters of Isis. He frequented their brothel, along with the other *scrutores*, bachelors and widowers; they were often seen there."

Claudia fought to regain her composure.

"He was much suspected," Helena murmured, "but nothing was proved. When we sent him to Byzantium, fearful that he might revert to his filthy practices," Helena smiled thinly, "as well as to keep an eye on that precious gang, Macrinus, former Tribune of the Vigiles in the Caelian quarter, was sent along as their keeper."

"In other words a spy?"

"Yes, in other words a spy." Helena smiled.

"And now?"

The Empress hitched her stole closer about her and made to rise.

"You, Claudia, are my keeper. Discover the truth behind Attius' death. I do not intend," she snapped, "to buy the secrets of the blessed Peter's tomb from some outlaw, a ruffian from the slums." She leaned forward and grasped Claudia's wrist, squeezing it tightly. "Find the Icthus casket and what it contains . . ."

CHAPTER
TWO

*He once more attempted to stimulate his courage
with the damnable art of Magic.*

"'Dead men are free from fickle fortune. Mother Earth
has room for every one of her children, and a corpse,
bereft of an urn, has the whole sky to cover it.' Do you
recognise the quotation?" Charon, lord of Rome's
underworld, turned to the witch squatting on his left.
In the light of the full moon she looked what she
claimed to be, a patched mourning mantle thrown
about her, bony naked feet painted black, her narrow
face the colour of boxwood under its coat of filth whilst
her grey hair, streaked with white paint and adorned
with dirty ashes, tumbled down to her shoulders. The
crone of the night just bared yellowing teeth in a
hideous grin. Charon turned to Cerebus, his lieutenant,
squatting a little to his left. He was well named,
reflected Charon, with his round bald head, mastiff
mouth, snub nose and darting eyes. A true dog of the
underworld! Charon laughed quietly to himself and
stretched his hands towards the fire, watching the
sparks burst up above the burning bracken and gorse.
He heard a whimper from the great thorn bush just
beyond the pool of light and glimpsed the hysterical
gleam in the staring eyes of the man bound, gagged and

imprisoned there. He could almost smell the man's sweaty fear, but that did not matter. The Lord of the Underworld stared up at the starlit sky, the blackness which housed the flowers of heaven.

"What I quoted comes from Lucan's *Pharsalia*," he murmured. "A great work. I studied it in the schools, copying it out on my wax tablet with a reed pen and ink made from soot, my backside thrashed till it was red as the dawn. If he was alive, I'd take my old magister and put him in a thorn cage and burn him too." Charon bit into an apple, his strong teeth crushing the fruit's white flesh. Lost in his own thoughts, he hummed a tune and reflected on the past. So many years, so many deeds, so many thoughts! Now he was here amongst the tombs of the great cemetery along the Appian Way. Nearby stood the sepulchre of some tribune of a long-forgotten legion, benefactor of this and that. Who cares? Charon thought. He believed in all the gods yet none. The past and the future were interesting, but the present was most important. In truth he had no regrets, no scruples, no soul; all that had died, crumbled to dust. Tonight he was waiting for his mysterious guest, someone who'd promised to make him richer still. Charon had come unarmed, but amongst the rotting tombs and sepulchres, the crumbling houses of the dead, lurked his horde of *inferni*. They would wait for his signal to attack if any danger threatened.

Charon wiped the sweat from his face and ran a hand over his closely shaven head. He breathed in deeply and stared across the fire into the darkness. He liked the harvest his power reaped — wealth, women and wine — but what he truly loved was the danger, the unexpected twist that was more attractive than anything else. He had agreed for his name to be used against the August Ones. The gamble had begun; now Charon waited for the next throw of the dice.

"He comes," Hecate the witch whispered, sniffing the air like a dog.

"As he said he would," growled Cerebus, leaning forward and peering into the night.

A shape emerged from the darkness, gliding like a ghost to the other side of the fire. The arrival was hooded and masked. He sat down, shaking out his cloak.

"Lord Charon, I greet you."

"I could kill you now."

"Of course you could," came the mocking reply, "and I would kill you. My lord Charon, I know the labyrinths of the catacombs, the hiding places, the caverns of the lost, the dismal chambers of the dead. All the places you hide. So, my lord, I have left certain papers with a well-respected merchant. If I do not drink honeyed wine with him tomorrow before the sixth hour, these papers will be sent to the secret office on the Palatine. However," the visitor spread mittened hands, "we are here not to threaten each other, but to negotiate. You received a copy of my letter to the August Ones?"

"You used my name."

"I also advised you to wager not on Scorpus in the recent race but Pausanias."

"You were responsible for that?"

"Of course. Gold and silver can loosen a wheel."

"A great deal of gold and silver!"

"And your wager brought great profit, Lord Charon."

"Yet you still used my name."

"And you shall be rewarded for that. Three million gold solidi in the new currency, to be delivered at a certain time in a certain place. Hence I need you."

"And I receive half?"

"Of course!"

"Why shouldn't I take all?"

"Because of my earlier threat." His visitor laughed.

"Who are you?"

"I am Valentinian, former deacon of the Roman Church."

"You have travelled far, my friend. You no longer believe in your own code, or even in old Seneca's axiom, 'For mortals to aid mortals is divine' or Martial's epigram, 'Man is sacred to man'?"

"Man is wolf to man," came the mocking reply.

Valentinian turned and looked over his shoulder at the unfortunate imprisoned in the cage of thorns. The captive had now fallen silent, eyes glazed from the drugged wine he'd been given.

"So why do you need me?" Charon asked.

"As I said, to collect the solidi. Here amongst the dead along the Appian Way, you have a legion of the damned to help you."

"And?"

"I keep hidden. The gods only know when I might have to act again."

"And?"

"The divine bitch Helena might try to interfere."

Hecate, sitting next to Charon, leaned over and whispered in her master's ear. He nodded.

"Did you murder Attius?"

"Oh yes. I can kill as I wish."

"And you have the Icthus casket?" Charon played with the ring in his earlobe. "I know all about that."

"I have it, hidden away."

"And the others?" Charon chuckled. "The *scrutores mortuorum?* You see," he spread his hands, "I too know what happens on the Palatine."

"Nonentities," came the rasping reply. "Frontinus, Attius' freedman, is lazy and stupid. The rest are old soldiers longing for a place in the sun, to be left alone to enjoy their wine and slave girls."

"So what is the danger?"

"Claudia, the little woman who lodges with her Uncle Polybius at the She-Asses near the Flavian Gate."

"I have heard of it, and of her."

"Watch Claudia," Valentinian hissed, "and if necessary kill her."

"That would cost more!"

"Of course."

"I've heard rumours." Charon scratched the side of his face. "That Attius was the Nefandus — the slayer of whores."

"I don't think so. You know the Nefandus has returned?"

Charon nodded. "What happens to common whores does not concern me. If he interferes in my interests," the ruler of the underworld gazed up at the sky, "then I will act." He glanced across the fire. "Can I trust you, Valentinian?"

"As much as I can trust you."

Charon grinned to himself. Trust had been the key to his life; trust, or the betrayal of it. For a moment he thought of her face, the one he had loved and lost, and those words of the poet Catullus came floating back: "You promised me eternal love, my darling. Heaven grant that this promise be true and that it lasts throughout our lives." Oh, it certainly hadn't! Charon felt the old pain, the deep loss, that terrible feeling of annihilation within. He whispered to Cerebus; his lieutenant plucked a brand from the fire, rose, walked over to the thorn cage and threw it in. The oil-drenched wood burst into flame, a sheet of roaring fire to consume both thorn and flesh. Despite the gag, the muted screams of the prisoner echoed shrilly, then died abruptly as the flames raced higher. Valentinian didn't turn or flinch, even when the foul odour of burning flesh drifted towards them.

"He betrayed my trust," Charon whispered.

"Fitting punishment," retorted Valentinian. "But trust me more. You think this is about a dead Jew, Lord Charon? Oh no!" He rose to his feet. "This is only the beginning. I have another secret which, if published, would cause a storm such as this city has never seen." Valentinian raised a hand. "Trust me and you'll see . . ."

★ ★ ★

The early evening breeze carried the fragrance from the flower beds and the small gardens hemmed in on each side by the elaborately carved peristyle. Between the pillars torches flared, drawing in the moths and flies which flitted from them to the lights in the array of brilliantly coloured alabaster jars along the ledges. Coloured lanterns added a festive feel as the *scrutores* gathered after their evening meal of milk-fed snails and hot boiled goose. Together with Macrinus, their military guardian, they lavishly praised the imperial chefs as they trooped from the *triclinium* to enjoy the evening air, downing goblets of watered wine mixed with honey, myrrh and aniseed and munching on small cakes of *mustaceae* to settle their stomachs.

Helena had dismissed Claudia just as the sun was setting. The Empress immediately withdrew into her private apartments to consult with Presbyter Sylvester, who looked far from happy; apparently some private matter in dispute between himself and the August Ones. Claudia and Murranus had to kick their heels for a while before joining the *scrutores* after their evening meal. Claudia was glad to be out in the open. Uncle Polybius, she reflected, would have loved to inspect this garden, with its clipped box hedges, marble statues of the gods, bronze cupids and water fountains. Despite the pleasant surroundings, however, Claudia was insistent on the business in hand. The *scrutores*, together with Macrinus, sat in a semicircle on the low marble garden benches. They looked like siblings: of medium height, with tough weathered skin and sharp eyes, faces clean-shaven, hair closely cropped. Claudia had met their type, former soldiers, all over Rome. They were dressed in simple linen tunics, hard-soled sandals on their feet; the occasional piece of jewellery, finger rings, bracelets, necklaces and chains, sparkled in the lanternlight. They were openly contemptuous of her, resentful at her presence, betraying their feelings by the occasional smirk or sideways glance. These men were veterans; the only thing that indicated their present calling was their ink-stained fingers. They showed Claudia only the barest respect out of fear of the Empress; they were also wary of Murranus' dominating presence. The former gladiator slouched beside Claudia, dwarfing her diminutive figure, exuding a menace won by his reputation as well as his silent, brooding look.

Macrinus was different from the others, more courteous. The former Tribune of the Vigiles was of medium height, thick-set, with a balding head and a sorrowful face, hollow-cheeked and deeply furrowed. His rather sallow features were disfigured by the cut branding his right cheek, a legacy, so he explained, of a *sicarius*, a city dagger-man. He wore no jewellery but was dressed in a linen military tunic with a belt rather than a cord round his waist. He was the only one to clasp Claudia's hand and immediately asked if she knew Horace's *Ode to Lalage*. When she replied that she didn't, Macrinus insisted on quoting the first few verses. The others smirked at this. They apparently regarded Macrinus as both their bodyguard and their keeper and tended to ignore him as they did Claudia. When she first joined them, they insisted on talking to each other in the lingua franca of the camp, deliberately excluding Claudia and Murranus from the conversation.

Frontinus, Attius' freedman, arrived late. He was short, rather plump, head and face closely shaven. He was pleasant-featured, with smiling eyes, his fat cheeks bulging with the grapes he'd stuffed into his mouth. He apologised for being late, breathing his excuses as he squeezed himself on to the end of a bench and peered short-sightedly at Claudia. She winked quickly at him and went back to her study of the rest. They knew she was here on the Empress' authority and that she'd be aware of their past. Eventually, they were forced to accept her, and relaxed a little when Claudia admitted she was not a Christian. She then skilfully drew them into conversation. Like all veterans, they were proud of their achievements, eager to talk about their past. True, they admitted, they had served under Maxentius, and true, they had ransacked Rome for Christian hiding places, shrines and tombs, but so had many others now serving the August Ones. They quoted that classic defence so beloved of those on trial: they'd only acted on orders, and if they hadn't, others would have done the task more ruthlessly. Under a brilliant starlit sky, the garden air heavy and warm with fragrant scents, they grew more garrulous as Claudia nodded understandingly at their litany of excuses.

"You searched for the tomb of Peter the Galilean?" she asked abruptly.

"Of course!" Narses, their self-appointed leader, answered swiftly. "But the Christians hid it well. We

47

know the sepulchre lies somewhere in the area of Vatican Hill, but Domina," the flattering title slipped off his tongue, "that part of Rome is marshy, a warren of old caverns, tombs and caves."

"Did you ever encounter the Christian deacon Valentinian?"

"No." Narses shook his head. "Of course, we've heard the name, but Domina, we were searchers for the dead, not the living."

"How did you know he was alive?"

Narses just shrugged and sipped from his cup.

"Our mandate," Severus spoke up in a slightly screechy voice, "was very clear. We were to search for this or that. Some tombs we found, some we did not. The records still exist."

"We followed orders," Philippus growled.

"As we do now," Gavinus added.

Claudia caught a twinge of an accent. "What province are you from?"

"Illyria," replied Narses.

"And Attius?"

Narses sniffed. "Oh, he came from somewhere in the north."

"Did he discover the Galilean's tomb?"

"He may have done, but if he did, he never told us," Narses quipped.

"Attius was a good master but very secretive." Frontinus beamed like the moon. He picked up the jug of wine and poured himself a generous cup. He lifted this, toasted Claudia and sipped noisily, smacking his lips, ignoring the contemptuous looks of the rest. "A very good master. He paid me well and never hit me. I had a slave girl, my own narrow chamber —"

"You served Attius for how long?" Claudia asked.

"Oh, longer than I care to remember. Always him, always me."

"Did he ever mention the Galilean's tomb?"

"Yes, he often cursed the fact that he could never trace it. Amongst the Christians, the knowledge was apparently confined to a few, and they were very difficult to find."

"And Valentinian?"

Frontinus just shook his head.

"And the Icthus casket?"

"Mistress, I swear by Apollo's penis, until he was murdered I never realised the casket was so important. My master kept it close, the key on a cord around his neck, but that wasn't my business."

"We would say the same," Narses intervened.

"So Attius was very secretive?"

"Oh yes."

"And you know nothing about the Galilean's tomb or the Icthus casket?"

"Mistress," Severus bleated, "we've answered that. We've told you Attius was secretive."

"Was he secretive when he visited the whores and brothels in the Caelian quarter?" Claudia smiled falsely. "And isn't it true you often accompanied him on such outings?" Her voice turned hard; men like these had raped her and killed her brother. She had no pity for them. "Weren't you," she accused, "the Emperor Maxentius' bully-boys, his favourites, allowed to do

49

anything on your evening forays, looking for pleasure here or there?"

A chorus of shouted denials and angry looks greeted her question. Narses made to rise, but quickly sat down when Murranus threatened to do the same.

"Well, did you or didn't you?" Claudia asked.

Baleful looks were their only reply.

"Did you see them?" Claudia turned abruptly to Macrinus. "After all, you were in charge of the *vigiles* in that quarter."

Macrinus had leaned back against the ivy-covered trellis which screened the garden bed behind. He masked his face with his goblet.

"Well?" Claudia asked.

"I saw them, mistress," Macrinus answered politely. "As I saw many, many people."

"But Attius was well known. He liked to hurt the girls."

"So it was rumoured," Macrinus whispered.

"No rumour!" snapped Claudia, tired of evasive answers. "Attius was well known amongst the Daughters of Isis as a violent man."

"But no one made a complaint!" Macrinus blustered.

"Because no one dared!" Claudia retorted. "He was one of you," she turned back to the *scrutores*, "members of the Schola Lunae, the School of the Moon, devotees of Diana and Dionysius." She fought to control her fury. "He wore the purple chalice emblem on his wrist, as you did; perhaps still do."

50

"One of many such guilds," Macrinus replied. "I too belonged to one."

"When you were Tribune of the Vigiles in that quarter?"

"Yes!"

"Did you turn a blind eye to your fellow associates?"

Macrinus lowered his goblet.

"That is unjust and unfair. You have no proof."

"Perhaps I do," Claudia replied heatedly. "Attius hurt whomever he liked. Did any of you join him in his games?"

Some of the faces stared boldly back.

"Did you, Frontinus, accompany your master?"

"Oh may the Gods be praised, I don't think so!" Frontinus waggled his fingers. Claudia caught the deliberate lisp in his voice and ignored the muted giggles from the rest. She couldn't decide whether he was hinting that he didn't like women or just playing the buffoon.

"But you all visited the Daughters of Isis."

"And other ladies of the night," Narses barked.

"So any of you could be the Nefandus?"

Again a chorus of protests greeted her accusation.

"Attius was a suspect, wasn't he?" Claudia pointed at Macrinus.

The former Tribune of Vigiles pulled a face. "There were many suspects," he replied slowly, "former gladiators, members of the School of the Moon, women-haters . . ."

"And the Nefandus, who gave him that name?"

"I did, or rather my wife," Macrinus snapped. "I am not a Christian, but my wife, may the gods take her to a place of light, certainly was. I told her about the appalling cruelty."

"Which was?"

"How the Nefandus ripped his victims open from crotch to throat." Macrinus twisted his fingers to demonstrate. "And if he could, he always gouged out their right eye."

Claudia swallowed hard. She'd heard of men who loved nothing better than humiliating and injuring a woman, a horror which sprang from the darkness deep within them.

"My wife quoted from the Jewish scriptures; she called him the 'Abomination of the Desolation standing in the Holy Place'." Macrinus blew his cheeks out and stared into the darkness, blinking swiftly.

Claudia glimpsed the tears in his eyes.

"Your wife?" she asked.

"She'd been ill; she died around the time Constantine became Emperor."

"Did you ever gain a description of the Nefandus?" Murranus asked.

"Nothing," Macrinus shook his head, "just vague sightings of an imperial officer." He spread his hands. "A few descriptions about a red cloak, an ornate helmet, the kind a member of the Praetorian Guard would wear. Believe me, I scoured every stinking alley, filthy nook, shabby courtyard, the most foul and fetid runnels and cellars of the Caelian quarter, but I found nothing!" His voice turned bitter. "Then Constantine marched into Rome, and chaos spread throughout the city. The Nefandus may well have been an officer in the imperial guard, because the murders abruptly stopped. He was either killed or just disappeared." Macrinus whipped the sheen of sweat from his face. "So many disappeared. I had a freedman, Crastinus, he too vanished. We were drawn into the chaos, the fighting outside Rome. By the time it was all over, I was finished, spent and exhausted. I could do no more. The August Ones asked me to continue in my post, but . . ." His voice tailed off as if he was weary of the topic.

"Yet now the Nefandus is back?" Murranus asked.

"Is he?" Macrinus replied slowly. "Is he really?"

"Two murders." Frontinus spoke up. "The Daughters of Isis must be panicking."

"I don't know anything about it," Macrinus slurred.

"I need to question you on that, tribune, as well as those *vigiles* who patrol the Caelian quarter; perhaps tomorrow about the third hour at the barracks?"

Macrinus picked up his wine goblet.

"Tomorrow about the third hour," Murranus insisted.

Macrinus quickly agreed.

"And your journey to Byzantium?" Claudia decided to change direction.

"The Augusta must have told you about that," Narses retorted. "We were to survey the fortifications of the city, a routine task."

"All of you?" Claudia asked swiftly.

Narses looked away. Claudia felt a shiver of apprehension, similar to when she was a member of an acting troupe, plodding up and down the roads of Italy from Ravenna in the north to Tarentum in the south. During a play, be it by Terence or Apuleius, particular actions were vital to the plot. So it was here: a suspicion that the journey to Byzantium was not just a simple surveying expedition.

"Did anything happen on your journey?" Claudia asked.

"Should it have?" Narses asked. "We went, we saw, we inspected, we wrote, then we returned."

"And you are now lodged here at the palace?"

"To finish our report. We were away for about fourteen days. We had to reach certain conclusions, make recommendations," Narses sniffed, "and that was it."

"But Attius returned a changed man," Macrinus declared. "We arrived back in Rome about two weeks ago. Attius didn't join us here. He claimed to be unwell; some contagion he'd picked up on his travels."

"A contagion?" Claudia asked. "Is that why he hid in that fortified vault in his villa?"

"Was he ill or terrified? Did you visit him?" Murranus asked.

"On the afternoon of his —"

"Murder!" Claudia interrupted. "Your colleague and friend was brutally murdered."

"We'd decided to visit him," Narses explained, "to see what the matter was."

"And?"

"Attius met us all out in the garden of his villa. He was quiet and withdrawn. We asked about his health.

54

We talked about the journey to Byzantium." Narses pulled a face. "Little else, then he retired saying he would join us soon."

"Was he frightened?"

"In Byzantium, no, nor on the journey back, but on that last day . . ." Philippus spoke, choosing his words carefully, "he did seem deeply apprehensive, withdrawn, nervous."

"So he was hiding from something or someone?"

"Perhaps, but whom?" Philippus shrugged. "I don't know."

"Did Attius know he was suspected of being the Nefandus?"

"Yes," Narses replied, "but he did not care a whit, at least in his prime!"

"Of course," Claudia breathed, "he was the beloved of Maxentius the Emperor, the destroyer of Christian shrines, quite the courageous bully-boy along the alleyways."

"He did have his virtues," Frontinus murmured.

Claudia rose to her feet. "Gentlemen, I'll leave you to your wine though, of course, I shall visit you again." She glimpsed Gavinus move quickly, as if shielding something beneath the bench, but all she could see was a rolled-up cloak and a pair of stout marching boots. She and Murranus made their farewells, which were coldly received, and left the enclosed garden. They went down colonnaded passageways. Lamps, glowing brilliantly in their niches, illuminated a line of paintings and murals extolling the exploits of the wolf's sons, Romulus and Remus.

"Little one, you're quiet."

"Little one is quiet!" Claudia paused in the light of a lantern. "Murranus, I'm tired, hungry and thirsty. I've been insulted, lied to, scoffed at, taunted . . ."

Murranus made to go back as if to confront her tormentors.

"No, no!" Claudia caught his arm. "This is not the arena, the gods be thanked!"

They turned the corner, making their way down to a side gate. Torches lashed to poles bathed the yellow paving stones in a golden glow. In the shadows stood the imperial guards in their ornate dress armour and plumed helmets. Behind them squatted groups of German and Samartian mercenaries. A place of beauty, Claudia reflected, but also one of terror and sudden death. Under the pavement beneath their feet stretched a warren of passageways, chambers and cells, the haunt of Constantine's deaf-mute torturers and executioners. Somewhere in the dark a horse whinnied, its hooves scraping the ground, accompanied by the creak of leather; torchlight flashed through the blackness. Some messenger, Claudia concluded, ready to take sealed pouches to a garrison or port or perhaps carry out the orders of the August Ones in the city. She and Murranus approached the gate, where a dark cluster of soldiers awaited them. Claudia undid the wallet on her belt and took out the small scroll carrying the powerful words, "The bearer of this enjoys the full favour of the Augusta . . ."

"Claudia?"

She whirled round. Presbyter Sylvester, garbed in a hooded cloak, slipped like a spectre towards them. In the pale light his face looked sepulchral.

"Valentinian," he murmured. "My apologies, I didn't wish to interrupt the Augusta when she was talking. I bring messages. First, Murranus, you will be excused from normal duties until this business is completed. Second . . ." Sylvester slipped back his hood and drew closer.

"You wanted to tell me something away from the Augusta's hearing?" Claudia teased. "About Valentinian?"

"He was a deacon of our Church," Sylvester replied, "but a strange man, surrounded by mystery."

"Do you have a description of him?"

"No. You see, Claudia, during the great persecution, the Christian community in Rome divided into units like the cohorts of a legion. It was important, indeed essential, that one group did not know anything about the next; such information could be extracted under torture. Now the persecution raged for over ten years. Christian communities flourished or died. People emerged as leaders, then disappeared. Valentinian was one of these. We do not know what he looked like or much about his background, except that his family came from Alexandria and his father was an architect. Valentinian proved to be a brilliant scholar, hence his appointment as deacon. Once the persecution ceased, some two years ago, we were able to carry out a census of the entire Christian community in Rome."

"And Valentinian?"

"We know that he and his community lived around Nero's gardens close to the Vatican Hill, but when the census was completed, it appeared that no one had survived." Sylvester cocked his head to one side, peering through the dark at Claudia.

"You find that strange?"

"Mysterious," Sylvester murmured. "Not one survived! As if the entire community had never existed; gone, Claudia, like a watch in the night, like snow beneath the sun." He stepped closer. "Yet stories, rumours and whispers persist how a spy betrayed them all, reduced that company of believers to nothing." Sylvester drew his cloak further about him. "Every one of the houses of those Christians was raided and stripped of all its possessions."

"Could Valentinian have been executed?"

"Many certainly were; just taken out and killed." Sylvester looked up at the sky.

"What are you fearful of, Presbyter?"

"For a community to be so betrayed, the names and places had to be revealed by someone in authority. Hence my suspicion that perhaps Valentinian, God forgive him, was the traitor."

CHAPTER
THREE

They were once human beings: tenants,
whilst they lived, of a mortal body.

Later that same evening, Julius Philippus and Petilius Gavinus slipped out of the Palatine Palace, informing Macrinus that they needed some refreshment. The tribune, lost in his own reverie, absentmindedly agreed. Both men were cloaked and hooded, short stabbing swords sheathed in their belts whilst they carried walking staves and sacks. Once outside the palace, they deliberately chose those streets still busy despite the late hour, the best way to hide from or shake off any pursuer. They entered the markets of the poor, where the sellers of beer and books, potions and perfume, figs and fish, savouries and salt still hoped to do business before the sun finally set. Grimy cookshops and shabby wine booths stood open for custom. Hawkers from Transtibernia offered sulphur matches. Sausage sellers and purveyors of dried fish bawled out prices as the steam billowed from their portable ovens to mix with other smells. Soon the curfew would be imposed. The sack-makers and other traders, the colourful shoal of people of every nationality would disappear down narrow, dark winding lanes and Rome would fall silent. At least in theory, for that would also be the hour for

Lord Charon's legions to emerge. Until then, the magicians in their booths offered spells against fever, red blotches and contagion as well as potions to stimulate conception or prevent hardening of the breasts or swelling of the testicles.

It was a stifling hot Roman evening, the air a fug of odours. Faces became sweat-laced, hands grew busy wafting away the flies and insects buzzing up from the mounds of filthy refuse lying about. *Vigiles* roamed, armed with their clubs. Slaves bound for the market, feet covered in white chalk dust to show they were new, hurried along in their chains. The gilded gleaming sedan chairs of the wealthy did battle with carts, packhorses and donkeys. Children shouted and screamed through windows. Dogs and cats fought over juicy morsels thrown out on to the street. An escaped monkey chattered on a sill. A group of gladiators with their painted, perfumed ladies joined in the shrieking and shouting to coax the animal down.

Gavinus and Philippus ignored all these. They crossed the Tiber by a narrow bridge; lights winked from boats, barges and punts beneath them. They were jostled and pushed, aware of a sea of faces in the light of crackling torches fastened to their iron clasps. The air stank of dried fish, wet wood and the pervasive odour from the ooze and mud of the river banks. On the other side of the bridge ranged more stalls. Gavinus and Philippus only paused at one to buy mallets and chisels, then hurried on towards the darkening slopes of the Vatican Hill. Here and there monuments reared up against the night sky: the beautiful obelisks Caligula

60

had brought from Egypt, the cornices of an old palace and the dark mass of various imperial buildings. The two *scrutores*, intent on their task, left the frenetic noise to slip down the narrow lanes leading into the Vatican cemetery, an unhealthy, bleak place, the breeding ground for snakes and other vermin as well as the supplier of the bitterest wine in Rome. The Vatican's only real asset was its clay for pottery as well as the gardens and plots former emperors had tried to develop. Gavinus and Philippus passed a temple shrine to two ancient fertility gods, moving on to the sombre slope of the Vatican Hill, which housed the ancient burial grounds of Rome. It was a stark contrast to the warm and colourful bustle of the city; a lonely, macabre spot with the branches of its cypress trees dark against the evening sky. A place of haunting silence broken only by the piercing shrieks of night birds and the heart-chilling scrabbling in the undergrowth. A repository of forgotten memories and dusty yesterdays, with its battered sepulchres and memorial tombs, the home of bat, fox and wild cat. The Vatican cemetery was also the meeting place for witches and warlocks, who lit their fires deep amongst the tangled undergrowth and made ghastly sacrifices to the spirits of the night.

Gavinus and Philippus, however, were old soldiers. They had fought on the burning sands of Numidia as well as the freezing, reed-fringed banks of the Rhine, and their only fear was of the living. Nevertheless, they were well armed, eager to discover not just the bones of some dead Jew, but a shrine that would bring them wealth and the favour of Caesar. They went deep into the cemetery, recalling the information they had memorised. At last they found the tomb they sought, near a clump of terebinth trees, a table-like monument to a long-dead tribune. Philippus put down the sack he carried, and brought out pitch torches and tinder. Sparks were struck and soon both cressets were blazing in the cool night air. Gavinus held these as Philippus pushed with all his might at the table-tomb top. The slab swung away easily. Gavinus felt a prick of suspicion and lowered his torch.

"The edges are clean and moss-free," he whispered. "Someone has been here recently."

"Perhaps a Christian prattler, one of their priests." Philippus grunted and climbed into the empty tomb, urging Gavinus to bring the torches closer. The bottom of the tomb was covered in dry bracken. Philippus pushed this aside, ignoring the pricks to his hands and arms, until he found the great iron ring in the wooden trap door in the far corner. He grunted, kicked away the rest of the bracken and pulled hard. Gavinus, leaning over the edge, once again grew cautious and wary. The trap door came up easily. He stared around; the darkness, now so deep, seemed to close in. Were there watchers amongst the terebinth trees? Did ghosts walk here? Was this a sacred site guarded by the lords of the air? He almost screamed as an owl, wings wafting, broke out of the darkness to glide like some spirit above him.

"I think we —"

"Come on!" Philippus mocked. "Are you a child to fear the things of the night?"

Gavinus climbed in. Philippus placed his torch in a small iron bracket in the inside wall of the tomb, and urged Gavinus to squat down with the other as he gripped the clasps fixed beneath the covering slab and moved it back into position. The space became hot and cramped. Philippus, followed by Gavinus, started down the narrow, steep steps revealed by the trap door. These had been hewn out of the rock and led down to a place which had nothing to do with Labienus' tomb. Even as they moved carefully from step to step, Gavinus and Philippus noticed the strange hieroglyphs on the wall, illuminated by the flames of their torches. At the bottom, hot and clammy, stretched a small cave-like chamber, its walls rocky and undressed; leading off from this were five tunnels about the height of a man.

"Which one?" Philippus growled.

"The two guardians standing on either side." Gavinus quoted the information they had learned. "The centre one!" They went down the tunnel, black as night. Here and there they glimpsed an old cresset torch pushed into a crevice. Some of these they lit to provide more light and comfort. Gavinus relaxed. He recalled what he and his comrades termed "the grand old days" when they pursued Christians through the catacombs like a pack of dogs would deer. Helpless men, women and children fleeing desperately, screaming in panic. Oh, Gavinus thought, the delight of the hunt, the glee of the pursuit, the satisfaction of the find! Women desperate with fear, ready to do anything.

Gold, silver and jewels waiting to be seized, bribes to be taken. Gavinus scratched at a bead of sweat. In truth the Christians had not concerned them; their altars and tombs did. Slabs to be smashed, plaster hacked from walls and the pathetic remains inside pulled out to be ground to dust and burnt. This, however, would be a different sort of hunt.

The tunnel was narrow, the ceiling barely above their heads. As they went deeper, Gavinus fought to control his excitement. This catacomb was special. Here and there the wall was smoothed and etched with crudely drawn figures, signs and symbols. Although they were difficult to make out in the poor light, Gavinus was certain they were Christian in origin.

"The Galilean must be buried here." Philippus paused to whisper excitedly. "These different tunnels are meant to confuse."

Gavinus swallowed hard. The air grew warmer, the darkness deeper. It would be so easy to become lost in a warren like this, never to escape. He was about to go forward when he noticed the twigs lying on the ground. Gavinus always prided himself on his sharp eyesight. He crouched down and picked them up; not twigs, but the desiccated stems of a bunch of grapes, dry and brittle but still recognisable. He twirled them in his fingers.

"Someone has been down here recently," he murmured, but Philippus was already marching off along the tunnel. Gavinus swore beneath his breath and followed. Philippus' shadow was dancing on the wall in front of him. Abruptly his companion stopped; Gavinus also. He felt a wet stickiness beneath his sandal and sniffed a familiar smell. Philippus was crouching down to examine the gleaming patch stretching in front of him, the torch he carried sparking. Gavinus realised abruptly what it was. He'd seen sappers use it to crack the foundations of a city wall.

"Oil!" he screamed, backing away.

Too late! Sparks from Philippus' torch floated down and the floor seemed to erupt into fire. Flames flicked around Philippus' feet. He screamed and dropped the torch. More flames leaped up, catching his sandals and cloak. He tried to beat out the fire, slipped and became a screaming human torch, legs and arms thrashing. He begged for help, but there was nothing Gavinus could do. He retreated back along the tunnel until, after what seemed an age, the screams subsided and the flames began to die. The air was red hot, reeking of burnt flesh; Philippus was reduced to nothing more than a blackened bundle.

Gavinus, fighting to control his panic, doused his own torch, then moved forward through the darkness, edging round the squalid mess with his back to the wall, using his feet to test the dryness of the ground. The foul smell stung his nose and throat. Skin slippery with sweat, he paused to control his stomach, to fight back the nausea. The blackness, the foul hot air closed in like a mist, but at last he was through. He rubbed his sandalled feet and crouched down; the ground was dry and hard. He stared back at the horror which had engulfed his companion. Small flames still flickered eerily. Gavinus opened his sack, found the tinder and carefully relit his torch. As he waited for the glow to grow stronger, he felt something slither across his foot. He carefully lowered the torch; the light glinted on the cold scales of rock vipers, attracted by the sudden heat, slithering out of their crevices. Gavinus panicked. He tried to retreat even as a viper struck, then another, their poison swiftly shooting up through his legs.

Claudia sat in Uncle Polybius' garden enjoying the morning coolness of what promised to be a beautiful autumn day. A faint mist still curled around the vines, the freshly dug oil press and, Uncle's pride and joy, the small orchard with Polybius' favourite tables, stools and benches, reserved for his very special guests. The grass of the well-kept lawn glistened wet in the strengthening light. Claudia watched the small drops of dew glitter then dry.

"You slept well, mistress?"

Claudia whirled round as Celades, Polybius' new cook, stepped out of the tavern kitchen. A Pict by birth, Celades looked like a warrior, with his dark skin, but as he often confessed, even when he held a club, he did more harm to himself than to anyone else. Now he was a freedman of Rome who had realised his lifelong ambition to be a chef, and had proved to be a very good one. He had shaved his head and beard and taken to working in Polybius' kitchen as if born to the position. As soon as he sat down on the bench next to Claudia, Caligula the tavern cat, a silent, deadly hunter, jumped on to his lap. Celades chattered to the animal, as he always did, in Pictish. Caligula gazed adoringly back at this constant provider of truly tasty titbits.

"You'll make him fat," Claudia offered Celades her beaker of crushed apple juice.

Celades shook his head and winked at her.

"He is still the terror of the vermin," he joked. "I feed him as a reward." He sighed. "As I did the rest last night. Oh yes," he continued, "Polybius and all his cronies: Torquatus the Tonsor, Petronius the Pimp, Simon the Stoic, Narcissus the Neat, Mercury the Messenger and, of course, Labienus." Celades nodded his head. "He's upstairs snoring like a toper. Gave them a banquet I did, fit for a Caesar. Hare in sweet sauce, ham in red wine and fennel, spicy lentils, Adriatic bread . . ."

"What were they talking about?" Claudia always kept a weather eye on Uncle, who lurched from one madcap scheme to another.

"Well," Celades took the beaker from her and drank noisily before handing it back, "plays! They talked of putting on a play here, perhaps a comedy by Plautus or one of Terence's or even a Greek —"

"And?"

"I don't know," Celades murmured. "Torquatus demanded a farce but one with a mystery which the audience could not solve. If they could, Torquatus wagered Polybius that he would provide everyone with a free meal and a hundred gold solidi for himself."

"Oh no!" Claudia groaned.

"Oh yes!" Celades whispered. "Both Polybius and Labienus accepted the wager. Labienus will write the play; Polybius even offered your help with the mystery."

"Oh no!"

"And then the farce deepened," Celades continued. "Labienus' troop arrived dressed in their stage costumes. I don't know their names, anyway they all became drunk and grew over excited about the play. A quarrel broke out over what should be done. The Skeleton attacked the Ape, the Ghost tried to seduce Januaria . . ."

Claudia closed her eyes. Januaria the tavern wench, with her flirting eyes!

". . . Oceanus," Celades continued drily, "lost his ear. You know the one bitten off in a fight . . ."

"Which he dried, pickled and wears around his neck." Claudia finished the sentence.

"Yes, but then he found it," Celades grinned, "and began to throw people out. Simon the Stoic was so drunk he had to pay Sorry —"

As if in a play, the rear door to the She-Asses was thrown open, and Sorry the kitchen boy stumbled out yawning and rubbing his eyes.

"Sorry," he mumbled, his constant excuse which had given him his nickname. He picked up some reed baskets, still muttering apologies, and staggered half asleep back into the kitchen.

"Well, you know what it's like," Celades continued. "Simon paid Sorry to throw stones at him, to encourage him to go home."

"And he did? So was it one excitement after another."

"Precisely." Celades rose to his feet. "What a night, mistress!" He gestured round. "Oceanus must have worked very hard to clear up the mess, here and inside. Now, may I tempt you? Carthaginian porridge with some rose honey mixed in?"

Claudia laughed and shook her head. Celades, carrying Caligula, wandered back into the tavern. A short while later, Murranus appeared, a piece of dried meat in one hand, a cup of watered wine in the other. He ate and drank quickly, apologising for oversleeping, which explained why he hadn't shaved. Claudia made him sit down, kissed him on the mouth and brow, then hurried away. She found a heavy-eyed, lurching Oceanus, scratching his balding pate and fingering his pickled ear, and asked him to bring Murranus' club and sword; even in the early hours of the morning the streets of Rome could prove dangerous.

Claudia and Murranus left the tavern and made their way down to the small dusty square where, as usual, Torquatus the Tonsor was setting up his barber shop under the spreading branches of a towering sycamore. He shouted his greetings then pointed to the nearby fountain, which was really nothing more than a high cracked bowl with an equally crumbling carved dolphin from which the water sluggishly poured, the bribe of some long-dead politician to buy the votes of the local citizens. A small crowd had gathered round, watching the two *vigiles*, Achilleos and Nereos, drag out the soaked corpse of a beggar who, during the night, had become drunk, fallen in and drowned. The *vigiles* lifted the cadaver on to the cobbles, loudly declaring that they had done their job, as the removal of a dead body was not their responsibility. Claudia vaguely recognised the pair. They were new to the quarter, and she recalled that they had also discovered the corpse of one of the recent victims of the Nefandus. Grabbing Murranus by the arm, she walked quickly to intercept them. They were shaking water off their hands, eager to make their way across to an itinerant cook who had set up a small stove. He was already laying out a string of sausages bought from a nearby butcher's stall, calling out that the meat was fresh and nicely spiced.

"Gentlemen, you are the *vigiles*?"

Both men turned. Achilleos was the younger. He was dark-featured with a squashed nose and thick lips, his ugly face unshaven; his greying hair was cropped close above ears which jutted out like jug handles. He spread his hands mockingly.

"No we're not!" he jibed. "We wear leather kilts, marching boots and sword-belts across our chests because we like trudging these filthy streets at whatever hellish hour our captain tells us . . ." He paused as Murranus stepped threateningly forward.

"Ah, I know who you are." Nereos intervened tactfully. "You're Polybius' niece from the She-Asses, and you, sir, must be Murranus, who won the crown of victory so many times in the arena." He extended his hand. Murranus clasped it and pointed to the beggar's corpse now sprawled in a pool of dirty water.

"A common occurrence." Nereos shrugged.

"Death certainly is around here," added Achilleos, chewing on the corner of his lip.

"Especially amongst prostitutes," Claudia added, "the Daughters of Isis. I understand you found a corpse?"

"Fausta." Achilleos blew his lips out. "A horrid sight, mistress, all bloody like a sheep on a butcher's stall, and that empty eye socket . . ."

"I need to question you about that. I am meeting Tribune Macrinus. You've heard of him?"

Nereos nodded. "Of course. He was once in charge of this quarter, wasn't he? Even our captain talks respectfully about him."

Claudia forced a smile and stared across at the beggar's corpse. The captain of the *vigiles* was one of Uncle's drinking cronies, a bald-headed tub of lard who took to bribery as a swallow to flying. Claudia peered up at the strengthening sun.

"We are to visit the barracks around the third hour, so you'd best come now." Claudia strolled on, leaving the *vigiles*, with the brooding presence of Murranus, no choice but to follow.

Claudia recalled how the *vigiles*' barracks lay on the other side of the quarter, a small castle-like structure similar to the forts along the great highways of Italy. She walked quickly. The streets were now growing busy, and she always liked to study the scenes and note faces. She often wondered if Helena dispatched other spies to watch her, and if not the Augusta, what about Presbyter Sylvester, whose word was law to many along these narrow, busy streets. Were any of these people spies paid to sit, watch and report? That wandering schoolmaster squatting on a plinth next to the battered shrine to Apollo of the Clouds? The base of the statue was covered in rotting flowers which the schoolmaster was busy sifting amongst. Then there was the hawker perched on a stool before the stone counter of that narrow wine bar which seemed to have been thrust between the two houses built on either side. Claudia blinked. Anyone and everyone could be both spy and trader.

Business was certainly growing brisk. The shaving booths were well attended, the barbers and their assistants dancing around customers with combs, razors, hot irons and bowls of scented water. Those who waited to be curled and shaved, drank and ate at the small wine and beer stalls set up by members of the barbers' families. Dogs and cats slunk in to hunt for scraps and occasionally clashed in hideous screeches and barks. The air was rich with many tangs and odours. The aroma from bakeries mixed with the stench of rancid bran strewn along the streets to disguise the odours from the slop pots and other messes. Claudia sniffed the bouquet of wine vintners, the sauces from the spicy fish stalls as well as the smell from the vats of urine used by the fullers in their stinking shops and mills. The crumbling pillars of the battered porticoes either side of the street were festooned with symbols of various trades: embroiderers, coppersmiths, knife-makers, potters and poulterers. Alongside these notices were posted of impending elections and crude street graffiti.

Claudia felt a sheen of sweat as she pushed her way through the throng. She glanced up at the house before her and recoiled at the sight of a witch standing at a window. The woman had thrust her head out, hair dyed orange, face covered in white paste. She wore a black cloth around her neck and clutched a small doll. Claudia felt sure she was searching the crowd for a victim. She broke from her reverie to stand quickly aside for a funeral procession. Musicians, professional wailers and mourners preceded the bier, the aged cadaver sitting up amongst the cushions. This was followed by the family, most of them still deeply inebriated from the funeral meal the night before. A young boy grabbed Claudia's hand and pointed to his father's stall, where lettuce, artichokes, peas, lentils and cabbages nestled invitingly in a bed of straw. She shook her head and smiled. Nereos and Achilleos had now drawn their clubs and went before them. They showed deference only to the occasional sedan chair or the groups of freshly bathed and coiffured clients nervously making their way up to their powerful patrons' houses near the Palatine; these professional beggars gabbled like a gaggle of geese about catching the eye of the nomenclator, who would decide whom their patron would favour that day.

At last they broke free from the tangled streets and crossed a stretch of wasteland. They passed the crumbling, blackened shell of an *insula* burnt down by arsonists. Three of these had been captured and crucified, beneath a sign proclaiming their crime, to some of the charred beams. Claudia quickly glanced away. The corpses were rotting, ravaged by a horde of black kites. Wild dogs and cats also circled, jumping over the mounds of rubble, drawn in by the stink of corruption. The remains of the crucified were too high to reach, so the scavengers waited for pieces to drop to the ground. Some of these dogs turned on the group as they passed, but when Murranus drew his sword and club, they slunk away.

At last they cleared the ruins, going down a narrow paved street which led under a yawning gatehouse into the cobbled yard of the barracks. It was already busy, thronged with soldiers, *vigiles* and servants. Carts rumbled backwards and forwards, dropping off supplies. Donkeys brayed, dogs yapped. A loud-mouthed groom shouted for space as he led out a string of horses to be trotted and exercised. In the shady peristyle on all three sides, clerks and scribblers squatted over their writing trays. Off-duty *vigiles* diced, gossiped or slept in whatever shade they could find. Murranus was soon recognised amongst these fighting men, former soldiers and self-appointed aficionados of the arena. Shouted greetings echoed across, and Murranus held his hand up in reply as Claudia, who disliked any encouragement for the amphitheatre, pushed her beloved up some steps into the captain's office.

It was a sparse, shabby room, many of its narrow windows still shuttered, the potted plants beneath them long faded. Pegs driven through walls were draped with dusty cloths, scraps of armour and harness. Dried onions hung from a beam and the small table just within the doorway was littered with bits of food and wine-encrusted goblets. In a corner stood a bed covered with a multicoloured damask quilt; a mat, similarly hued, was unrolled on the floor beside it, the only luxury the room could boast. Macrinus and the captain were sharing a crater of wine on stools behind a high desk littered with dusty documents. Both turned as Claudia and her escort entered. The captain roared at a slave clutching a broom of tamarisk twigs just within the doorway to bring up the bench then get out. Once this had been moved, with a little help from Claudia and Murranus, they sat down, Achilleos and Nereos standing behind them. Claudia suspected the captain used the bench for interrogation; it was splattered with bloodstains, whilst she'd glimpsed similar marks on the floor. Macrinus rose stiffly to attention and bowed before retaking his seat. The captain, however, eyes almost hidden in the greasy folds of his fat face, just grimaced in a show of yellowing teeth.

"I'm sorry," Macrinus rubbed his eyes, "but I've slept only a little. Gavinus and Philippus have disappeared."

"What do you mean?" Claudia asked.

"They went out last night and have not returned. They were glimpsed by *agentes* going down the Palatine and crossing the Tiber towards the Vatican Hill; after that, they simply vanished. The August Ones will want to know," Macrinus added pointedly, "but," he straightened up, "you're here about Attius Enobarbus?"

"Could he have been the Nefandus?" Claudia asked.

"Before my time," the captain slurred.

"No it wasn't!" Macrinus intervened. "You were a decurion, I was your commanding officer."

"All I am saying is that I wasn't in charge!" the captain snapped.

"No, you certainly weren't!" Macrinus leaned across the table. "Claudia, to answer your question bluntly. The battle of the Milvian Bridge took place over two years ago. For years previous to this a killer terrorised the alleyways of the Caelian quarter. We knew little about him except that his shadowy figure was occasionally glimpsed, dressed in the helmet and cloak of a Praetorian; that means he must have been an officer."

"The Praetorians supported Maxentius against Constantine, yes?" Murranus asked.

"Fiercely so. As you know, after Constantine's victory, they were disbanded for good."

"Was Attius a member?" Claudia asked.

"Of course, and so were the others. They may have served in the XXth Victrix but they were given honorary posts in the guards."

"What made you think Attius might have been the Nefandus?"

"He was violent. He could be cruel with the whores." Macrinus paused, wetting his lips. "He was known to use a knife or a whip. He liked to get his pleasure from listening to them cry and squeal."

"But you found no proof," Claudia asked, tapping the table, "to link him with those horrid deaths?"

"None whatsoever. You see, mistress, we had to be very careful. We knew that Attius was used by Maxentius for other work, secret work against the Christians, so it was a matter of diplomatic enquiries and tactful questions. Now and again I had him followed, but never once did we gather one scrap of evidence," he snapped his fingers, "to arrest him."

"Then the civil war broke out."

"And the killings abruptly stopped," Macrinus confirmed. "But by then Rome had changed, and so had my life. My wife was dead. A new master ruled Rome. I offered my resignation; it was reluctantly accepted. I retired to my house. I have a garden, a few books, some wine." He waved a hand.

Claudia turned to the captain. "Then the killings began again?"

"Twice," the captain replied, eager to exercise his authority. "A whore was killed at the beginning of September; another three nights ago. We've searched the Caelian quarter, we've bribed people, hired spies and informers, but never once did we even catch a glimpse of the killer."

"It's possible," Macrinus spoke up, "that Attius was the original Nefandus. He was protected by the Emperor, he could go where he wanted, do what he wanted. Then the civil war came, Maxentius was killed at the Milvian Bridge, Constantine swept into Rome and Attius realised he had to be very careful. I was brought out of retirement to act as the *custos*, the military adviser on the expedition to Byzantium. Never once did I see Attius do anything which would betray him as a killer."

"And the last slaying?" Claudia asked.

"The same day Attius was murdered," Macrinus declared. "Or so I gather." He pulled a face. "In a way, Attius' death proves he wasn't the Nefandus."

"It could have been another member of his group."

Macrinus shook his head. "Claudia, I watched them closely. I found no evidence for that. Moreover, they were all, Attius included, absent from Rome when the first woman was killed."

"It could be someone else imitating the former Nefandus."

"Perhaps."

"And you?" Claudia pointed at Nereos and Achilleos, now sitting on camp stools to her left. "You must have seen the first corpse."

"A Daughter of Isis," Nereos replied. "Cut from crotch to throat, her right eye missing."

"We gave her body back to her sisters," Achilleos declared. "They cremated it and the ashes were buried."

"And the second girl?"

"Fausta, also a Daughter of Isis." Nereos spoke up. "We found her corpse, but uncovered no clue to the murderer except the sighting by some beggar of an officer of the Praetorians dressed in helmet and cloak."

"But they've been disbanded."

"Mistress," Nereos replied, "Achilleos and I fought for Constantine at the Milvian Bridge. We killed

78

Praetorians. The Emperor promised that their like would never be seen again. This one certainly has."

"And Fausta's corpse?"

"Handed over to the Daughters of Isis. I believe her funeral may be later today or tomorrow morning."

"And these?" Claudia pointed to the manuscripts piled high upon the table.

"Reports," Macrinus replied, "the legacy of my failure."

"I would certainly like to read them."

Macrinus and the captain looked at each other, shrugged, rose and, followed by Nereos and Achilleos, left the room.

CHAPTER
FOUR

Then it may be truly said: the earth shed tears and the all-encircling heavens mourned because of the pollution by blood.

Murranus immediately declared he was still tired, then went across to the bed, threw himself down and promptly fell asleep. Claudia raised her eyes heavenwards, closed her ears to his snores and the sounds from outside, then pulled across the dirt-edged scrolls, unrolled them and began to read the reports. They were written in slang Latin by some scribbler or clerk. There were gaps in the accounts, particularly when the armies were gathered around Rome, and often the entries were hastily written; nevertheless, Claudia experienced a chill of deep apprehension as she read the details supplied by *vigiles* and the occasional report from Macrinus. Horrid murders, one after another, in the Caelian quarter and sometimes beyond. The victims were usually prostitutes; a few maid-servants or young women wandering where they shouldn't have been. All had been killed in a barbarous way. Bodies ripped open, right eyes gouged out. According to the reports, Claudia calculated that at least twenty-four young women had been murdered. She sat back. Now she remembered! After the attack on herself and Felix, Uncle Polybius had referred to other macabre killings,

80

but that had been during the days of the civil war when her world and that of the city had been overtaken by violent events.

As Claudia re-read the reports, she was surprised at what she learnt about Macrinus. He was no longer the tired, cynical official. Despite the illness of his wife, mentioned occasionally, he emerged as an energetic investigator who seemed to have spent every waking hour hunting the Nefandus, the title he himself had given to the killer. Despite all the chaos in the city, he had done his very best to pursue that barbaric slayer.

Claudia also learnt something else. This had not been simply the pursuit of a murderer, but a violent vendetta between Macrinus and the Nefandus. Small items, scraps of gossip indicated that. If Macrinus was hunting the Nefandus, the murderer was also hunting Macrinus, and openly baited the tribune with his failure to trap him. Certain sentences and lines mentioned *contumelia* and *irrisus* — taunts and mockery. She picked up one scroll and re-read the entry most carefully; there were references to such messages scrawled on walls even here at the barracks. Claudia clicked her tongue. Only an arrogant man would do that, someone confident of escaping. Attius? Yet Macrinus had made it very clear that while Attius may have been a brute, he was not a killer. Then there were the other slayings which had taken place this month. Attius had either been away from Rome or locked in his secure chamber, whilst the second murder had taken place on the very day he died. Claudia put the report down. There was another mystery: Macrinus had been a loyal, industrious, energetic official. He had spent years pursuing a killer, yet when the Nefandus ceased his depredations, Macrinus stopped his hunt, betraying no urge or willingness to pursue the matter any further.

Claudia rose, pushed away the scroll and walked across to Murranus. She leaned down and kissed him full on the mouth.

"Come, my beloved." She shook him. "Time to get up! A day's work still lies before us."

Murranus opened his eyes, groaned, rubbed his face and lifted himself up from the bed.

"There is something very wrong here." He put an arm around Claudia's waist and pulled her close.

"What?" Claudia teased. "You're hungry? You wish to go back and join that rabble at the She-Asses?"

"No." Murranus, much to Claudia's disappointment, took away his arm and sat on the end of the bed.

Claudia watched him closely. Her beloved liked to act as if he was all brawn and no brain. Claudia knew different. Murranus was a skilled, vicious fighter who owed his victories, his very survival, to his quick wits and nimble brain. She crouched down. "What's wrong?" She tapped him on the knee.

"Oh, the Nefandus! Why would a Praetorian guard go walking in the slums in dress armour? Was he killed in the civil war or did he just go into hiding? How many killers are there? And why was Attius chosen as the main suspect?"

"Stop!" Claudia rose to her feet and went back to the scrolls. She searched feverishly, then looked up and smiled. "Oh my great philosopher, I missed that." She picked up a scroll and let it drop. "Attius is hardly mentioned here." She came back. "And what else?"

"Why were Attius and his companions given a pardon, while others were disgraced, banished from the city."

"And?"

"Why were they sent to Byzantium on a surveying expedition? It is a common enough task; other engineers and architects in the city could have been used. Why them?"

"And?"

"Why send a military adviser like Macrinus? Was he their keeper, Helena's spy or their jailer? And there is something else." Murranus raised a hand and squeezed Claudia's wrist. "Presbyter Sylvester and Helena." He lifted a hand, two fingers locked together. "They are one, they pursue the same vision, yet a real difference has arisen between them."

"Over what?"

"The tomb of the Galilean Peter, I think, but there again . . ." he got to his feet, "I am supposed to guard doorways, not listen at them. It's just a suspicion. Strange." Murranus walked across to the window and stared out. "I know a little about the Christians. Once a hunted sect, they lived underground in the dark, yet now they enjoy the light of imperial favour. Already, Claudia," he glanced over his shoulder, "they have become very powerful. They've been given gold, temples as churches, land in the city, clerks and servants. Sylvester now needs a bodyguard, and other

Christian officials are demanding the same. If matters continue, the imperial court and the Christian Church will become one; it will be hard to distinguish between the two. Intrigue will flourish, life will become very complicated." He came back, walking slowly, placing one foot in front of the other as if measuring the distance between himself and Claudia. "Do you ever think," he peered down at her, "we should leave all this, Claudia?"

"Why?" Claudia felt her stomach pitch. Was Murranus becoming restless? Was he thinking of returning to the arena?

"No, I'm not." He smiled as if reading her mind. "I have no desire to go back. Moreover," he rubbed his stomach and stretched his arm, "I'm getting fatter and slower, but above all, I'm getting older. No matter how good I am, how much I dance, one day I'll meet someone faster, more deadly, and the crowd?" He pulled a face. "Fickle as moonshine; they'd demand my death as quickly as they used to shout my name."

"So what should we do?" Claudia went over and grasped his hands. "Become farmers, Murranus, or open a tavern like Uncle Polybius?"

"If you worry about me," Murranus kissed her gently on the brow, "I worry about you! We scurry along dirty streets. We investigate and probe the dark things of life."

Claudia squeezed his hands.

"Everybody, Murranus," she smiled up at him, "must have an obsession. Polybius' is the She-Asses and whatever featherbrain scheme comes his way. Celades' is cooking. Helena and Constantine dream dreams of empire, as does Presbyter Sylvester . . ."

"And you, Claudia?"

"You touched on it, Murranus: the dark things of life. I'm not a Christian, unlike my father and mother. I look around and see the cruelty and the devastation: those corpses nailed to the ruins, the Nefandus prowling the streets of the Caelian quarter. I find it difficult to believe a loving God is interested in each one of us, but I do believe this, Murranus: there are the dark things of life and there are those of the light. One day," she smiled, "perhaps sooner rather than later, we'll become farmers or own a tavern, but until then, I have a choice: to broaden the light or deepen the darkness. I'm not too sure what happened to the Nefandus; however, I too suffered an attack similar to those poor women. For them, justice must be done and seen to be done. Until I lose the appetite for that, then yes, we'll delve into the dark things, and in doing so, spread the light a little further. Now, my philosopher," she tugged at his hand, "let's talk to Macrinus."

Murranus left, and came back with Macrinus trailing dolefully behind him. The captain was eager to join them but Claudia made it very clear that she only wanted to ask Macrinus a few questions, then they would leave. The captain nodded, face all surly, and swaggered out. Macrinus eased himself down on the stool behind the desk; Claudia sat on the other, whilst Murranus lounged on the bench. Claudia studied the tribune's face: kind, she thought, though the expressive eyes were tired. She noticed the furrows down his cheeks and around his mouth; his skin was rather pale except for the reddish scar.

"Any news of Gavinus and Philippus?"

Macrinus shook his head. "I told the other two," he growled, "to send a messenger here if they returned."

"Tribune Macrinus," Claudia leaned forward, "I like you."

He half smiled.

"No, I do. You strike me as a brave soldier, a good investigator, an able administrator, a man committed to justice. I doubt if you ever took a bribe or bullied or oppressed anyone." She pointed to the bench and the floor. "I've seen the bloodstains. I don't think that was your work."

Macrinus just gazed steadily back.

"I think you've told the truth. You try and walk in the way of truth. So let's begin again. You are a former soldier?"

"I was a leading centurion in the Xth Gemma, later promoted to tribune. I received many military crowns and I was honourably discharged. Even though my wife was a Christian, the Emperor appointed me as Tribune of the Vigiles in the Caelian quarter. His ministers gave me a salary as well as a pension. They asked me to impose order, so I did. If you ask your uncle . . . true, it was a little before his time, but I was feared by those who preyed on others. I enforced the law. I kept the peace. If I promised something, I carried it out."

"Until the Nefandus emerged. You truly hated him, didn't you?" Claudia asked. "Why?"

Macrinus glanced away.

"Why, Tribune?"

"Oh, it wasn't just the cruelty, the barbarism, the slaying of innocent young women; he enjoyed it! He knew I was hunting him — I'm sure you've discovered this — and he began to taunt me. Messages were left scrawled on walls as if he and I were playing some childish game of hide-and-seek. Now and again he had the impunity to send a message here, neatly written out on a piece of parchment as if it was a shopping list."

"And these messages?"

"I got rid of them. You can imagine. Some I destroyed immediately; others I kept but later burnt."

"And what did they say?"

"Oh, the usual! How incompetent I was for stumbling about in the dark."

Claudia gestured at the pile of manuscripts.

"So you were unable to catch him?"

"Apparently."

"You had suspicions, but you collected no evidence against anyone?"

"I have already answered that: none whatsoever."

"So why did Attius become a suspect?"

"I have also answered that: because of his reputation."

Claudia gently pushed the pile of manuscripts towards Macrinus.

"You're a good soldier, a competent official. You pursued this killer with a vengeance. He baited you, and despite your wife being ill, you spent every waking hour trying to track him down."

Macrinus nodded in agreement.

"The civil war breaks out, the killings stop, you retire. Weren't you curious about who this murderer was? Why didn't you still pursue him?"

"I've told you. My wife had died. The situation in Rome had changed. Above all, the killings had stopped."

"Yet you accepted the commission to leave Rome and accompany Attius and the rest to Byzantium."

Macrinus pulled a face. "You get bored sitting under your vine tree, tending your flower beds, drinking wine, visiting old friends. It was only a short journey. I've served in Greece and elsewhere. It's good to travel again. It's interesting."

"What was wrong with your wife?" Murranus asked.

Macrinus patted his stomach. "Some growth deep inside her; she took a long time to die."

"Why did you accept the commission to travel with Attius?"

"As I said, times have changed. It was good to travel and be paid for it."

Claudia shook her head. "I find your answer difficult to accept."

"I'm afraid, mistress, that is the only answer you'll get."

Claudia stared down at the floor. She was certain Macrinus was not lying but, like a typical old soldier, only telling her what he had to, what he felt would satisfy her.

"Do you know, Macrinus," Claudia scratched the back of her ear, "I think you accepted this commission because you hated Attius. You suspected he was the

Nefandus. You thought if you travelled with him perhaps you could study him closer, discover a little more."

Macrinus gave a lopsided smile. "The thought did cross my mind."

"Tell me," Claudia leaned her face against her hand, "you hunted the Nefandus for almost four years. Did you ever wonder why he killed like he did?"

Macrinus chewed the corner of his lip. He stared up at the rafters, then across at the window. "I'm a soldier. I have served in the legions. I have fought in battles. I have taken towns. Your friend," he gestured at Murranus, "will tell you the same. I killed because I had to. I killed to defend myself or to carry out orders. Where possible, if an enemy surrendered and threw down his weapon, that was the end. I can honestly swear to any gods you name that never once in my career did I kill a woman or a child. However, and Murranus would agree, there are other men who just love killing. They join the legions or enter the amphitheatre solely for that, for no other reason except the pleasure of killing another human being. I have served with such men, I've even promoted them. They were brave, they were ruthless, but it was the killing they lived for. They reminded me of animals, like a hungry wolf or a tiger in the arena. They had no choice in the matter, they had to kill."

"But young whores in the back streets of Rome?"

"I've met soldiers who openly boast they cannot have sexual pleasure unless they take a woman by force, and after they've finished, they will despise her, and abuse her. The Nefandus was much more dangerous; he wanted to kill and humiliate them."

Claudia hid a tingle of excitement. Macrinus was drawling, trying to speak slowly, but watching his eyes, she could see the interest there, the excitement he had experienced in pursuing the Nefandus, in getting to know more about this barbaric killer. "And the cut," she asked, "from crotch to throat?"

"I did wonder. Could he have been a butcher? After all, that's how they carve the carcass of an animal. I've also seen soldiers do that to enemy women. A deep slash here," he gestured with his hands, "in the soft part of the belly, and up. No one ever survives such a cut. It disfigures the body and humiliates the dead."

"And the right eye?"

Macrinus picked up the wine bowl from the desk and tipped the dregs into his mouth. "I can only speak about my own experiences."

"Then speak!"

"I've been a soldier for decades. I've served with men who took offence just at the way someone looked at them. You take our captain; he is a good enough fellow, but the gods help anybody he dislikes. A subordinate who speaks to him in a fashion he deems unacceptable. If he can, our captain will think of some way of retaliating."

"And the Nefandus?"

"I suspect he didn't like the way women looked at him, their alluring glances and coy expressions. He wanted to stop that, destroy it."

Claudia half listened to the sounds from outside, the neigh of a horse, the shout of a man, the clink of pots and pans.

"You hunted the Nefandus for years?"

"Yes."

"You used your men, spies and informants, whilst the ladies of the night would be only too willing to supply any details they thought might help you in your hunt?"

"Of course."

"And yet you never caught him?"

"Apparently not."

"You must have planned and plotted, prepared ambushes, traps?"

Macrinus nodded. "Of course," he murmured again.

"Yet never once did you even catch sight of this killer."

"I've told you that."

"So, did you begin to suspect that the Nefandus might either be someone very powerful or, perhaps, someone who worked with you, a member of the *vigiles*?"

Macrinus blinked and glanced away, but Claudia glimpsed it, just a look, a brief shift in the eyes. Macrinus certainly knew more than he was conceding.

"With whom did you discuss your hunt?" Claudia insisted.

Macrinus took a deep breath. "I'd go home at night and discuss it with my wife. Although she was ill, she was very interested in my work, horrified at the reports she heard. That's the way we were." He smiled. "A happy couple. Whatever happened, I always told her. She gave me good advice."

"And who else?" insisted Claudia, refusing to be distracted.

"Well, there is the present captain." Macrinus put his goblet down. "He was a decurion then, my lieutenant. I needed to consult with him; he had to know what happened."

"And . . ." Claudia gestured at the manuscripts. "Some reports are missing?"

"Yes, they are," Macrinus answered quickly. "I had to report to Attius Enobarbus." He spread his hands. "You see, Attius was a Praetorian. He had the ear of the Prefect of Praetorians as well as the Emperor. He would often come down to the barracks and, as he put it, discuss my work. He'd insist on reading reports and finding out how I was progressing."

"He could do that?"

"He was favoured by the Emperor, Claudia; he could do whatever he wanted. He was my superior. Moreover, he often frequented the Daughters of Isis. It was easy for him to say he had a special interest in them."

"Even though he abused them?"

"No one complained. Attius was a man who paid for his pleasures. He may have abused the girls, but he also rewarded them." He smiled thinly. "Don't forget, certain ladies of the night specialise in such matters; a few knocks and bruises, what do they care? If it's a gold piece, perhaps a little gift, as well as the favour of a man like Attius . . ."

"Ah . . ." Claudia rose to her feet and stretched. She pulled the leather belt around her waist tighter. "I can see why Attius became your leading suspect. On your journey to Byzantium you studied him closely?"

"Of course, but I discovered nothing untoward. He was surly, withdrawn, regretting what he called 'the good old days', he and the rest. I didn't like them and they didn't like me. Now and again I would join them for a meal, but in the main I left them alone. We journeyed overland, stopped at hostelries, taverns and inns. On one occasion we slept out in the open. I could use imperial warrants to requisition food, horses and supplies. It was very much like a military expedition. I carried out my orders."

"What were those orders, Tribune?"

"If you want the answer to that it's best if you ask the Augusta."

"I will, but why can't you answer? Were you there as their keeper, their guardian? Were you given orders about what to do if one tried to escape?"

"They weren't prisoners."

"To my mind they certainly were. Look how agitated you are about Gavinus and Philippus' disappearance."

Macrinus drew a deep breath as if he was about to speak. Then he closed his mouth and rubbed his face with his hands.

"I was given very clear instructions," he muttered at last. "I was to guard them, protect them and keep an eye on them."

"And if one tried to escape?" Murranus asked.

"Why should they do that? Where could they go?"

"Answer my question," Murranus insisted. "If one tried to escape?"

"I was to arrest him and send him immediately back to Rome."

"And those same rules," Claudia asked, "apply now? They were confined to barracks?"

"Yes, you could describe it so. I understand my orders," Macrinus continued. "After all, they were Praetorians, supporters of Maxentius, so why should Constantine trust them?"

"But he did," Claudia replied. "He sent them on a special expedition to Byzantium. Why?"

Macrinus just shrugged, becoming more interested in the empty wine bowl.

Claudia realised he had told them everything he would for the moment; they could take the matter no further. She thanked him, patted him gently on the shoulder, and then unleashed the questions she'd kept hidden like arrows in their quiver.

"Macrinus?"

He glanced up wearily.

"The Nefandus' victims were Daughters of Isis, a guild of prostitutes?"

"That's right," he agreed. "They have a house, two or three storeys in an *insula* on the corner of Janus Street."

"And in a period of four years," Claudia declared, "they lost perhaps twenty-four women?"

"I would say between twenty-five and thirty. I am not too sure." Macrinus replied. "However, before you ask, Claudia, remember that for many poor girls there is only one way of advancement. The Guild of Isis is popular. The Domina looks after her girls, or at least tries to. She protects them, hires a physician for their ailments, so there is always a queue of young ladies eager to take up the call of the night."

"Even when those same girls are being barbarously murdered?" asked Murranus.

"You of all people should know! How many men wish to be gladiators? Yet how many men survive their first fight? How many last longer than a year? This is Rome," Macrinus' voice turned bitter, "life is cheap. People value a donkey more than a young girl or a young man."

"And my next question."

"I thought you were leaving?"

"All these victims were, in the main," Claudia said evenly, "Daughters of Isis; others were young women in the wrong place at the wrong time. Could you tell if their attacker had intercourse with them?"

"On a number of occasions a physician was called, and dried semen was noticed on their thighs and between their legs."

"So these girls," Claudia continued, crouching down to face the tribune, "must have agreed to take custom, even though they knew a killer was stalking the alleyways?"

"A gold or silver coin can soon dispel any sense of danger," Macrinus declared.

"But still," Claudia persisted, "what I'm saying is that their attacker must have been someone they trusted; despite the lure of gold or silver they felt it was safe to be with that man. You must have thought that yourself. It's not unknown for prostitutes to refuse custom if they feel danger or sense a threat."

"I did consider that," Macrinus agreed. "Possibly one of us, a soldier, someone they knew, a priest? A visitor to their house on the corner of Janus Street? I don't know, but yes, someone they trusted."

"And this description of a Praetorian officer, did that come early in the investigation or later?"

"I don't know." Macrinus replied. "One of those rumours which floated along the alleyways like a breeze; the last time one of the girls had been seen she'd been with such a man."

"But you found no hard evidence? I saw nothing in the reports."

"True, true."

"So it could have been just a rumour?"

"Possibly."

"One final question . . ." Claudia paused. "The killer always gouged out the woman's right eye; was that left with the corpse or taken?"

"Oh, always taken . . ."

The House of Isis stood on the corner of Janus Street. It looked well tended, the brickwork clean, the wood freshly painted. On either side of the great oaken door with its copper studs were vivid pictures of Isis receiving the semen of Horus into her hands. Above the door gleamed the Wadjet, the Ever-Seeing Eye, to ward off danger and evil spirits. Four burly oafs dressed in the colours of the guild, green, gold, scarlet and blue, and armed with wicked-looking clubs provided more practical protection. These immediately recognised Murranus and ushered him forward as if he was Horus Incarnate. He and Claudia entered a world of ostentatious luxury. The outer vestibule was decorated with paintings in eye-catching shades of gold, ochre, green and blue describing the virtues and strengths of Isis. To the right of this room stood a small altar carved in the form of an Egyptian temple; above it was a statue of a serenely smiling Isis completely naked, her hands extended in welcome. Around the base of the statue were strewn sprigs of fresh flowers, herbs, pieces of fruit and bowls of fragrant smoking incense as well as a row of different-coloured alabaster oil jars, their dancing flames creating a shimmer of light. The floor was tiled in red and white with small designs placed within these. Only when she looked more carefully did Claudia realise that these depicted an exotic variety of sexual positions and poses.

The black lattice screen at the far end of the room was quietly slid back. Three more oafs appeared escorting a young lady. She was overdressed in white linen robes, silver-edged reed sandals on her feet, a scarlet band wrapped tightly around her chest, her painted face framed by an old-fashioned veil edged with red stitching. She moved so serenely she reminded Claudia of a priestess. She bowed low, the bracelets and coloured chains around her wrists jingling noisily, the rings on her fingers reflecting the light.

"Claudia, Murranus," her voice was almost a whisper, "my name is Silvana. I welcome you. The Domina waits."

CHAPTER
FIVE

Such was the conduct displayed by this woman.

They went deeper into the house, Silvana in front of them, the oafs trailing behind. According to a proclamation above the doorway, they were entering "The Arbour of Love", its walls decorated with erotic pictures extolling the love life of Isis and her help in Horus' eternal war against Seth the Destroyer. On either side of the passageway stood narrow cedarwood doors which Claudia reckoned led into private chambers. At the end of the passageway they crossed a richly caparisoned *triclinium* furnished with gleaming tables and luxurious couches. Scented oil lamps glowed everywhere, and the air was sweet with the fragrance of a summer garden. Hanging ornaments tinkled softly; somewhere a lyre and flute provided melodious music. A pleasant place, Claudia reflected, if it wasn't for the oppressive feeling of being always watched, and she wondered if the walls held eyelets and spyholes. They were about to leave the *triclinium* when a shadow to her right caught Claudia's attention: an eerie masked figure moved jerkily at a crouch through the half-light. Despite its strangeness, the figure was vaguely familiar. Claudia shook her head and moved on.

They were taken through the back of the house into a small garden enclosed on three sides by a high red-brick wall with cruel spikes embedded along the top. In the centre of the garden stood a peristyle built out of cedarwood, its columns painted a brilliant green and gold, its sloping roof a deep ochre. Silvana led them down the path past the flower and herb beds and into this. The centre of the roof was open to the sky; directly beneath it was a square, green-tiled pool with a fountain in the centre carved in the shape of a lotus lily. Flowers floated on the light blue water and Claudia glimpsed the glitter of golden carp darting about. A woman dressed in a similar fashion to Silvana sat on a stone bench on the far side. She rose as they entered and gestured to two cushioned stools nearby. Claudia and Murranus sat down. Silvana offered them food and drink; both refused.

The Domina kept her head down as if studying the silver-edged tiles around the rim of the pool. Only when Silvana and the oafs disappeared did she look up. A strong, harsh face, the hair iron grey, the eyes black and resolute, the nose imperious, the mouth thin-lipped. Unpainted and free of any jewellery or decoration, Domina Agrippina, as she introduced herself, reminded Claudia of the Empress Helena. They exchanged pleasantries, before Claudia moved swiftly to the purpose of their visit. She asked the same questions as she had of Macrinus and received virtually identical answers. The Guild of Isis was famous. The Domina looked after the girls as best she could. They entertained guests here, but there again, the Domina explained, the girls were free to wander the streets seeking custom; only the favoured ones stayed behind for what she called "special clients". The Domina was shrewd enough to realise that Claudia already knew a great deal about the Daughters and the murders. With a touch of dry humour, she asked Claudia to tell her what she'd learnt. As Claudia did so, the woman sat nodding, rocking slightly backwards and forwards. When Claudia finished, she held up a hand.

"I have nothing much to add," she declared. "Those poor girls went out in the street. I warned and advised them but they went their own ways. Over four years I would say at least twenty-four were murdered."

"At least?" Claudia asked. "You don't know the exact number?"

"Three disappeared completely," the Domina replied. "They may have run away or been kidnapped." She shrugged. "I don't know. Girls come and go. They entertain our visitors but they are not slaves, they are not prisoners. Any one of them could have walked from this house and out of the Guild whenever they chose."

"Did you have any suspicions about a possible killer?" Claudia asked.

The Domina pursed her lips and shook her head.

"But Attius?" Claudia insisted.

"Attius?" The Domina laughed quietly to herself. "Yes, he was a frequent visitor. We all knew about his violent ways, and yes, now and again, in the street he'd take a girl and push her against the wall of an alleyway. But he came here because . . . well, now he is dead I'll tell you: he had a share in this house."

"What?" Claudia exclaimed.

"Yes, he invested money, but after Constantine's victory at the Milvian Bridge, I bought him out. Attius had lost power. He was no longer interested in me, the Daughters of Isis or this house."

"Did he ever come here?" Claudia asked. "I mean, after Constantine marched into Rome?"

"Never!"

"So you don't think he was the Nefandus?"

"No, I don't."

"Yet as I said," Claudia insisted, "the girls must have approached the killer, they must have felt comfortable with him."

"Tribune Macrinus thought the same, but there again, some of the girls are desperate for money, and an officer from the Praetorian — yes, I've heard the rumours — would be a favoured customer. How long," she turned, "does it take to kill a girl? A knife to her stomach? They know the risks. Every time they go out on to the streets they face danger."

"And you can offer no protection?" Murranus asked.

"Protection?" The Domina smiled. "What protection? Life is cheap; flesh is like grass to be trodden underfoot or wither." She shook her head. "I know nothing about the deaths of my girls. I take them in, I bathe and feed them, I dress them in their scarlet bands, I teach them what I know. Yes, the Nefandus may have been someone the girls trusted. Yes, Attius was a suspect."

"But what do you think?"

"Me, Mistress Claudia? I think the Nefandus was never caught. He is a liar, a two-faced creature who loathes women, who has reflected deeply on the lines of Semonides of Amorgas."

"I'm sorry?"

"Haven't you read his poetry?" The Domina laughed, then stared up at the ceiling and closed her eyes. "How does that verse go: 'From the beginning the gods fashioned the mind of a woman, a thing apart, one they made from a long-haired sow who wallows in the mud and rolls about the ground.' " She opened her eyes. "You should read the poem, Claudia. It goes on and on about how women's minds are fashioned from a dog, the entrails of a bitch or those of a wretched weasel." She pursed her lips. "Such a man, who hated women, killed my girls and thoroughly enjoyed doing so."

"And Macrinus?"

The Domina looked away. "A good officer," she murmured. "Yes, one of the few."

"He never visited here?"

"Very rarely." The reply came too fast, too smoothly.

"You are sure of that?" Claudia insisted. "I mean, his wife was very ill. Men do have their needs . . ."

"Not him!" the Domina snapped. She flailed a hand. "I can tell you no more. Attius was a boar, rampant and vicious. Now he is dead, yet the Nefandus has apparently returned." She picked up a bronze hand-mirror beside her and stared at the image. "I can tell you no more."

"I think you can!" Claudia retorted. "Those two last victims?"

"Marina and Fausta?"

"They were Daughters of Isis, members of your Guild, and therefore both must be part of the funeral club set up for your girls."

"Yes." The Domina's unblinking gaze held Claudia's.

"Marina has been cremated," Claudia continued, "but Fausta?"

"In a cellar below." The Domina licked her fingertips and pointed to the ground. "All prepared and prettified; well, as best as the Anubis can do." She licked her fingertips again, as if she'd just picked up a piece of sticky honey cake; a rather macabre gesture, as though she was distancing herself from the events she was describing.

"Anubis?" Claudia asked.

"Our embalmer, the funeral master."

"I would like to speak to him." Claudia recalled the strange figure she'd glimpsed as they crossed the *triclinium*. "He must be here," she insisted. "Fausta's funeral will surely take place soon?"

The Domina sighed, picked up her goblet and slurped from it, her heavy-lidded eyes never leaving Claudia.

"Now," Claudia insisted. "If I don't speak to him now, I'll return with Augusta's Germans."

The Domina yawned and slammed down the goblet. Claudia wondered if it was laced with some form of opiate. The Domina stretched beneath the marble seat, picked up a hand bell and rang it. This time Silvana

104

came running down the path, the folds of her gown flapping. In other circumstances Claudia would have laughed; the spell was broken. The atmosphere of this serene house of love was like a wine to be savoured not drunk. Everything was an illusion; underneath it lurked tension and secrets like turbulence beneath the placid surface of a stream. Silvana stopped, gasping for breath. She no longer looked so pretty or composed. The Domina spoke swiftly to her in a guttural dialect Claudia couldn't understand, a patois common to the brothel. Silvana nodded, hurried off and returned with a grotesque-looking creature dressed in a leather kilt and sandals; around each arm, from shoulder to wrist, curled a bronze replica of Apep, the great snake of the Underworld. On the man's face was the black and gold dog mask of Anubis, the Egyptian God of the Dead. His chest was festooned with blue and red tattoos. Claudia gazed suspiciously at him. There was something very familiar about that skinny body and bony knees, the rather jerky movements.

"You are Anubis?" she asked.

"I am." The voice behind the mask was deliberately sepulchral.

"No you're not!" Claudia snapped. "Narcissus, take off that mask."

"I . . ."

"Take it off!"

The mask was doffed and Narcissus the Neat, the finest embalmer in Rome, or so he proclaimed, stared mournfully at Claudia, his thin face suitably wreathed in a tragic look. He fingered a bead of sweat on his cheek, then scratched his thinning hair.

"Sit down," Claudia ordered quietly.

He came round the pool and squatted before her. Claudia narrowed her eyes and stared at him. Narcissus was a fine embalmer; according to him, the best in Syria until he was captured during an uprising. Once a slave, he was now a freedman of Rome. Oh yes, Claudia smiled to herself, and one of Uncle Polybius' closest cronies. Narcissus had been freed by Helena as a reward for services rendered. He had moved to the She-Asses and, with Uncle Polybius' help, had bought an apartment in the same *insula*.

"A joint venture," Polybius had proclaimed. "I look after the customers in life, Narcissus the Neat in death."

"Well?" Claudia was trying to ignore Murranus' laughter.

"I got lonely, mistress," Narcissus pleaded. "I visited the Daughters . . ." The embalmer moved his head from side to side. "One thing led to another."

"So it seems," Claudia replied.

"We hired him," the Domina intervened harshly. "He is most skilled."

Claudia felt sorry for Narcissus and decided to move to the business in hand.

"You dressed the corpses of the two girls slain by the Nefandus?"

"Cut open, right eye missing," Narcissus replied, relaxing. He was now talking about something he knew. "They were definitely raped," he added. "The amount

106

of semen on both was more like from a bull than a man. I also prepared their nails. Claudia, I can tell you this. The first fought for her life; Fausta, however, died more quickly."

"How can you tell that?" Murranus asked.

"Marina had hair under her nails, as well as dried blood; she'd scratched her attacker. Black hair, a few white. Fausta not so; her nails were clean. She hadn't time to fight."

Claudia stared at the pool. She couldn't ask Macrinus such questions. She suspected the Nefandus' former victims were quickly bundled up and cremated as the tribune hunted their killer.

"Narcissus is definitely skilled," the Domina repeated. "The other girls were dressed for burial and that was it. Nothing was ever found."

"Did Attius ever inspect any of those corpses, the other ones?"

"No! Strangely enough he said he could not bear to."

"Did you discover anything else?" Murranus asked. "Anything at all?"

Narcissus blinked quickly as he tried to recall. He was nicknamed "the Neat" for a good reason: with the living he was lugubrious; he only came to life when he talked about the dead.

"The first victim," he declared carefully, "had scratches down her back, nasty ones. She must have been pressed up against an alley wall, its brickwork rough and cutting. Fausta had no such marks, almost as if she had rested against a cloth or a rug."

"No bindings, no ligatures?"

"None on either." Narcissus shook his head. "There is really nothing else except that the blade which cut them was two-edged, very sharp and pointed."

"Did Attius know those two girls?"

The Domina shook her head.

"And Macrinus?"

"No." The Domina was most emphatic. "Tribune Macrinus never comes here. Certainly not in the last few years."

"And the *vigiles* of this quarter, Achilleos and Nereos?"

"Typical." The Domina smirked. "Everything for free or else . . ."

"Just like at the She-Asses," Narcissus added quickly. "You know how they eat and drink free of charge."

The Domina picked up her goblet, crossed her legs and stared at Claudia. "There is nothing else, the day is dying. We have work to do, mistress."

Claudia and Murranus left the House of Isis and adjourned to a nearby tavern, a sprawling shabby affair which offered Cappadocian lettuce, leeks, tuna garnished with sliced eggs and small sausages in lettuce leaves followed by Syrian pears and Neapolitan chestnuts. They ate in silence. The food was barely edible and the wine sour; the table was grease-caked whilst the stools had a life of their own. Claudia eventually had enough and pushed her plate away.

"One thing I have learnt," she murmured, touching the tip of Murranus' nose.

"Yes?" Murranus was famished. He swiftly devoured what was on his platter before turning to Claudia's.

"I believe," Claudia stared at some graffiti on the tavern wall, "that Macrinus and the Domina were locked in a fierce conflict with the Nefandus, whatever they say. Now they seem placid, exhausted, as if the Nefandus was a relic from the past rather than the present, and yet he has killed again! I do wonder." Claudia finished her wine. "But come, my beloved, Attius' villa awaits." She continued to stare at the scrawled graffiti, then burst out laughing.

Murranus turned and looked at the words that had caught her attention: "I was not, I was. Now I am not and I care not."

"Come." Claudia grinned at him. "There is more to life than that." She shoved back her stool and got to her feet, and was about to caress Murranus' head when an urchin appeared, smutty-faced and garbed in dirty goatskin. He stood before her, grinning, pushed a piece of parchment into her hand then promptly disappeared. She unfolded the sheet and read the blackened scrawl:

I invoke you, Headless God, one with sight in his feet, who releases lightning and thunder. It is you whose mouth pours out fire. It is you who commands! Necessity, I invoke you against the woman Claudia. Destroy her mind. Ravage her soul, weaken her will. Bring all she does to nothing.

Claudia glanced around. No one was staring at her. She clutched her stomach even as she handed the curse to Murranus, then walked out of the tavern door and stared up at the sky. The sun was still hot, though noon was long past. Claudia tried to regain her poise. She intended to visit Attius' villa but she'd had enough of the dead. Murranus joined her, swearing under his breath. He thrust the scrap of parchment back at Claudia and walked a little further down the street as if he might glimpse its sender in the crowd milling about. Claudia put the parchment into the small leather wallet on her belt then went and slid her hand into his. Murranus stared down at her.

"Who?" he asked.

Claudia forced a smile. "I've certainly caught someone's attention." She sighed. "But," she squeezed his fingers, "only from the darkness. Let us rest from all this," she whispered.

Later that day, as the shadows lengthened, Drusilla, former mistress and bed servant of Attius Enobarbus, hurried through the narrow streets of the Caelian quarter. Night was falling. Shops' shutters were going up. The crowds were dispersing, the narrow trackways falling quiet as the hucksters grabbed their trays and headed for the nearest tavern or cookshop. Drusilla began to regret her haste, but the letter she had received had been most explicit. She now had it clutched in her bejewelled fingers. Its writer apparently knew Attius' killer and the whereabouts of the Icthus casket, as well as the source of the foul rumours regarding her master. Drusilla had not told anyone else about the letter. The writer had demanded that she keep it secret and meet him at the She-Asses tavern around the tenth hour. She had left immediately, even though it was growing late. House lamps burned eerily behind their grilles as doors and shutters were slammed closed. Shadows flitted across her path; strange odours billowed. Smoke and fire curled like a dirty mist. It was bat-wing time, between light and dark, the strange hour when the day's work was done but that of the night had yet to begin. A beggar whined from a shadow-filled nook, a skeletal hand thrust out which Drusilla knocked away. She rounded a corner and almost collided with the two *vigiles*, Achilleos and Nereos, walking quietly, swinging their clubs. She stepped back in alarm.

"I am sorry," she gasped, "but I must be at the She-Asses . . ."

The *vigiles* looked her up and down.

"Who are you?"

"Drusilla, freedwoman of the house of Attius Enobarbus. I know," she added hastily, "Macrinus the tribune."

The *vigiles* were already nodding understandingly. They could tell from her dress and her voice what she must be. They warned her to be careful and asked her if she needed an escort. Drusilla refused reluctantly, so they gave her directions and waved her by.

Drusilla hurried on. She reached the top of a needle-thin alleyway, and in the glow of a bonfire at the far end glimpsed the cracked fountain in the square leading down to the She-Asses. She saw a figure move, a small boy; no one else. She hurried down, the laughter of the *vigiles* carrying faintly behind her.

"Gods be thanked, you've come!"

She stopped abruptly at the narrow mouth to a runnel leading off to her left.

"It's safe," the voice whispered.

She heard a tinder strike. A torch spluttered into life and dazzled her. She stepped into the dark.

"Come, come!" the voice urged. Drusilla felt a hand grasp hers, and she was roughly pulled down on to the cruel tip of a two-edged sword . . .

On their arrival late in the evening at the villa of Attius Enobarbus, Claudia and Murranus found the heavy double doors closed; laurel branches and sprigs of pine were nailed to them to show the dead lay within. Servants, their face and clothes grey with ash, led them up the path through more funereally decorated doors into the atrium full of the mournful music of pipe and lyre. Lamps glowed, their flickering light making the shadows dance. The air was heavily scented from the wreaths placed at the feet of statues and before the closed doors of the *naos* holding the household gods or *lares*. The faces of statues and busts were veiled whilst the cupboard holding the yellowing oil-stained masks of Attius' ancestors had been opened in preparation for the formal funeral procession the following morning. In the centre of the atrium lay Attius in his costly coffin, feet to the door, face waxen under its mop of greying hair. He was tended by servants and those who would maintain the nightly vigil, making offerings to the gods so Attius' journey through the Underworld would be trouble-free. The air was cold due to the unshuttered windows, open to allow the soul of the dead easy passage; only a few charcoal braziers provided some warmth. Next to these squatted three professional mourners, keening softly though still eager to keep warm. Frontinus came out of a side chamber wringing his hands, fat face all anxious.

"It's Drusilla," he moaned as soon as he greeted them. "She apparently received a letter just before dusk and has not yet returned. There is a vigil to be kept, the funeral tomorrow and . . ." He wiped his eyes with the back of his hands as he realised the slaves were staring at him. "You'd best come," he whispered. "You wish to see the chamber?"

Claudia nodded. Frontinus beckoned them forward as if they were fellow conspirators, and led them through a darkened peristyle garden where a few lamps glowed, picking out the colours of the flowers, the glinting water of the pool and the shady outlines of statues. The back of the house was cold and dark, still reeking of the natron and spices the embalmers had used to prepare the corpse. Frontinus stopped at a shabby recess, fumbling for his keys as he explained how the villa had once been a farmhouse, and that these were the cellars of the old building. He unlocked the door and went quickly down the steps, pausing occasionally to light cresset torches. At the bottom stretched a paved path which led past iron-studded doors. More torches were lit and flared to reveal a long, grim-looking passageway. Frontinus stopped before Attius' chamber, its broken-down door pulled aside. He went in and lit the lamps, calling out to them to follow.

Claudia was surprised at how large and cavernous the chamber was, its ceiling quite high and ribbed with black beams. In the far corner, near the top of the wall, a brick grille fixed into the stone provided air. The walls were smooth and whitewashed. It was a stark but comfortable place, with woollen coverings strewn on the floor, while small tables of gleaming acacia carried lamps carved in fantastic shapes: a griffin's head, a snake, the god Bes, a stork, a dragon.

"My master collected those," Frontinus declared mournfully.

Claudia picked one up and moved to the broad bunk bed in the far corner of the room just beneath the grille. The sheets, blankets and headrest had been removed but the feather-stuffed palliasse still bore a broad dark bloodstain.

"Attius was found here, sprawled on his face, head slightly turned," Frontinus declared, "a knife thrust deep into his back." He gestured at the great oaken desk with a large camp chair behind it. Claudia crossed over and picked up the dagger; it boasted a copper hilt with a cross guard and a long serrated pointed blade. All bloodstains had been wiped off.

"Whose dagger was this?"

"My master's; he always kept it close."

"Why?"

Frontinus stepped out of the shadows. "My master was a supporter of Maxentius. He hunted Christians, or at least their shrines. He amassed a fortune. He had enemies, those who didn't like him and those who envied him."

114

"Such as?"

Frontinus spread his hands. "Not even his companions, especially Macrinus, liked him. I suppose the only two people who had any affection for him were myself and Drusilla."

Claudia stared down at the great desk carved out of oak. The writing tray in the centre contained black and red ink pots, reed pens, sander and cutting knife. On each side of it lay a pile of manuscripts neatly stacked. Nothing out of place.

"Attius' will?" she asked.

"I understand that Drusilla, myself and others receive bequests but the bulk of Attius' wealth, including this villa, will go to a nephew in Massilia, his native city. Attius was of Gallo-Roman descent."

"So." Claudia walked back to the door. It leaned against the wall, wrenched off its pivots. The bolts at top and bottom were undamaged, but the lock was shattered. The key was still inserted on the inside. Claudia eased this out, inspecting the lock and the surrounding wood. To all appearances the door had been firmly locked and so had to be forced. She turned back.

"Attius was sent to Byzantium?"

"Yes." Frontinus shrugged. "Nothing untoward happened."

"Nothing?"

"After the Emperor's victory at the Milvian Bridge, Attius settled down, tending his gardens, keeping to himself until the August Ones chose him for that expedition."

"His companions welcomed that?"

"They were relieved to be accepted by the Emperor and his august mother."

"And the tomb of the Galilean, the Icthus casket?"

"Domina," Frontinus replied respectfully, his face creased in an ingratiating smile, "scrutinise the records. I come from Iberia, a slave though a very educated one. Years ago Attius bought me then freed me. I am good with manuscripts, columns of figures, managing affairs. I am a steward, Attius' servant. I looked after his needs. I followed him into the city when he visited the whores. I stood beside him when he ate, but as for his private life, his hunt for the tombs of Christians . . ." he spread his hands, "I cannot tell you."

"And the Icthus casket?"

Frontinus pulled a face. "Attius was secretive. He kept many things to himself. Mistress Claudia," the freedman stepped forward, "I am not being evasive, but when my master worked for Maxentius, his task was clandestine. He could not trust anyone. Many slaves and servants were Christians; some were educated, and could read and write." Frontinus tapped the side of his head. "Attius kept his secrets to himself, even from me, nor did he trust his companions."

"Why not? Of course." Claudia smiled, answering her own question. "Rewards were offered for finding those shrines. Attius kept such information to himself, including the whereabouts of Peter the Galilean's tomb, if he discovered it."

Claudia stared across to where Murranus sat on the edge of the bed.

"And in the last days before his death?"

"Ask Drusilla," Frontinus replied, "when she returns. Once my master came back from Byzantium, he was not changed but just . . ."

"Frightened?"

"More cautious, sly. He kept himself here, in a chamber he'd furnished after Maxentius had fallen. It provided comfort and reassurance."

"And what did he do here?"

Frontinus gestured at the documents piled high on the table as well as those on the shelves and coffers standing around the chamber. "He went through these. As I've said, ask Drusilla."

"Did he meet anyone?"

"Only his companions on the afternoon of his death. He spoke with them out in the garden. They left after he adjourned here."

"Could any one of them have followed him down here, or been waiting for him in the passageway outside? It is dark, shadow-filled?"

"It's possible, but that door was locked from the inside." Frontinus drew a deep breath. "I am sure Attius came here by himself. I was supervising servants in the garden. Drusilla later tried to rouse him; she knocked and there was no answer. She knelt down, peered through the lock and glimpsed the key on the inside. It's a special one, unique; only Attius held one. He never let it out of his sight. Drusilla became concerned and summoned me. There was still no answer, so the door was forced. Inside the lamps had burnt low. Attius lay sprawled face down on the bed,

117

Drusilla went across to the desk and immediately exclaimed that the Icthus casket was missing." Frontinus sat down on a stool. "Mistress," his voice was almost a wail, "I can tell you no more. My master's funeral awaits, there's the vigil . . ."

"You'd best go. Wait!"

Frontinus turned.

"Drusilla?"

"She'll be back soon. She'll answer any question."

"No, you answer it. What was she to Attius?"

"He bought her many years ago. She was apparently very beautiful. He freed her. She became his bed companion and confidante."

"Did she stay here with Attius?"

"Sometimes. Look, Drusilla and I do not like one another, we merely tolerate each other's presence. At times she can be friendly and I respond. She rarely mentioned Attius' secrets. I think she was under strict instruction not to. She began to talk more during the last few days; she was growing deeply concerned at Attius hiding down here. By the way, did you know that Attius was born a Christian?"

Claudia shook her head.

"I'm not too sure what Drusilla was, but she recently claimed that Attius, well before he died, wasn't so much fearful as haunted, as if something was threatening him from the past. He talked of ghosts. He quoted from the Christian scripture about some deadly thing fastening on him and how those who lived by the sword died by the sword." Frontinus wetted his lips. "Yes, that's the best way to describe Attius, haunted, as if he was hiding from something."

"Could Drusilla have murdered him?"

"It's possible." Frontinus scratched his head and came back to where Claudia sat behind the desk. "I know sometimes Attius abused her. She'd become very angry and curse him but she always maintained she could never leave him, that he had his qualities."

"Who else do you think could have killed him?" Murranus asked, getting off the bed and walking over.

"Tribune Macrinus hated him."

"Why?"

"I think Macrinus suspected he was the Nefandus, though I have no proof of that, but there again, Attius' companions weren't too fond of him either. They regarded him as boorish and overbearing; apparently he always took the lion's share of any reward. And then, of course, there is the Nefandus himself."

Claudia stared at him.

"You see," Frontinus leaned against the desk, "Attius knew he was accused of those awful murders. He just laughed. He mocked the Nefandus, proclaiming how he should try his sword on a man rather then some alley girl. It was a taunt. According to Drusilla, Attius once received a threat from the Nefandus."

"What?" Claudia exclaimed.

"Yes, a threat that one day perhaps he might try his luck with Attius, but that was all. Mistress, is there anything else?"

Claudia shook her head.

CHAPTER
SIX

There might be no sacrifices consumed by fire, no demon festivals, nor any of the other ceremonies usually observed by the slaves of superstition.

Frontinus lurched out of the room. Claudia asked Murranus to bring the lamps closer. She patted the manuscripts. "I'll study these. You search this chamber for any secret entrances in the floor or walls." She pushed away the writing tray and pulled the pile of manuscripts towards her. Some were fresh and cream-coloured, others yellow, blackening with age and dog-eared. Upstairs echoed the faint mournful sounds of lyre and flute, the invocation of prayers, the chanting of hymns. Now and again Murranus would curse as he pulled rugs up and pushed aside chests and coffers.

Claudia went through the manuscripts carefully: bills of sale, documents showing Attius' investments in shipping wine from the north, corn from Egypt or fish oil from the Greek islands. Everything was carefully annotated. Once she'd finished the manuscripts on the desk, she went through similar documents from the chests and coffers, but they all told the same story. Even the scraps of litter in the reed baskets revealed nothing about this mysterious cold man who lived such a secretive life. Claudia suspected that Attius was a born spy. A man who either hid away or burnt any incriminating document. He had served in the legions, but the bulk of his wealth came from goods seized from Christians. He also seemed fascinated with sex and had acquired a number of manuscripts from Alexandria, the best in Egyptian erotica. Once she'd finished her searches, Claudia sat in the camp chair and stared across at the bunk bed. Murranus was still busy in one corner moving rugs, feeling the cold paving stones. He sighed and got up.

"Nothing at all," he murmured and pointed to the grille high in the wall. "Apart from the door and that, there is no other entrance to this chamber. Attius designed it to keep himself secure and safe, but from what?"

"From the past, maybe," Claudia murmured. "He must have been responsible for the deaths of many Christians. He destroyed their shrines, he supported Maxentius, he was disliked by his colleagues, by Tribune Macrinus, perhaps even by Drusilla and Frontinus." She rose and walked to the door. "Undoubtedly Attius was murdered, stabbed in the back. Now this may have happened when he was lying down, drifting off to sleep, or he could have been surprised, stabbed in the back and staggered to the bed."

"In other words, he is attacked," Murranus murmured, "he staggers to the door, locks it, then goes back to the bed, collapses and dies."

"Perhaps," Claudia agreed. "The assassin also took the Icthus casket from the desk."

"If that was the case," Murranus asked, "why didn't Attius raise the alarm?"

"He was shocked, frightened. Perhaps he didn't have enough strength. He panicked. He made a mistake. He locked the door instead of going out to look for help."

"That's possible," Murranus agreed.

"The other possibility," Claudia continued, chewing her lip, "is that the killer stabbed Attius then locked the door, but how did he did do it? The key in the lock fits; it's the only one." She went down on her hands and knees and crawled across, taking the shortest route, towards the bed in the corner. She stopped at one of the rugs, picked it up and asked Murranus to bring a lamp closer. "There," she exclaimed. "Look, specks of blood. Perhaps I'm correct. Attius was stabbed. The killer grabbed the casket and fled. Attius locked the door behind him, then, still dripping blood, staggered back to his bed."

"Or the blood could have come from the killer," Murranus declared. "Yet that doesn't explain how the door was locked from the inside."

"Perhaps the killer never left." Claudia smiled. "Look around, Murranus, this chamber is full of shadows and dark corners. Can you imagine it, the door being forced, Frontinus and Drusilla rushing in, their eyes only for Attius? The killer could have crept out or stayed hidden for a while, then mingled with everyone else."

"Dangerous," Murranus declared, "very dangerous indeed!"

122

Claudia rose and walked across to the bed. She picked up the small mat beside it, inspected it carefully, then threw it down before lying on the bed. She stretched her arms out; her right hand felt the gap between the edge of the bed and the wall.

"Murranus," she swung herself up, "drag this away from the wall."

He bent down, seized the wooden frame and pulled. The bed moved, then stopped. "It's fastened!" he gasped. "I cannot move it any further."

Claudia, kneeling on the bed, slid her hand down. She felt the leather thongs connecting the bed to small rings driven into the wall. Murranus brought across the dagger from the desk and sawed through these, then pulled the bed clear. Claudia carefully examined the strip of floor between the bed and the wall and found it: a scrap of parchment. She picked this up and went back to the desk, trying to control her excitement. She undid the small scroll, using weights from the writing tray to keep it flat, and pulled it closer. With Murranus leaning over her shoulder, she carefully scrutinised the small, ill-formed letters written in black ink.

"It's in Attius' name, the draft of a letter to Presbyter Sylvester," she exclaimed excitedly. She plucked up a reed pen, its point blunt and worn, then picked up the other pens and studied them closely. Some were sharp, others well used.

"Attius was writing," she said, "drafting a letter and destroying whatever he composed. I think this was his last attempt, just before he was killed." She paused as the professional wailers recommenced their mournful chant. "Murranus, if the door at the top of the steps is open, close it."

Murranus left the chamber. Claudia took a good reed pen and carefully transcribed what was written on the scroll. When he returned, she held up a hand.

"I have it!" she breathed. "It's not much." She continued with her writing throwing down the pen when she had finished.

"Well?" Murranus asked.

"Nothing new under the sun," she whispered. "Our friend Attius," she smiled, "was drafting a letter to Presbyter Sylvester. He admits he is frightened, terrified of something. He knows the Nefandus has returned, but listen." Claudia picked up the manuscript. "Attius writes: 'An even greater demon lurks in the darkness to haunt me. However, if you are agreeable, I shall describe how Caesar's old friend holds the secret of the Galilean's tomb.' " Claudia put down the manuscript. "What did he mean by that, eh, Murranus? Caesar's old friend holding the secret of Peter the Galilean's tomb? This might prove," she got to her feet, "that the Icthus casket did contain secrets. I suspect Attius was going to trade that information for better protection. He'd written this draft. He prepared it probably time and again using many pens. He must have burnt the other drafts but kept this one tight in his hand, even when he was dying, and in his death throes thrust it down the side of the bed. So, Murranus, my fellow philosopher, we have a number of riddles. First, how was Attius killed in this chamber? How did his assassin escape? What is this greater demon which lurks in the darkness? Someone more fearful than Nefandus who apparently terrified Attius? Finally, what does Attius mean by Caesar's old friend holding the secret?"

"Is he referring to Constantine?" Murranus asked.

"Perhaps. Go and call Frontinus away from that awful noise upstairs. Tell him I have other questions to ask."

Murranus left, returning in a short while with a rather ridiculous-looking Frontinus, the funeral wreath resting lopsided on his head. The freedman cradled a brimming goblet apparently to assuage his grief. Claudia handed the scrap of manuscript over and asked him to read it. Frontinus did so, lips moving soundlessly, then glanced up.

"What does it mean?" he demanded. "As far as I know, mistress, Attius had nothing to do with Presbyter Sylvester. It's a riddle."

"Well at least we have found something." Claudia stared round. "Is this chamber as it was when Attius was murdered?"

"Of course, mistress, though we have tidied it up. We moved the corpse, and the blood-soaked blankets. I arranged the manuscripts on the desk. Oh yes, one other thing. I removed a small money coffer. However, I assure you, I've kept very careful accounts. I have only taken out what was needed to run the household and meet the costs of my master's funeral."

"Did Attius keep much money and wealth here?"

"Oh no, mistress, just enough. In the casket there were a few hundred solidi, a little bit more perhaps. As I've said, I have kept careful accounts."

"With whom did your master bank?"

Frontinus smiled. "I think you know his name, mistress! Ulpius the banker; he has a shop on the approaches to the Palatine Hill."

"Ah yes, Ulpius," Claudia declared. "I have indeed heard of him. My uncle Polybius was warned not to do business with him."

"Yet a good banker," Frontinus declared. "Attius trusted him completely."

"Your master was a wealthy man?"

"Very much so, mistress."

Frontinus was about to make his excuses and leave when there was a commotion upstairs, people shouting. He hastened to the doorway, and was almost knocked aside by a servant who threw himself in and fell to his knees.

"Master Frontinus!" He pointed at Claudia. "Mistress, you must come, you must come!"

"What is the matter?" Claudia asked.

"It's Drusilla," the servant wailed. "She's been found dead, a victim of the Nefandus. Her body lies at the She-Asses . . ."

Murranus and Claudia, together with Frontinus, gathered their possessions, left the villa and hastened up the road towards the towering Aurelian walls. On either side of the approaches torches lit the night sky, whilst fiery braziers glowed around the postern gate. Claudia showed her pass and they were let through along the thoroughfare to the next gate. It was a rather cold night, yet once they entered the city, they found the streets still busy. Revellers were returning from parties, grotesque masks of satyrs and other animals over their faces. A group of whores, hair painted red, faces all white, were dancing in a pool of torchlight, castanets clicking, sandalled feet beating the cobbles as onlookers clapped, urging them along. A man lay sprawled in a pool of blood outside a tavern door. The light was patchy and full of smoke. Two beggars offered to do a dance as they begged for a coin. Murranus drove them off, pushing his way through the throng. Claudia turned and glimpsed the witch she had seen previously that day. The woman, her horrid face framed in its mask of tangled hair, hurried out of a tavern clutching a boy by the hand. Claudia wondered if he was the one who had delivered the message, but she could not be sure. A group of gladiators noticed Murranus and shouted greetings. He held a hand up in reply. Frontinus was quietly sobbing, talking to himself: "What shall we do? What shall I do? The master's funeral tomorrow, and now Drusilla? The gods be cursed!" He continued to lament dolefully as far as the square leading down to the She-Asses.

Polybius had lit torches and placed them by the side of the doorway above the grinning Hermes. The dancing flames illuminated the statue of Minerva holding her pet owl above the lintel, as well as the huge knocker shaped in the form of a phallus resting against the heavy wood. Claudia, hastening ahead, pushed her way through the crowd and tried the door. It wouldn't budge. Lifting the knocker, she brought it down with a resounding crash. Oceanus, his face laced in sweat, threw open the door. He was about to curse when he glimpsed Claudia and quickly beckoned her, Murranus and Frontinus into the dining hall. Claudia immediately recognised something was wrong. The usual placards advertising the dishes of the day, a magnificent array since the arrival of Celades, were missing, as were the notices listing the prices of drinks and warning wandering warlocks, wizards and pimps to take their business elsewhere, unless they had the specific permission of Polybius, the She-Asses' proprietor. The dining hall, however, was still packed, people grouped around tables looking down towards the kitchens and the rooms beyond. They tried to question the barrel-chested, pot-bellied Oceanus as he pushed his way through like a barge along a river, but he knocked aside hands, refusing to answer. He led Claudia and her companions round the counter into the kitchen, which was bereft of any sweet smells — no crackling charcoal on the hearth, a stack of unwashed pots perched on the floor, the two great ovens standing open and cold — then took them across to a stone building where the *insula*'s hypocaust had once been stored.

Mercury the Messenger, the tavern gossip, stood on guard; half drunk, he was already reciting to himself the news and descriptions he'd later spread through the entire quarter. This self-proclaimed herald kicked open the door, and Oceanus led them down into the mildewed darkness lit by fluttering torches. The chamber at the bottom was full of people peering over each other's heads. The usual rogues had gathered: Simon the Stoic, Petronius the Pimp, Januaria the tavern wench and others of their ilk. In the next chamber cresset torches and a ring of smoky oil lamps circled a funeral bier resting on a stone plinth. Claudia stared at the horror, gagged and turned away. Frontinus would have collapsed if the two *vigiles*, Achilleos and Nereos, hadn't caught him in time. Polybius and Poppaoe stood some distance away, arms around each other. Poppaoe was sobbing quietly. Narcissus crouched by the mangled remains of Drusilla, trying to wash away the black blood encrusted over her face like some horrid mask. The poor woman was drenched in gore; it saturated her clothing as if she floated in a pool of red from that dark, hideous slash which had sliced her body from crotch to throat.

Claudia heard a sobbing from a shadowy corner and walked over. Celades crouched there with Sorry and Caligula. Claudia had never seen the tavern cat so subdued. She felt her own stomach pitch and stood waiting for it to settle. When she turned round, Murranus was whispering to the *vigiles*, who stood half listening as they stared at the gruesome sight. Claudia abruptly clapped her hands.

"You must not stay." She swallowed hard. "This is the stuff of nightmares. It's a shock which both fascinates and repels. You mustn't stay! Come, Murranus, Oceanus." The two gladiators, used to such macabre sights, immediately began to usher everyone away from Drusilla's corpse. Claudia told Narcissus to stay and do what he could to clean the remains, and have Drusilla removed immediately to his own embalming shop. Then she went over, took Sorry by the hand and led him out of the cellar, Celades following mournfully behind. Once back in the kitchen, she decided to impose order.

"Murranus and Oceanus, get rid of everybody. This tavern is closed for the night; there'll be no more food or drink."

Both hastened to obey. Shouts and cries echoed from the dining hall. Fat-bellied Labienus, the acting troupe manager, burst into the kitchen. Round-faced and round-bodied, with balding head, protuberant eyes and fleshy cheeks, he always reminded Claudia of some plump cherub. He was dressed flamboyantly in a spangled gown, with soft red boots on his feet and a silver girdle round his waist; in his left ear a large ring shimmered in the light.

"I can stay, surely?" he intoned dramatically.

"Of course you can." Claudia smiled. Assisted by the *vigiles*, she ushered them all into the dining hall, which was now strangely quiet. Poppoae, assisted by Januaria and a pale-faced Sorry, briskly cleared the tables, rearranging the lamps. Celades busied himself in the kitchen, loudly assuring everyone that honey omelette, bread and peas would settle their stomachs. Polybius, now recovered, brought out his best Samian ware and opened a jar of his finest Falernian. Everyone sat round, and Claudia allowed the ordinary things of life to clear away the disgusting spectacle. Sorry, his mouth full of food and cradling Caligula for comfort, told everyone what had happened. He spoke softly, the terrors he'd experienced being replaced by the importance at being the centre of attention. He explained how he was sent out by Polybius on some errand or other, but forgot it, so returned. He then left the tavern again, and was going up the narrow street when he saw someone hastening out of the needle-thin runnel which ran off it.

"What did he look like?" Claudia asked.

"Oh, he was a soldier," Sorry spluttered. "Definitely a soldier. I could tell that from his gleaming helmet, and he had a big red cloak which billowed about him. Anyway, I went up and looked down the runnel. A torch lay spluttering on the ground. I saw the woman's jewellery glinting. It was horrible, disgusting." Sorry stretched out for another piece of food.

Polybius slapped him gently on the hand. "Wait till you finish speaking," he warned.

"I have," Sorry replied. "There is nothing more. I've told you everything."

Polybius pushed the platter towards the boy.

"It's like he said. He came back here white as a ghost, screaming his head off. So I sent Oceanus up to see what had happened."

"It made me sick!" the former gladiator confessed. "Blood splattered everywhere, like a fountain springing up from the dirt. I came back to organise the bier. Nobody else would come, so Polybius and I went and brought the poor wretch back to the cellar. Then we summoned Narcissus, and he advised we send for you."

"How did you know it was Drusilla?" Claudia asked. "Did she carry any document, a letter?"

Polybius shook his head.

"We recognised her." Nereos spoke up. "We were doing our patrol and we passed her. Naturally we stopped and asked her business. She said she was from the house of Attius and had to go to the She-Asses."

"Did she say why?"

Nereos shook his head and glanced quickly at his comrade. "That was all, wasn't it? We walked on."

"We thought it would be a quiet evening," Achilleos declared, "until Polybius here said there was something we had to see. We arrived, took one look and sent a message to Attius' villa."

Claudia paused as Celades brought in fresh platters of bread and cheese, the omelette neatly diced. He portioned this out with his knife. Claudia took hers and ate, as did the others, mouths crammed with food, talking amongst themselves about the horror and who might be responsible.

"Well, she certainly wasn't raped."

Claudia looked up. Narcissus, hands and arms all bloodstained, came into the dining hall. Polybius immediately told him to clean himself up.

"No, stop, just stay there!" Claudia demanded. "You are sure she wasn't raped?"

"Killed like the rest, ripped open, right eye removed, but definitely no rape."

Polybius roared at him, and Narcissus hastily retreated into the garden to wash himself in the rain tub.

"What on earth," demanded Claudia, "was a woman like Drusilla doing coming to the She-Asses tavern. What business did she have here?"

Silence greeted her question.

"And why did she leave Attius' house alone, making herself so vulnerable at night?" Claudia looked at Polybius. "You found nothing on her?"

"No, no reason as to why she should be coming here. After the *vigiles* spoke to me, I asked around. Nobody here knows Drusilla."

Claudia stared at Frontinus. He had now stopped quivering, drinking one goblet of wine after another. He caught Claudia's gaze and shook his head mournfully.

"I cannot tell you, Mistress Claudia. I was busy with my master's funeral." He put his finger to his lips. "I must go back there soon; the funeral is tomorrow."

"Never mind that," Claudia soothed.

"All I know," Frontinus continued, taking another slurp of wine, "is that I was busy. Apparently a message was delivered to Drusilla — a letter, according to one of the servants — and then she left. I told you, I was expecting her back."

"How long ago was that?"

"How long? Oh, some two or three hours before you arrived."

Claudia stared at the flame of a nearby oil lamp and tried to follow the logic of events. Drusilla had left the villa, hastening into the city, eager to get to the She-Asses, yet why, and whom she was supposed to meet, remained a mystery. She'd been murdered nearby. If it hadn't been for Sorry, the corpse might not have been discovered until daylight. Now it had been brought here, Claudia could imagine the hubbub that ensued.

"That is not the problem," she said aloud, startling everyone. "The real problem is what she was doing here in the first place. Can anyone answer that?"

Again silence.

At last Frontinus rose to his feet. "I'm sorry." He wiped his mouth with the back of his hand. "Mistress, I am very sorry, but I must go." He opened his purse and placed some silver coins on the table. "Polybius, that is for your trouble. Once my master's funeral is over tomorrow, I shall arrange Drusilla's. If you could have her corpse dressed . . ."

"Leave her here," Claudia declared quietly. "Don't take her back to the villa until Narcissus has done his best. No one else should see what we have seen tonight."

Frontinus looked fearfully at the door. The *vigiles* offered to escort him, an offer he quickly accepted, and they left. Polybius announced that they had all had enough excitement for one day. Everyone agreed and began to drift away. Claudia insisted that Sorry take a few mouthfuls of wine and patted him gently on the head.

"It will make you sleep," she said. "It's best if you don't see it again. Try and forget it as quickly as possible." Even as she spoke, images of poor Felix's corpse sparked a memory. She rubbed her stomach. The wine she'd drunk was turning sour. "I think I will retire," she declared. She absentmindedly kissed Murranus, did the same to Poppoae and Polybius, wished the rest a good night and went up to her own chamber, where she locked the door behind her and

134

leaned against it. Then she sighed, moved across, lit a lamp and squatted down on the floor, staring around. She was glad to be alone. One part of her wished to go back, sit next to Murranus, perhaps discuss the day's events, but there again, this was the time for reflection, here in her own room.

She stared around. Polybius had done his best to make the chamber comfortable and pleasing. Tapestries displaying leaping ibex hung against the walls above furniture from a craftsman's shop: a bronze tripod, an acacia-wood stool, a proper table and chair as well as two carved Egyptian chests where she stored her belongings. She got up, walked over to the lavarium, poured out some water and carefully washed her hands and face. Then she took off her belt, tunic, sandals and undergarments and, using her precious sponge, daubed on some ointment and carefully cleaned herself. Once she'd finished, drying herself off with a linen towel, she put on her night tunic, which covered her from neck to toe, and sat on the edge of the bed. The small charcoal brazier had been fired hours ago; its coals now glowed dully. She lay back on the bed, staring up at the ceiling, searching for that cobweb she'd noticed the morning before. It fascinated her, the spider scurrying in and out; now it was hiding in a darkened corner.

"Like so many things," Claudia muttered. She sighed, swung her legs off the bed and went across to the small writing desk Polybius claimed to have borrowed from a nearby temple. She opened her writing book and recalled the piece of parchment found in Attius' chamber. She retrieved this from her wallet, lit the large lamp on the corner of the table and re-read the cryptic message.

"What, in the name of all the lords of light," she whispered, "did Attius mean about Caesar's old friend holding the secret of the Galilean's tomb?"

She carefully put the piece of manuscript away, and prepared a roll of vellum, taking out the reed pens, sharpening them, stirring the ink in its pot. Her mind became a blizzard of memories: that curse, the little boy with his smutty face, the grotesque witch staring at her, Drusilla's mangled remains, Attius' lonely chamber, the clever, subtle looks between Helena and her son.

"I must impose order," Claudia murmured. Her gaze was caught by a small carving of a Greek hoplite, a present from Murranus. She picked this up, smiled and offered thanks to any spirit hovering close that Murranus had given up the amphitheatre. He was now a bodyguard, with clever ideas of building up a business with a cohort of former gladiators and army veterans. The imperial court had its own guards, but the Christian Church, with its hierarchy of priests and officials, was also eager, even greedy, for the trappings of power. Claudia's smile abruptly faded. Presbyter Sylvester had dispensed with Murranus' service for a while so as to assist her. Was something happening between the presbyter and the Empress which that enigmatic priest did not want Murranus to witness?

"I can guess, guess and guess again." Claudia sighed and put the carving down. "Let's see what happens when we impose order."

CHAPTER
SEVEN

*The tyrants had shamefully plundered and sold
the goods of godly men.*

Claudia sharpened a reed pen, dipped it into the ink
and carefully began to write:

Primo: The Nefandus. The Abomination, the
hideous killer who for years had terrorised prostitutes
in the Caelian quarter. Those brutal slayings had
abruptly stopped when Constantine marched into
Rome. Now, two years later, in this month of
September, the Nefandus had returned. During his first
spate of murderous attacks he had struck down at least
twenty-four young women, probably raped, certainly
cut from crotch to throat, their right eyes removed.
Most of his victims were from the Daughters of Isis,
prostitutes who'd left the safety of their brothel to
search for custom on the streets. Rome swarmed with
such girls touting for business. They would certainly
have been frightened or cautious, yet they had a stark
choice: to find customers or starve. They'd be careful,
but the Nefandus had proved to be more cunning.
Rumour had it that the Nefandus had been dressed like
a Praetorian guard. These were now disbanded, but
Sorry had seen something similar: an imperial officer?
Was that how the Nefandus beguiled his victims,

137

dressed in disguise or as someone rich in status? The street girls would be drawn to such a person like a moth to a flame.

Tribune Macrinus, probably with the help of the Domina at the House of Isis, had waged war against the Nefandus using his men, spies and informers, but with little success. There were hints that the Nefandus had learnt confidential information about Macrinus' plans. So was the Nefandus a member of Macrinus' staff? Claudia paused, closing her eyes, and thought before writing on. Macrinus' task would have been very difficult. The Caelian quarter was a warren of streets, runnels and trackways, some no wider than a man. A slum dominated by towering shabby *insulae* with countless doors, gates and windows, an ideal place for any assassin to lurk or strike. Yet the killings had suddenly stopped two years ago, only to begin again. Was it the same Nefandus, or had he been killed in the sectarian fighting around Rome? Was someone imitating him?

Claudia knew all there was to know about the Schola Lunae, the society which boasted the purple chalice as its emblem. Someone very similar to the Nefandus had killed her brother Felix and raped her. Rome was full of such men who'd take their pleasures where they wanted, bloating themselves on sex and violence. Those last two victims from the Daughters of Isis had definitely been raped. According to Narcissus they'd been covered in semen as if ravaged by a bull! Fausta had died quietly, but Marina had fought for her life, her back scarred, nails blood-encrusted with traces of black and white hair. What were these? Human hair, or threads from some cloak or piece of clothing? And suspects? Attius had been one, but as regards these two most recent killings, he had been out of Rome for the first and murdered himself on the afternoon before the second. Moreover, and Claudia made careful note of this, scoring her words, if Attius had been out of Rome when the first slaying had taken place, so had his four companions, as well as Frontinus and Macrinus. All had been sent on that mysterious surveying expedition to Byzantium.

Helena had asked her to investigate the mystery of Attius' death and discover the secrets of the Icthus casket, yet — Claudia pursed her lips — the Nefandus was part of all this. Claudia was determined to do all in her power to trap the perpetrator of these horrid slayings. Poor Drusilla, lying in the tavern cellar like a piece of meat on a butcher's block! Why had she left the security of Attius' house, hurrying by herself to the She-Asses? Was it a mere coincidence that she had met the Nefandus, or something else? Claudia sighed, drew a line and moved on.

Secundo: Attius Enobarbus. A veteran, a centurion, a hard man — perhaps not the Nefandus, but certainly one who liked to humiliate and hurt women. He'd been Maxentius' bully-boy, hunting Christians in the catacombs, destroying their shrines, and in doing so had made a handsome profit for himself. Constantine and Helena had pardoned him and the other *scrutores* because they might have learnt the secret whereabouts of Peter the Galilean's tomb, as well as to use them on that mysterious expedition to Byzantium. A number of puzzles here. First, how could Attius die, stabbed in a room locked from the inside? How had his killer escaped with the Icthus casket? As regarded the secret tomb, Constantine and Helena had been correct: Attius did know the secret, or at least where it could be found. So, why hadn't he used such information before? Who was the greater demon he was so fearful of? Who was the old friend of Caesar who knew the actual whereabouts of the tomb? Why had Attius waited two years? Why write to Presbyter Sylvester now?

Tertio: Drusilla. Attius' concubine, who, earlier that day, had received a letter, no longer extant, and hurried into the night eager to reach the She-Asses only to have the ill fortune to run into the Nefandus. Or was it as simple as that? Who was Drusilla really? Was she the greater demon? What did she know about Attius? Claudia chewed her lip. Whatever secrets the dead woman held, she had carried these to the grave.

Quatro: Tribune Macrinus. A man of integrity, a high-ranking officer who'd resigned his commission and became commander of the *vigiles* in the Caelian quarter, an honest official who'd done his best to unmask the Nefandus but failed. He'd resigned his post once Constantine swept to power, only to be invited back to be bodyguard and keeper of Attius and the other *scrutores*. Was this because Helena knew Macrinus suspected Attius of being the Nefandus? What was the link between Macrinus and the Domina? She'd been rather evasive when his name had been mentioned. Finally, why had Macrinus, who had

140

worked so zealously to catch the Nefandus, now become so resigned, showing very little interest in these recent killings?

Quinto: The Scrutores. A group of former soldiers; Maxentius' henchmen, pardoned by the August Ones just in case they knew something about the Galilean's tomb. They too had been dispatched to Byzantium. Why? And now, according to Macrinus, two of them had disappeared. Claudia shook her head.

Sexto: Charon, Lord of the Underworld. He apparently knew the location of the tomb the Empress was searching for and was offering to sell it. How had he learnt this? Valentinian? Was the former deacon of the Roman Church now a member of Charon's cohort, or was he Charon himself. And why had the offer been made now? Had Charon sent that curse warning Claudia off? She racked her memory for what she knew about this king of Rome's underworld, a mysterious, sinister figure with more spies and informers than the imperial palace. Yes, he could have sent that curse, warning her not to pry where she shouldn't.

Claudia heard a guffaw of laughter from downstairs. She rose and stretched, walked over to the windows, pulled open the shutters and stared down into the garden. A single coloured lantern glowed against the night.

"I must not forget them either," she whispered. Uncle Polybius and his schemes! Labienus offering to write a play at Torquatus' behest! Claudia liked the barber, but he was a man who took an impish delight in enticing Polybius into one mad scheme or another, always with an eye for his own advancement.

Claudia closed the shutters, stretched her neck and stared back at the writing table. She would stay here tomorrow. She needed to think, to find some answers to these questions. She also needed some help. She'd send for Sallust the Searcher and have those other two *scrutores*, Severus and Narses, brought here for questioning; they must know something! She went over and sat on the bed. Although she wished to concentrate on Attius' death, the image of Drusilla all bloodied and torn dominated her thoughts. She lay down and stared into the darkness, and memories of those she loved drew close, particularly young Felix. How, she pleaded, can I trap the Nefandus?

Valentinian, former deacon in the Roman Church, hummed the tune of an ancient hymn his mother had taught him as he studied the mangled, sordid remains of Decurion Philippus. Most of the flesh was charred black lumps, though rather eerily, the left side of the dead man's face had remained untouched by the oily fire. Gavinus, a little further on, looked truly abominable, his face and legs all swollen and mottled. Valentinian, still humming the tune, squatted down carefully, moving the shuttered lantern, its polished horn sidings gleaming in the stygian darkness of that narrow tunnel.

"Very wrong!" Valentinian waggled a finger like an irate schoolmaster. "Very wrong indeed!" He stared at Gavinus' glassy dead eyes pushed into slits by the swollen cheeks, mouth open, the stubbled chin stained by the stream of dried mucus which had poured through the puffy lips. He patted the heavy plank which now sealed the tunnel, protection against the vipers. Nevertheless, he had taken no chances; he also wore thick leather leggings and stout marching boots.

Valentinian sighed, rose, took a coil of rope out of the sack he carried and dragged the remains of the two dead men out of the tunnel and down another one. He pushed Gavinus' corpse over the blackened remains of Philippus. Once positioned correctly, he drew his sword and, expertly as a flesher, sliced off Gavinus' head. He shook this, wrapped it in the dead man's cloak and pushed it into his sack, then went back to the other tunnel and cleaned away any traces of the violent deaths which might alert other trespassers. Afterwards he crouched in the small antechamber munching on a bunch of grapes, taking generous sips of wine from the skin he carried. Trespassers! If Gavinus and Philippus had discovered this place, did others know? He squatted, spitting out seeds and pieces of grape skin, and stared around. Gavinus and Philippus were gone. Attius' corpse, that bag of spite and malice, had been consumed by flames just after dawn this morning. Drusilla was no more. The little bitch Claudia might be dangerous! Valentinian sucked on his teeth. He would have to do something about her.

The former deacon smiled to himself. He would have been a great actor. He could have summoned up dreams, visions for his audience; instead, his harsh-faced mother had forced him into the Christian faith, lecturing him constantly about a loving God. Well, Valentinian had seen little of that in his life: so many people, so much evil! Lives snuffed out like the wick of an oil lamp. Ah well. He finished off the grapes. The door to a new future was opening, and what did he fear? The *vigiles*? He laughed quietly to himself. The August Ones? Presbyter Sylvester? Fools stumbling around in the dark. Attius' household? He'd certainly taken care of that. Lord Charon? Perhaps, but there again, Charon, with his legion of imps, was sorely needed at the moment. Valentinian had spent years in the catacombs and knew Rome's underworld. If Charon tried to trick him, punishment would be swift. The Nefandus? Valentinian scratched his chin. Who could that be? He returned to Claudia. She was another matter. The She-Asses must be kept under close supervision, and for that, he needed Charon.

Valentinian extinguished the lantern horn, picked up the sack and scurried down the tunnel leading to the small entrance chamber and the steps going up into the old tomb. As he emerged carefully into the fresh morning air he stared around, but sensed no danger. He pulled back the covering of the table-tomb, then, delving in the sack, took out a mask and placed this firmly across his face, tying the straps tightly behind his head. He peered through the slits around this haunted place of the dead, then squinted up at the sun. Soon it would be noon. He eased his short stabbing sword from its sheath and, clutching the sack in his other hand, wormed his way around the crumbling memorials, through the spiky, tangled gorse and rough long grass.

Birdsong echoed eerily. The cry of a jay cut across this, harsh and insistent. Valentinian smiled, it reminded him of so much of his early years when he believed in the Lord Christ and led his congregation across the lonely scrublands of the various cemeteries and catacombs around Rome. It was on a day like this that he'd been captured and dragged into the filthiest cell at the Tullianum. Terror-filled days and nights had followed, when he'd prayed and begged for solace. None had come, and Valentinian had peered into the blackness and realised there'd been nothing there in the first place.

A furious scrabbling amongst the undergrowth made him pause and crouch down. A dog fox trotted by, a rabbit's carcass dangling from its bloody jaws. Valentinian went on towards the ancient holm oak where he'd agreed to meet Cerebus, Lord Charon's lieutenant. He approached the spot and sat deep in the shade with his back to the treetrunk. He had warned Cerebus which way to approach. He looked to the left and right. He knew this place better than anyone; the paths, the empty tombs and memorials where he could hide. All those derelict sepulchres which would lead him underground as well as the places where he had secretly placed bags of oil and sharp tinder to create fire and mask his escape. The long, coarse grass directly opposite him suddenly parted, and Cerebus emerged, ugly face watchful, nosing the air like a hunting dog.

"*Salve*," Valentinian sang out. "All hail, my friend! You have come alone?"

Cerebus held up his right hand, five fingers splayed.

145

"As long as they stay where they should," Valentinian warned. "You, however, may draw closer."

Cerebus did so.

"Any news from Rome?" Valentinian asked. "Has the imperial bitch replied to your master's letter?"

"No." Cerebus shook his head.

Valentinian, hiding behind his mask, ground his teeth but concealed his disappointment. "Then perhaps it's time for a second letter." He fished inside the sack, took out a copper scroll-holder and threw it. It fell close to Cerebus and rolled towards him; he picked it up.

"My master says the *agentes in rebus* are busy; that little chit Claudia is snooping about."

"So she is, and —"

"My master has warned her," Cerebus declared. "He also says two of the *scrutores* working in the Palatine palace have disappeared."

"So it seems."

"My master has spies in the imperial writing office. The two other *scrutores* have been invited to the She-Asses. Claudia, the little bitch, wishes to interrogate them there."

"And so it seems again." Valentinian was grateful that the mask concealed his panic. In truth he had no knowledge of what Cerebus had just told him. "If that happened," he declared flatly, "it might be dangerous. Perhaps your master should take care of the problem, in the one place all at the same time."

"You mean visit the She-Asses?"

"Of course, tonight. There is plunder to be had, dangers to be confronted, risks to be nullified. Your master would also be sending the august bitch a clear warning, as I do." Valentinian pointed at the copper scroll Cerebus had tucked into his waistband.

"You say my master should visit the She-Asses?" Cerebus repeated.

"Why not? A place not patrolled by imperial troops, only two drunken *vigiles*. What danger do they pose?"

"Would you be there?"

"Of course not!" Valentinian scoffed.

"My master will have to reflect."

"Tell him to do so, swiftly. True, there are risks," Valentinian shrugged, "as in any business venture, but also a great deal to gain. If you follow my advice, your master will demonstrate his power in Rome."

"That is my master's business. He does wonder if Attius took the secret of the Galilean's tomb to Hades with him. Indeed, did he have the secret in the first place?"

"Oh no, Attius had the secret, and now it is mine."

"Do the others know?"

Valentinian laughed. "They did, and two of them have paid the price. Show this to your master, but first, if Lord Charon decides to visit the She-Asses, let me know the time."

"How?"

"Leave a notice amongst the many handbills in the Portico of Venus in the Caelian quarter; a bill of sale for she-asses, with the time on it. Tell him to do it swiftly. Time is of the essence."

Cerebus nodded. "You have something to show me?"

Valentinian undid the sack and, shaking loose the bloodied cloak, sent Gavinus' severed head rolling towards Cerebus. "Look at it well."

Cerebus lunged forward and grabbed the grisly token from where it come to rest against a stone.

"Petilius Gavinus," Valentinian declared. "Former decurion in the XXth Victrix, *scrutor* for the late but not lamented Emperor Maxentius. He was bitten to death by rock vipers."

"And the other *scrutor*, Julius Philippus, where is he?"

"Burnt to a cinder."

"You killed them both?"

"No, the tomb did! Tell that to your master."

"And Frontinus, the freedman?"

Valentinian sniggered softly. "Soft blubbery Frontinus? He watched his master being cremated here just after dawn, a man of straw, full of fear. He even cancelled the funeral banquet due to a family crisis."

"What?"

"Oh, haven't you heard?" Valentinian was now enjoying himself. "Drusilla, Attius' concubine? If she knew anything, she has also gone to Hades. She was killed last night by the Nefandus near the She-Asses. Do tell your master that."

Cerebus stared down at the severed head, its face a hideous blueish-white colour. When he looked up again, the grotesque masked figure crouching in the shade of the holm oak had gone.

Gemellus Severus, former decurion in the XXth Victrix, also wished he could be gone. He crouched over the table in the chamber adjoining the imperial writing office which lay at the heart of the Palatine and bitterly regretted his part in all of this. He glanced across at the far wall; the maenads painted dancing there seemed to be mocking him with their extravagant rejoicing around the welling wine press. The artist had depicted the dancers in a variety of poses, heads all garlanded, feet and hands splashed with the purple grape juice over which they danced. In the centre of the painting the wine god Dionysus, swathed in purple skins, sat enthroned, a flute in one hand, a jewel-studded goblet in the other. Severus bitterly wished he could escape all this, even if it meant drinking one deep bowl of Falernian after another. He wanted to be away from Rome. Oh, to be free from the plans for Byzantium, the past with its haunting secrets, the present dangers and future threats!

Severus cursed the day he'd volunteered to be one of Maxentius' henchmen. He had become enmeshed in the hunt for the Galilean's tomb. Narses and Attius were to blame, especially Narses. He was a stranger brought into the legion late in his career with the rank of decurion, and had soon proved to be an enthusiastic hunter and destroyer of all things Christian. Now Gavinus and Philippus had disappeared, and that old spy Macrinus had been furious. Severus knew where they'd gone: pursuing moonbeams, seeking the Galilean's tomb. Hadn't they learnt their lesson? Attius had been murdered; the hunt for that shrine brought the darkest ill-luck. Now Narses had gone searching for his colleagues, or so he'd said, leaving the palace at an early hour. Macrinus had told them they could only leave the palace one at a time. Had Macrinus followed Narses? Severus hadn't caught a glimpse of the tribune since daybreak. He glared at the secret plans laid on the table. No wonder he and the rest had been pardoned by Constantine! They would pay a heavy price for that.

He heard footsteps in the corridor outside. Narses, wet with sweat, his tunic rather soiled, came into the chamber and went straight across to the lavarium to wash his hands and face.

"Nothing," he declared, turning round and wiping himself with a napkin. "I went across as far as the Vatican Hill; no sight or sign of them."

"Could they have fled?"

"Fled?" Narses snapped. "Where to, with what?"

"To Licinius in the East?"

Narses walked across and leaned over his comrade. "Use your wits, Severus!" he hissed. "They went looking for that tomb; you know that, I know that! I think they are dead, as we might be. I will have nothing more to do with that tomb. Attius is now a jar of dust, Gavinus and Philippus probably likewise . . . Oh, by the way, have you heard the rumours?"

Severus shook his head.

"Drusilla, Attius' concubine, is dead. Slain last night by the Nefandus. The news is all over the city."

"Who could the killer be?" Severus bleated. "Frontinus?"

"Frontinus! Attius told us all about him; a timid schoolmaster."

"And Macrinus?"

150

Narses pulled a face, turned his back and walked across to the lavarium. Or you, Severus wondered, the stranger in our midst? He went to rise but the door was flung opened and Macrinus marched in.

"Where have you been?" Narses asked.

"None of your business really, but looking for you and the others," Macrinus snapped. "Anyway, I bring a message from the Augusta."

Severus groaned at Macrinus' withering glance.

"The woman Claudia wishes to question you, but not here. We," Macrinus smiled falsely, "are to be her special guests at the She-Asses tavern in the Caelian quarter tonight."

"Why?"

"I don't know," Macrinus retorted. "The request came in to the imperial writing office. The Augusta has agreed. Scribes have drawn up your passes." He clapped his hand on Severus' shoulder. "It's an invitation you cannot refuse . . ."

Claudia slept late that morning. She'd had a troubled night and just before daybreak sent Oceanus into the city with messages for the Augusta and Sallust the Searcher. Now she rested in the tavern garden, Narcissus seated beside her. He briefly explained how Drusilla's remains had been removed to his embalming chamber and that he had nothing else to add about her killing.

"Why do you think the Nefandus removes the right eye of his victims?" Claudia asked.

"If you'd asked me that yesterday," Narcissus replied, "I would have been unable to answer, but working on that poor woman's corpse, I recalled something from my days in Antioch. Now that city is built on three of its sides along thickly wooded steep hills. In my time, women were found strangled out beneath the trees, bellies ripped open, both eyes removed, very similar to these killings by the Nefandus. I'd forgotten all about that," he mused, "until last night." He smiled at Claudia. "I try not to remember anything about my former life; just the thought of my wife makes me angry. Anyway, the killer confessed how he hated women but claimed it was their eyes which taunted him as much as their bodies, and that was why he killed the way he did. Cruel bastard! The governor crucified him near the bridge over the Orontes; it took days for him to die, and even then they had to break his legs."

"How did they capture him?"

"Oh yes," Narcissus screwed up his face, "how did they?" He grinned. "Very simple: whistles!" he exclaimed. "The kind used by centurions in battle. Whistles and criminals."

"I'm sorry?"

"The governor visited the city prison. He offered a pardon to eight condemned women. They were to dress as whores and frequent the streets close to the Aleppo gate, the same quarter from where the other victims came. As in Rome, whores throng near the city gates in search of customers and a comfortable nook for their trysts. In Antioch it was easier: nice hilly countryside close by with plenty of cover amongst the trees and thick vegetation."

"And?" Claudia asked, now deeply interested.

"The prisoners were dressed and painted, then given those whistles. At the same time the governor deployed a cohort of mountaineers, Illyrians, along the wooded slopes. They were given rations and told to stay well out of sight. The condemned women were eager for a pardon. Despite the paint and clothes, they were tough and resolute, unlike the poor girls who'd been murdered. Claudia, they captured the attacker almost immediately. The chosen victim fought like a tigress and blew her whistle; her attacker fled but the Illyrians caught him."

Claudia stared across the garden. A ripple of excitement made her stomach pitch. Of course, there were two ways to hunt: to search and to trap. Why hadn't Macrinus attempted the latter? Why couldn't they do that now?

Murranus came out chewing on a piece of chicken, and informed her that a message had come from the Palatine: the *scrutores*, together with Macrinus, would be here just before dusk. He mumbled something about visiting Torquatus the Tonsor and wandered back into the kitchen. Claudia got up, walked across the grass and sat in her uncle's favourite seat, staring up at the branches. A thought occurred to her: she must see Presbyter Sylvester and seek an audience with Helena. The Nefandus could be trapped.

She heard her name called, and whirled around as Sallust the Searcher, grey-faced, grey-haired and grey-garbed, came strolling across the lawn, hands extended. Claudia rose to greet him, kissing him on each cheek, inviting him to sit down. Sorry came trotting behind with a tray bearing a cup of Polybius' finest wine, some bread, cheese and a sliced apple. Claudia let Sallust break his fast then told him what had happened and what information she needed. Sallust just nodded, now and again squinting up at the sun or fingering the corner of his mouth. Claudia had every confidence in him. Despite his appearance, he was the best searcher in Rome. He and his legion of assistants — sons, cousins, uncles, nieces and nephews — spread like a huge spider's web throughout the city. If there was information available, Sallust and his people would find it. Claudia trusted him implicitly. Sallust had backed the wrong side in the recent civil war, and it was only due to Claudia's intervention that imperial disfavour had been avoided. Even so, he had lost a great deal and was eager to make up such losses.

Once Claudia had finished, Sallust got to his feet. He promised to do his best but said he could give her no guarantees. Claudia thanked him and watched him go, then went back and opened the leather writing satchel she'd left on the garden seat. She had so much to do, yet she still had no answers to the questions she'd listed the previous evening. Murranus called her and she recalled that he was about to meet Torquatus; that was another matter! She went back into the tavern. Polybius and his fellow conspirator, Labienus, squatted in a shadowy recess, heads together like the conspirators they were. Claudia, unannounced, pulled up a stool and sat down.

"Uncle," she began, "I have warned you time and again to avoid wagers and madcap schemes. I've heard all about Torquatus' offer. You cannot accept it. No! No!" She held a hand up. "Listen, I am going to give Torquatus a puzzle; if he can solve that, then the play goes ahead. If not, he will fund a banquet here at the She-Asses."

Polybius made to object, but Labienus, who now apparently regretted such foolishness when they were deep in their cups, sided with Claudia, and Polybius reluctantly agreed.

"Good," Claudia exclaimed. "Now it's time for Torquatus."

"What will you tell him?" Polybius asked.

Claudia leaned down and kissed her uncle on the forehead.

"Uncle dearest, if I told you that, I might as well advertise it throughout the Caelian quarter and pin a notice on the tavern door. You'll just have to wait and see."

"You've thought of a story?" Labienus asked.

"I've thought of a riddle," Claudia replied.

She went into the kitchen, where Murranus, cradling Caligula, was watching Celades preparing the evening meal. Both man and cat seemed transfixed by the delicious odours from the pans. Celades was making a hot sauce for roast pork, stirring in peppers, dried almonds soaked overnight, honey, wine, olives and chopped leeks, whilst at the same time preparing another sauce for boiled chicken. Now and again Murranus would nibble absent-mindedly at the piece of dried bacon Celades had placed in a freshly baked scone, or nod understandingly as Celades lectured both man and cat on how not to prepare a sauce. Claudia took Caligula out of his arms and dragged Murranus out of the tavern, pushing him up the street towards the great sycamore where Torquatus held court. It was mid-afternoon, so business had grown slack before the usual rush of those who'd finished their day's work and sought Torquatus' attentions before resorting to the wine booths or baths. Torquatus grandly ushered them into his "sanctuary", as he called the partitioned area with its stools and tables, the latter covered with razors, scissors, curling irons, and jars of cassia, cinnamon and other perfumes. Next to these were stacks of white napkins, silver bowls and pans of water which Torquatus would heat over a portable stove.

Felicitations and introductions were exchanged. Murranus walked to the stool, a napkin tucked around the neck of his tunic. Claudia stared at the mirrors hung on the side of the screen. She sniffed at the bowl of spiders' webs soaked in oil and vinegar which, Torquatus assured her, was the best cure as laid down by Pliny if, the gods forefend, he cut a client's face. Scissors in one hand, Torquatus began to clip Murranus' close-cropped hair, assuring him that he would never grow bald, whilst Murranus' distaste for a beard was "the height of fashion". Oh yes, Torquatus declared, better to be shaved with razor and hot water than use creams such as ivy gum, asses' fat, she-goats' gore, bats' blood or powdered viper to remove hair. Whilst he chattered, Claudia read the epigrams of Martial written on various parchments and hung on the screen for the delectation of customers. She laughed at one: "While the slow barber goes round your face and trims your cheeks, a second beard grows."

"I like that too." Torquatus stopped his clipping and smiled at Claudia. "But are you here," he picked up a small Spanish whetstone to sharpen the blades, "to watch your beloved have his hair cut or, perhaps, to request my ministrations yourself?"

Claudia stuck her tongue out and went back to reading the epigrams.

"You know why I'm here, Torquatus: your wager with Uncle Polybius and Labienus." She turned and faced him squarely. "You wanted them to write a play containing a riddle or a mystery which the audience cannot solve. Now you know that's impossible! Whatever they concoct, they must give to the actors, and actors certainly talk."

Torquatus grinned. "I'd thought of that myself," he conceded. "I was going to see Polybius."

"Well I've got a different wager," Claudia stepped forward, "and it's this. I will now give *you* a riddle, a mystery for you to solve. If you can, and I know you trust me, Uncle Polybius will invite you to a feast at the She-Asses. However, if you cannot solve it within four days, it is you who will be our host at the tavern."

Torquatus wiped his fingers on a napkin and stretched out his hand; Claudia caught and clasped it.

"Agreed," he declared. "And now this mystery?"

"Oh, very simple: a man locks himself into a chamber which has no hidden entrances or passageways. His steward and concubine try to rouse him. The concubine clearly believes that the key is turned in the lock from inside; the steward reports the same. They have no choice but to force the door. Once inside, they find their master sprawled on his bed, a dagger thrust into his back."

"You are talking of Attius Enobarbus? I've heard the story."

"Yes, I'm talking about Attius Enobarbus. If you can solve how the assassin entered that chamber, killed his victim and left, locking the door from the inside, then, Torquatus, you deserve every cup of wine you can down."

"Ah, but wait." As the barber splashed hot water on Murranus' face, the former gladiator winked at Claudia; she just grimaced back at him. "I want to make this very clear," Torquatus continued, sharpening the razor on the whetstone. "No tricks! The chamber has no other entrances, the door was certainly locked and the key was found on the inside. First question: could there be more than one key?"

"There is only one key; both steward and concubine claim it was still there when they broke the door down."

Torquatus ran the razor lightly along the side of Murranus' face.

"Second question: did the assassin have some form of device that could turn the key from the outside?"

"Impossible," Claudia replied. "The lock was heavy and deep, the key embedded in it. There was no other

158

entrance to that chamber except through the door, and it was secured by a heavy lock; the key was found on the inside; there was no second key."

Torquatus slapped more warm water on Murranus' face.

"It's possible," he said, turning his back on Claudia to concentrate on Murranus, "that the assassin struck, drove his dagger into the victim's back and fled the chamber. The victim didn't die immediately but staggered to the door, turned the key, went back and collapsed on his bed."

"It's possible," Claudia conceded, "but if that was the case, why didn't he go to the door and cry for help? There was very little blood; only a few drops found between the door and the bed. I think such a solution is highly unlikely. The dagger was thrust so deep, he must have died immediately. What I wager, Torquatus, is this: either you give me an answer which is acceptable to both of us, or I will give you one, also acceptable to both of us. Our wager is based on trust and honesty, the best guarantee." She smiled. "Do you wish to continue?"

Torquatus nodded.

"And if I win," Claudia added firmly, "discuss with me any future project you wish to propose to Uncle Polybius before you even dream of talking to him!"

CHAPTER
EIGHT

Unsparing as the thunderbolt, he continued his career of slaughter.

Torquatus just laughed and continued with his shaving. He began to interrogate Murranus about Attius' murder, but his customer could only repeat what had already been said. Claudia decided to leave the booth and sit on a stool outside. She stared around. The square was quiet; a light breeze sent the dried leaves whirling across. She gazed up at the blue sky. The weather was changing, gods be thanked! Slowly autumn and all its full glory would be here. The mornings and evenings would grow cooler, and that dreadful stifling heat would disappear. She watched the usual sights: a boy pushing a wheelbarrow full of freshly severed meat, a tramping hawker sitting in the shade, two children playing round the fountain, a beggar hopping behind a merchant, scrawny arms extended, weeping for alms. Petronius the Pimp strolled by with two of his girls; he glimpsed Claudia and raised a hand in greeting.

Claudia was about to move back inside the booth when something caught her attention. She was always interested in the various characters and scenes of the quarter, and that huckster with the tray tied around his neck was definitely new; she hadn't seen him before.

160

She rose to her feet and walked round the booth. There were more strangers: people just idling, servants sheltering in the portico, a man playing with a dog, teasing it with a stick, a youth carrying a water jar, a pedlar laying out his movable store, individuals Claudia couldn't recognise. She felt a slight prick of unease. Why here? Why now?

Her name was called and she went back into the booth. Murranus, now standing up, was thanking Torquatus, dropping coins into his hands. He and Claudia strolled back across the square towards the She-Asses. Murranus paused and stared down at her.

"What's wrong, Claudia? One minute you are chirping like a sparrow on a branch; now you have fallen silent, watchful. You're not regretting the wager with Torquatus?"

"Look around, Murranus," she whispered. "Look around and tell me what you see."

He did so. "Hawkers, walkers, people taking the shade against the sun. Come on, Claudia, I want to go back and watch Celades do that sauce. There's nothing as tasty as crisp pork."

"Look around, Murranus," she repeated.

He sighed, scratched his freshly cropped hair and did what she asked. He was about to turn back, then looked again.

"Yes." He stared up at the sky, then winked at her. "A lot of people here I don't recognise. You can usually tell the time of day by the drunks stumbling down for a free drink, or Petronius the Pimp looking for custom. *Agentes in rebus?*" he added. "Helena's agents? You're bringing those two *scrutores* down here tonight, aren't you?"

Claudia nodded.

"That could explain the strangers. They are spies being paid by the imperial treasury to keep an eye on the tavern, that's all. Come on, let's go."

Once back at the She-Asses, Claudia excused herself and went up to her own chamber, locking the door from the inside. She moved across to her writing desk and once again studied what she'd written, but any solution to the mysteries eluded her. She still felt uneasy about what she'd seen in the square. The wager with Torquatus would have to wait; once she'd resolved the mystery of Attius' murder, she'd have her answer.

Claudia lay down on the bed and stared at the ceiling, searching for that cobweb and the spider scurrying about. From downstairs echoed the sounds of laughter. Simon the Stoic was, once again, declaiming one of his mournful poems. Claudia drifted off to sleep, and when she woke, immediately recalled what she'd glimpsed in the square. She splashed water over her face, put on her sandals and ran down the stairs and out of the front door of the tavern. Two Sarmatians stood there, mercenaries dressed in leather kilts, their hair braided and oiled. They were studying the scribble on Polybius' blackboard offering the delicacies of the day: boiled chicken, roast pork, hot lamb stew, truffles followed by peas à la Celades, lentils with chestnuts, julienne potage and patina of elderberries.

"Are you hungry?" she asked.

162

"Very," one of them growled, looking her over from head to toe, "and not just for food."

Claudia pointed to the other notice, warning pimps, witches and warlocks not to seek their custom in the tavern.

"The food is delicious," she said, "and so is the wine, but that is all you'll get in this house."

The two Sarmatians laughed, one of them patted her on the shoulder and they went into the dining hall, bawling for service. Claudia followed them; mercenaries on their day off, looking for a girl and a bite to eat, often frequented the She-Asses, and these seemed no different. They swaggered in and commandeered a table, clapping their hands, shouting for Polybius to bring a jug of his best wine and a beaker of clear water. Claudia pretended to busy herself at the counter. She noticed how the two strangers were extremely curious about the She-Asses. One of them got up and walked to a window overlooking the garden; the other came across to the counter, before wandering off to inspect Murranus' shield and sword, which Polybius had placed on a wall as a mark of honour. Claudia's unease deepened. She went out to the garden and sat for a while, but felt restless and returned to her chamber, where she washed and changed. She'd hardly finished when she heard a roaring downstairs, followed by shrieks of laughter and Januaria's squeals.

"Burrus has arrived!" Claudia whispered to herself. She raced down the stairs. The Sarmatians had gone. Burrus and six of his Germans seemed to dominate the dining hall, great shaggy bears in their furred cloaks, hair and beards all tangled; the war belts strapped tightly round their waists sported dagger, sword and a small throwing axe. Burrus had already seized a platter of roast pork whilst his companions, torn between the prospect of food and Januaria's plump, bouncy tits, snuffled like boars eager for mischief. Polybius had apparently taken Claudia's guests out to the garden. Burrus glimpsed Claudia and, his mouth still stuffed with pork, roared his greetings, then advanced on her, arms extended, to deliver a warm, tight, breath-stifling hug. The German reeked of sweat, meat and ale. He stepped back, his icy blue eyes full of pleasure at meeting what he called his "little spear maiden", woman to the great warrior Murranus, special friend of the Augusta, whom Burrus and his gang of ruffians regarded as a goddess incarnate. Then he turned to roar greetings at Murranus, who brought other platters on a tray from the kitchen. He took one, promptly refilled his own, then laughed over his shoulder at his companions.

"Burrus?" Claudia stood on tiptoe. "You and your lovely lads! I want nothing missing, platters or knives, statues or goblets. This is my house; you are my guests!"

Burrus nodded solemnly. The Empress Helena had given him and his companions a similar lecture as they'd knelt in front of her in the imperial gardens. They were to deliver Macrinus, Narses and Severus and then return immediately to the palace.

"No mischief!" Helena had warned. "No dilly-dallying on the way, you great hulking brutes, or you'll have my cane across your shoulders. No fighting, no thieving, no wenching, no drinking! I don't want you back here in the early hours drunk as pigs, roaring out one of your disgusting songs. Now give my love to Claudia, but . . ."

The lecture had gone on and on. Well, Burrus peered down at Claudia, they'd been good boys so far, only one drink on their way here, and another on the way back. The German stuffed more pork into his mouth and studied Claudia intently. She was distracted, peering round as if looking for someone. He thrust his platter at Januaria as she passed, simpering at him, then smacked her bottom and grabbed the goblet Murranus brought, thanking him and raising it in toast.

"Claudia," Burrus leaned down, "you want to talk to your old friend Burrus. What is wrong?"

Claudia touched him on the tip of his nose. "Outside," she whispered. Slipping round Burrus' companions, also eager to hug her, she went out of the front door, then turned as if studying the menu posted there.

"What is it, little one?"

Claudia glanced sideways at Burrus. He was no longer playing the rough, drunken buffoon. The German's face was solemn, eyes watchful. Claudia knew him to be as nimble-witted as he was quick on his feet.

"What are your orders, Captain? To bring your guests here and return later this evening to escort them back?"

"Yes, the Augusta declared she did not trust us to remain sober here."

Claudia laughed. "Go back to the Augusta." She pointed to the notice as if describing it. "Ask her if she has *agentes* here."

"At the She-Asses?"

"Yes. Ask her if she is being watchful."

"And if she isn't?"

Claudia turned. "Ah, don't worry, my great bear, the Augusta will know exactly what to do." She grabbed Burrus' paw of a hand. "It is time we went back."

Claudia remained in the eating hall, laughing and talking with Burrus' escort, before wishing them farewell. Then she went to Polybius, whispered that she was not to be disturbed and walked out into the late evening sunshine, across to where Macrinus, Narses and Severus sat in Polybius' favourite place. The shadows were now lengthening, and all three had finished a platter of roast pork and boiled chicken and were busy helping themselves to a bunch of grapes. They'd also drunk deeply on the fine Falernian Polybius had served. Claudia was halfway across the lawn when she heard her name being called. She stopped, sighed and turned. Polybius stood at the kitchen door, waving her back.

"You have another guest," he declared. "Frontinus; he is in a bit of a state but he has brought us a present."

Claudia went back into the eating hall. The Germans had left. Frontinus slouched forlornly at a table, before him a beautiful figure of Artemis, modelled on the statue at Ephesus; next to it was a small cask of wine.

He jumped to his feet as Claudia approached. He looked the very picture of woe, face unshaven, eyes red-rimmed with crying, fingers all dirty.

"I should have stayed," he stammered, "I should have stayed at Attius' house, but it's a hall of ghosts now. He's gone . . . Drusilla . . . I . . . I . . . thank you and Narcissus for your work. You are both very kind. I needed a little company, I had to escape that house. I cancelled the funeral banquet, you know?"

"Frontinus," Claudia squeezed his hands, "relax, you're here with friends." She nodded at the statue and the cask of wine. "It was very kind of you to think of us. Stay here, have something to eat and drink. Murranus will escort you back." She glanced across to where Murranus stood chatting with Polybius near the door; he nodded in agreement. "I have other business," she said, "but please, feel at home here."

Claudia whispered to Murranus to keep an eye on Frontinus, then rejoined the others out in the garden. They'd finished their meal and were now enjoying the last of the sunshine, the birds chattering and fluttering in the branches above them. Claudia slipped on to the bench and smiled around.

"You enjoyed your meal?"

Murmurs of satisfaction answered her question.

"Why did you bring us here?" Macrinus asked. "Did you think the wine would soften us?"

"I brought you here," Claudia retorted, "because I might be able to save your lives." The smile faded from her face. "Narses and Severus, you were *scrutores* for Maxentius. You searched for Christian tombs and destroyed them. So did Attius; he is now dead, murdered. Two of your colleagues, Gavinus and Philippus, have disappeared. I doubt if they've fled; they wouldn't get very far. They have either been kidnapped or killed. I suggest the latter. Why? I suspect it's connected to the tomb of Peter the Galilean, so I ask you now, do any of you know anything about that?"

Narses closed his eyes. Severus, however, flushed with wine, leaned forward over the table. "Claudia, you have been blunt with us. I'll be equally blunt back. We destroyed tombs. We carried out the orders of the Emperor. Naturally, the great prize was the tomb of the Galilean. I suspect Attius Enobarbus may have learnt its whereabouts; he may have shared such information with Gavinus."

"Did they also share that secret with you?"

Severus laughed and shook his head. "Of course not! I don't know if Attius wrote it down. I suspect he did, and kept it in that damnable Icthus casket. Gavinus may have written it down or committed it to memory."

"Why didn't they share it with you?"

"For the same reason," Narses opened his eyes and leaned his elbows on the table, "he didn't share it with the August Ones. He told us that we should keep it — or rather he should — until times changed and we could use it to our advantage. Moreover, he pointed out that as long as the Emperor thought we knew the secret, he would keep us employed!"

Claudia nodded in agreement.

"Otherwise," Narses continued, "we might end up like so many of Maxentius' former supporters, thrown

168

out to fend for ourselves. Yes, yes, we are prisoners. Tribune Macrinus here is our jailer, our keeper, but at least we are comfortable, we are paid, eat regular meals and have a good place to sleep. For the time being, that is enough."

"We all now know," Claudia replied slowly, "that Attius was not the Nefandus. We have also established that he did know the whereabouts of the Galilean's tomb. He probably kept that information in the Icthus casket. However, in his last days Attius became very frightened. I found a scrap of parchment; he was preparing to write to Presbyter Sylvester offering to share the secret of the tomb. In that letter he talked of an even greater demon than the Nefandus, who terrified him. Did he share such information with you?"

"Yes," Narses replied. "He was very frightened. Just before he was killed, I asked him why."

"On the day he was murdered? Please," Claudia continued, "tell us the truth. Did you follow Attius from the garden down to his chamber?"

"Yes, he did," Macrinus intervened, "because I went down as well."

"Why didn't you tell me this before?"

"I can't speak for him," Narses gestured at Macrinus, "but Attius was murdered. I didn't want to be suspected."

"Then tell me," Claudia invited. "Tell me the truth now!"

Narses took a deep breath. "In Byzantium, Attius became even more withdrawn and kept to himself. He did what he was asked but rarely talked to us. To me he seemed frightened, fearful of something, lost in the past. Anyway, we returned to Rome. Attius refused to come to the Palatine Palace, claiming he was unwell. I suspected he was hale and hearty enough but fearful of something. The day he died, I and the others went to meet him in the garden of his villa. He left us and went down to his chamber. I followed. Attius had locked himself in. I knocked on the door. He answered and let me in. I asked him what the matter was." Narses paused. "You say he was about to write to Presbyter Sylvester?"

Claudia nodded.

"Possible," Narses murmured. "Perhaps he wished to confess. Perhaps, tired of the tension and the fear, he wanted the protection of the Christian Church, but I didn't know that at the time."

"On that day in his chamber?" Claudia insisted.

"Dark," Narses replied, "a few lamps burning. Attius sat behind his desk, what must have been the Icthus casket to his right. I challenged him, saying that we should either look for the tomb of Peter the Galilean ourselves or hand the secret over to the Augusta. He said that was a matter for him to decide. He believed Gavinus knew some of the details, but he would have to think. I argued with him; I admit I became angry." He waved a hand at Macrinus.

"Narses had excused himself in the garden," Marcrinus declared. "I thought he'd gone to relieve himself, but I became suspicious and followed him. I came down the steps and along the passageway to Attius' chamber. I could hear raised voices. I knocked

170

on the door. It was locked. Attius opened it and asked me what I wanted. I demanded to know what was happening, but he," Macrinus gestured at Narses, "and Attius refused to answer. So I left. I went back along the passageway and up the steps into the garden. A short while later, Narses rejoined us."

"And you have no knowledge of the Galilean's tomb?" Claudia asked.

"Oh, Gavinus made reference to it," Narses replied. "He talked of a code which would lead you through to the heart of the mystery. I thought he was only teasing us." He pulled a face. "Anyway, he and Philippus were determined to find the tomb and hand its contents over to the Augusta. They thought they'd be lavishly rewarded and allowed to return to ordinary life. I must admit, I was tempted to join them. Now that they haven't returned, I no longer wish to have anything to do with that dangerous mystery. Mistress," Narses peered at Claudia, "that is all I know."

Claudia glanced at Severus, now deep in his cups.

"I agree with everything he said," Severus slurred. "I just want to go home. I'm tired of this; I have been for years."

Claudia stood up. "Gentlemen, I'll leave you to your wine." She walked a few paces away, then turned. "Oh, Macrinus, may I have a word with you?"

The tribune got up and came towards her.

"Macrinus." Claudia glanced up at the sky, then down at the moon-washed grass. Darkness had crept in, and all was quiet except for the chatter of the birds.

Claudia still felt a deep unease, as if was she was being watched from the shadows.

"How can I help you?" Macrinus asked politely.

"You hunted the Nefandus," Claudia declared. "There are two ways to hunt, Tribune: one is to search the alleyways; the other is to lay a trap, a bait. Did you ever consider that?"

"Of course we did!" Macrinus snapped. Claudia caught a flicker in those tired eyes, as if she had touched on something sensitive. "But how could it be done?" he blustered. "We tried a few times but failed. It really wasn't successful, I assure you."

Claudia had her answer. She thanked him and walked back across the garden, passing Frontinus sitting on a bench talking to Sorry, in one hand a goblet of wine, in the other a piece of chicken. Claudia could see that the freedman was deep in his cups, cheeks drenched with tears. She smiled at Sorry and hurried on into the tavern. Murranus and the rest were grouped round a table exchanging funny stories. Claudia excused herself and went upstairs to her chamber. She thought of lying on her bed, but she did not wish to sleep, so she went to the window and looked down. Frontinus, now hunched over, was listening to Sorry tell some tale. Caligula, however, had moved into the arc of light thrown by the lamps and was staring down the garden to where Macrinus, Narses and Severus still sat at the orchard table, gossiping amongst themselves. Claudia wondered whether it was Caligula she had sensed watching from the darkness. She stared at the trees and vineyard behind the three men. Nothing but a wall of blackness, but then she caught a glint of steel, a sliver of light. Was someone lurking in the garden? Caligula, already alarmed, was trotting backwards and forwards, tail high, fur all ruffled. Sorry also had sensed something wrong. Unlike the rest he hadn't drunk, and he sprang to his feet, staring into the night. Claudia leaned out of the window and caught another glint of metal shining through the gloom.

The garden was surrounded by a high brick wall; at the back of it ranged Polybius' vines, orchard, vegetation and a few outhouses. A host of men could secretly gather there to attack the tavern. The sounds below were dying. Out across the grass, Macrinus had risen to his feet. Sorry abruptly grasped Caligula and ran shouting into the kitchen. Claudia screamed at Macrinus and the others to flee. Macrinus and Narses moved swiftly; Severus staggered drunkenly behind them. Downstairs the alarm had been raised, with shouts and cries and the crashing of shutters against windows. An attack by the *inferni*, the outlaws of Rome, on a prosperous tavern like the She-Asses was not unknown.

Claudia stood back and stared. Dark shapes were now streaking across the grass, hideous figures, heads and faces hidden by animal masks. Macrinus and Narses had almost reached the back door of the tavern. Severus, however, stumbled. Macrinus turned to go back to help, but someone, probably Murranus, pulled him in. Claudia watched in horror as Severus tried to rise but a masked figure brought his two-edged axe down, splitting the back of his head. She pulled the shutters closed and ran to join the rest downstairs. Petronius the Pimp and Simon the Stoic, followed by others including a drunken Frontinus, were already fleeing through the front door. Oceanus slammed this shut behind them, rolling down the thick piece of protective leather inside. Others were being organised by Murranus. Most of the lamps were extinguished. Polybius had opened his weapons chest, and Macrinus and Narses took out bows and quivers of arrows. Polybius and Poppaoe brought spears from the cellars. Others were given axes. Celades brought his cleaver from the kitchen, whilst Claudia grabbed a bow and a few arrows.

"They won't attack the front!" Murranus yelled. "Too public and too hard. The kitchen door will hold for a while; watch for fire! The shutters are the weakest." As if in response, a dull thudding began against the heavy kitchen door, whilst axe blows rained down on the shutters. The assailants were trying to force as many entrances as possible. One shutter fell apart with a crash and a grotesque figure pushed its way through. Macrinus loosed an arrow and the attacker fell back. More gathered. Murranus sprang forward, sword whirling as if in the amphitheatre. He stabbed and jabbed and the attackers retreated with screams and yells, but another shutter was weakening. Celades screamed that smoke was curling beneath the kitchen door. Claudia notched an arrow to her bow, then raised it and loosed at the blackness where the shutter had been. She did not know if she hit her mark,

174

for the strident wailing of war horns cut through the din.

"More attackers!" Narses yelled.

Claudia, however, recognised the sound. Burrus had arrived! The wail of horns came again, followed by screams and yells. The attack on the tavern eased, and instead the hideous din of battle echoed from the garden, above this the blood-chilling fighting chants of the Germans. Celades opened the kitchen door. Murranus went out, sword in one hand, a makeshift shield in the other, kicking away the burning branches outside. Claudia joined him. Polybius' elegant garden had been turned into a battlefield. The attackers had now broken and were trying to flee over the walls, but Burrus had planned well. He'd formed his entire cohort into a semicircle and they'd simply moved like reapers through a cornfield, sword and axe falling, no mercy being shown. The yells and screams, the cries of horror eventually subsided. Corpses strewed the ground. No more attackers, just Burrus and his Germans standing, sobbing for breath, swords and axes dripping with blood. Burrus lifted his sword and intoned his paean of victory, echoed jubilantly by his companions, then he swept across the garden to greet Murranus and Claudia.

"You were correct, little one." Burrus, splattered with blood from head to toe, went to embrace her, but he caught the look on her face and stepped back. "There is still work to be done," he agreed. "Murranus, you'd best join us."

Polybius and the rest filed out into the garden. Murranus and Burrus, however, were determined to secure prisoners. Those attackers beyond any help were given a quick cut across the throat. Poppaoe saw this, screamed, retched and fled back into the tavern, followed by Januaria and other customers. Now the crisis was past, they wished to renew their courage with generous cups of wine. Murranus shouted for more light. Polybius brought out poles and lashed cresset torches to them; the pitch was fired and flared into flame to reveal a truly gruesome sight. Corpses lay across the garden; some had their heads severed, others arms and legs.

"The scum of Rome," Murranus whispered to Claudia. "There's no need for you to stay here."

Claudia swallowed hard and shook her head. "I'll stay, I want to."

"Whoever they were," Murranus added, "they were no match for Burrus and his Germans." He grasped Claudia by the hand and walked on to the grass. "How many?" he called.

Burrus came shuffling towards them, pausing to wipe his sword and dagger on a corpse. "Forty to fifty. About ten escaped, some of them wounded. Most of these are dead, or wounded beyond recovery." He paused as a hideous scream shrilled through the darkness. "We have some prisoners. Come!"

Polybius came out of the tavern again, determined to clean up what he called his "little paradise". Once he'd inspected the mangled remains, he strode back into the tavern to ask his customers for help. The small side gate from the garden was opened, Polybius had the tavern cart brought out and the corpses were unceremoniously thrown on to be taken to one of the burial pits just outside the walls. Burrus had six prisoners. Now disarmed and stripped of their masks, they didn't look so dangerous or fearsome; just men trembling at the prospect of a hideous death.

"It will be crucifixion for you." Burrus declared, walking up and down. "They'll take you outside the Aurelian Gate and crucify you along the Appian Way. You'll be shown no mercy, but before that you'll be flogged and tortured. Who are you?" Burrus yelled.

The prisoners shuffled uneasily, looking over their shoulders at Burrus' Germans gathered behind them.

"Who are you?" Burrus repeated. Going to one of the poles, he took down a cresset torch, then walked up to the nearest prisoner and thrust the flames straight into the man's face; he screamed and fell to his knees. "Who are you?" Burrus moved to the next prisoner.

The man knelt, hands extended. "We were sent by Lord Charon."

Another prisoner, further down the line, objected. Burrus walked towards him.

"Are you the leader?"

The man gazed sullenly back. Burrus thrust the burning brand towards his face, and the prisoner nodded.

"I'll tell you what." Burrus marched up and down the line, ignoring the screams of the burnt prisoner. "If your leader here confesses the truth and you bear witness to it, adding anything else you know, it will be a

177

swift end, a warrior's death. Your heads will leave your shoulders like flowers being culled. Do you understand? Offer resistance, tell lies, attempt to deceive and I'll make sure that it takes you days to die on the cross."

He walked back to the leader and the questioning began. Burrus threatened him with sword and fire, now and again moving down the line to seek confirmation of what was being said. In the end they didn't tell him much. They were Lord Charon's men, two cohorts brought together and given strict orders to attack the She-Asses after nightfall. They were to kill everyone they found. When asked why by Murranus, the leader just shrugged; even when he had his shoulder burnt by Burrus he could only scream that he'd had his orders and followed them faithfully. The interrogation continued. Burrus asked where Lord Charon was. The man couldn't reply, even after he was tortured again. Others agreed with him. They lurked in the slums or out in the great cemetery along the Appian Way. They'd received their orders, assembled at a certain point and been given instructions to attack the She-Asses and kill everybody; more than that they couldn't say. Claudia, despite the effects of shock after the attack, listened intently. Eventually Burrus tired, turned towards her and shrugged.

"Little one, we've done enough."

"Three more questions." Claudia stepped forward. "Was my name, Claudia, given?"

The prisoners shook their heads. Up close, Claudia realised they were pathetic-looking, lean-faced, with thin-ribbed bodies and birthmarked skin, their tunics and sandals scuffed and stained.

"They are simply foot soldiers," she whispered to Burrus. "They know nothing, but I must at least try. Do any of you know anything about the tomb of Peter the Galilean?"

Again shakes of the head and loud denials. The prisoners themselves were tired of this; they wished matters to be finished.

"And the name Valentinian, does that mean anything to you?" Claudia's voice carried through the darkness. She felt the cold night breeze ruffle her hair and shivered at so much death around her. She wanted to be away, back in the warmth of the tavern.

"Valentinian!" she repeated, "Does it mean anything to you?" She expected no reply, but abruptly one of the prisoners stepped forward. He was young, narrow-faced, his right eye covered with a patch, his left cheek badly scarred. In the flickering torchlight Claudia also noticed the old wounds on his legs beneath the knee; a man who'd apparently been tortured. "What do you know?" she asked.

The other prisoners began to mutter amongst themselves. Burrus ordered them to be quiet.

"I know Valentinian." The prisoner's voice was strangely cultured.

Claudia approached the man. His face had once been handsome; now it was unshaven, dirty and cut, yet the good eye was clear, his voice resolute.

"Valentinian?" Claudia asked, "What do you know about him?"

"I was with him."

"What is you name?"

"My name is Decius. I was once a member of Valentinian's community around the Vatican Hill, before they all died and the good deacon disappeared."

"And what can you tell me?"

The good eye shifted to Burrus, the lips curled in a smile. "In Rome, so it is said, everything has a price."

"And what is your price, Decius?"

"My life, one gold solidi, a knife and free passage."

Burrus strode closer. "Little one, I could torture him, then he'd talk."

"Torture me?" Decius jibed. "Look at these scars, my legs, my face. I've been tortured and tortured again. Do so and she will learn nothing."

Claudia nodded at Burrus. "The rest I am finished with," she said quietly.

Burrus shouted at his men, and the prisoners were led away, the Germans forming a ring of steel around them. They were pushed across the garden and out of the side gate. Claudia knew what Burrus planned. He'd take them to the nearest piece of wasteland, make them kneel and sever their heads.

"You'll join them," she peered up at Decius, "if you lie or try to mislead me. You will be crucified above their corpses."

"Domina," Decius replied, "I'm a raptor, a thief, a killer; that's the way life has turned. I lived out in the

180

cemetery along the Appian Way. I have glimpsed you before; I know your name. There is no need to threaten me. For a goblet of wine and some food, I'll talk all the more swiftly."

CHAPTER
NINE

*But especially abundant were the gifts the
August Helena bestowed on the naked and
friendless poor.*

Murranus and Oceanus seized hold of Decius, took
him across to the kitchen then into the dining hall.
Polybius was now restoring order as well as soothing
nerves with generous cups of wine and whatever scraps
of food were left. The door had been barred. Polybius
loudly declared how those cowards who'd fled would
not have a bite to eat or a drop to drink. The rest were
celebrating. They looked strangely at Decius, then went
back to their own conversations. Murranus and
Oceanus tied Decius' hands and placed him at a table
in the far corner, his back to the wall. Claudia sat
opposite him.

"I asked for wine and something to eat."

"And you shall have it," Claudia agreed. "Tell me
swiftly what you know."

"My name is Decius. I was once a Christian. My
brother and I were part of the community around the
Vatican Hill. Our leader was the deacon Valentinian."

"What did he look like?"

"He was thin-faced, a mop of black hair, very much
the dandy in many ways."

"What do you mean?"

"Although he was a powerful member of our Church, his hair was always crimped and curled, his moustache and beard black and neatly oiled."

"Any other distinguishing mark?"

Decius shook his head.

"His voice?" Claudia asked.

"Very sharp, like that of an officer, as if used to giving orders."

"And what happened to him?"

"The gods only know," Decius answered. "My brother and I were Christians; like the rest we were eventually captured. Our dwellings were searched and ransacked. No doubt about it, we had been betrayed. We suspected each other. My brother was killed. I and others who escaped began to live out amongst the tombs on Vatican Hill. Valentinian, however, seemed to survive. He used to come and go. He'd always give us confidence, assure us that one day our fortunes would change."

"So you believe there was a traitor in your midst?"

"Oh, looking back, certainly. I suspect it was Valentinian."

"But did he give you that impression at the time?"

"Of course not!" Decius shook his head. "Valentinian could inspire you with confidence. He could quote the Christian scriptures verse by verse. A fount of spiritual comfort was Valentinian."

"And the tomb of the Galilean?"

"It undoubtedly lies somewhere in that sprawling cemetery around the Vatican Hill. Valentinian might have held the secret. There were rumours." He paused.

183

"That he had made the entrance to the tomb even more dangerous. Whispers that he was an Egyptian by birth, that he knew something about architecture and had prepared traps for anyone stupid enough to enter the tomb, very similar to the devices used to defend the ancient sepulchres in Egypt." Decius licked his lips. "I am hungry . . ."

Claudia looked over her shoulder. "Cut his bonds," she told Murranus. "Bring him a goblet of wine, some bread and meat."

Murranus obeyed. Oceanus brought the wine and slammed it down on the table, a platter of food beside it. Claudia had never seen a man eat so quickly. When he had finished, Decius took a generous sip of wine, cradling the cup in his hands.

"These are all rumours," he continued, his one good eye studying Claudia closely.

"But you never knew where the tomb actually was?"

"Oh no, Valentinian kept that to himself."

"And then what happened?"

"Valentinian disappeared completely. Oh, it must have been two or three years before Constantine's victory at the Milvian Bridge. He was never seen or heard of again. Shortly afterwards imperial troops ringed our last hiding place. I was captured and tortured. Eventually I apostatised, I rejected the Christian faith; after all, what had it brought me? I was released, the only survivor of that community. I drifted and became a raptor in the Appian cemetery, a member of Lord Charon's horde. At least I had protection, some food and drink, and now and again the occasional coin.

I forgot about my past, and then one night recently, Cerebus, Lord Charon's lieutenant, told me I was to be part of an escort; Lord Charon was to meet someone deep in the Appian cemetery. I don't know what happened, mistress, I was some distance away. I saw a figure approach the fire, an outline, one more shadow amongst the rest until I heard that voice. It was definitely Valentinian."

"You are sure of that?"

"As I am that I am sitting here."

"What was the meeting about?"

Decius pulled a face. "I couldn't hear, but rumour talked of an alliance between the two: of a letter sent to the August Ones in my master's name. Lord Charon agreed, I think, though he warned Valentinian."

"How do you know that?"

"Lord Charon was displeased with one of his men; he'd betrayed his trust. At that meeting my master had him imprisoned in a thorn bush and burnt alive as a warning to us all, including Valentinian."

"Why should Charon ally with Valentinian?"

"Profit! Again, rumour has it that Valentinian warned Lord Charon about the recent chariot race at the Circus, not to wager on the favourite, Scorpus, but Pausanias."

Claudia stared down at the table. She'd heard tavern chatter on the same topic: how Pausanias' victory, or at least Scorpus' defeat, had been unexpected, a great surprise even to the experts.

"Is there anything else, Decius?"

He shook his head. Claudia opened the purse on her belt, took out a coin and slid it across the table. Decius seized it.

"And a knife?" he asked.

Murranus went outside and brought a dagger taken from one of the dead. He handed this to Decius, who thrust it into his belt. The raptor smirked at the sword Murranus held in one hand, a loaf of bread in the other. He took this and nodded at Claudia. Oceanus opened the front door, and Decius walked out into the street.

Decius heard the door slam behind him and hurried up towards the square. He had no idea where to go. He was just eager to be away, relieved at his near escape from death. He almost crashed into the figure who slipped out of the ribbon-thin runnel to his right. He staggered back, hand searching for his knife, but it was too late.

"Decius?" a voice mocked. "Decius, have you forgotten me?"

"Valentinian!"

Decius pulled at the dagger hilt, but he wasn't swift enough. Valentinian's knife cut through the air like a scythe, neatly slicing his throat.

Claudia knelt on the marble floor of the Alexander chamber in the north-east section of the Palatine Palace. Her knees hurt, so to distract herself from the soreness as well as Helena's baleful silence, she gazed at the floor mosaic of Alexander the Great depicted as a warlike Apollo. She shifted her gaze to the beautiful pastel colours on the walls, the vivid paintings describing the exploits of the Great Conqueror. On her right knelt Murranus; to her left Burrus, whose stomach kept rumbling like a drum. Claudia stifled a giggle; this recalled childhood lessons with old Magister Sulpicius when Felix could almost make his tummy rumble at will. She composed herself and peered up at Presbyter Sylvester, dressed in a white tunic, a dark red cloak draped about his shoulders, a silver chain boasting the chi-rho symbol around his neck. The presbyter did not look too happy, lips moving soundlessly. Was he praying? Helena certainly seemed intent on playing the role of the angry Goddess Juno, hair piled high on her head, a pure white gown with a purple-fringed stole adorning her shoulders. Claudia just wished the imperial feet in their silver sandals would stop tapping the floor so noisily. Burrus' stomach rumbled again. This time Claudia laughed out loud.

"Do you wish to add something to your dismal report?" Helena snapped.

"Yes, Augusta, two things." Claudia glared up at the Empress. "First, Burrus needs a meal. Second, my knees need a rest."

Presbyter Sylvester grinned.

"You may sit."

All three sighed as they sat on the stools behind them.

Helena pointed at Claudia. "Those criminals should not have been executed. They could have been tortured, interrogated."

"Augusta, they told us all they knew. They were simply the foot soldiers, not the leaders; their task was to kill, burn and retreat."

"And Decius?"

"He was pardoned because he could give us information. Much good it did him; his corpse was found near the tavern, throat cut from ear to ear."

"Why was he killed?" Helena asked.

"I suppose some of Charon's men may have stayed to watch. Decius was allowed to leave; they must have known he'd talked, so they killed him." Claudia shrugged. "That's what I suspect."

"Why the attack in the first place?" Presbyter Sylvester spoke up.

"Oh, I think I know," Claudia replied. "Possibly to kill me, to stop my prying and snooping. I suspect they also wanted to kill Narses and Severus. This is about the tomb of Peter the Galilean. Attius knew the secret; he is now dead. Gavinus and Philippus went looking for it and they have disappeared; they must be presumed murdered as well. Severus died last night. Narses remains, yet he would take the most solemn oath, and he is a very frightened man; he knows nothing about the tomb."

"Lord Charon, when he is caught," Helena muttered through gritted teeth, "will certainly hang on a cross. I want to watch him die. The sheer insolence of the man! I've just learnt that Gavinus' head, all rotting and decomposed, was left in a basket on the palace steps."

Claudia just stared back.

"And there's more." Helena brought out a scroll placed between herself and the side of the silver-edged stool. She leaned across and handed it to Claudia.

The vellum was of the highest quality, the letters perfectly formed in expensive ink. It began with the usual arrogance: "Lord Charon to the Augusta, greetings and blessings." Charon, who titled himself *Imperator Infernorum*, "Emperor of the Damned", indulged in a few pleasantries before going to the heart of the matter. He deeply regretted that the imperial court had not responded to his former letter. He threatened that if the Augusta did not wish to purchase "certain sacred goods", he would sell them elsewhere, which would be a major blow to her "plans to create a new Rome". The last two words were underlined. Lord Charon concluded that he expected to receive the Augusta's reply, as described in his first missive, to be posted in Caesar's forum within five days. Claudia handed the letter back.

"And what will the Augusta do?" she asked.

Helena sprang to her feet and stood over her. "Claudia, your Augusta will do nothing! I do not negotiate or barter with thieves, rapists and murderers. I will find, or you will, the secret of the Galilean's tomb and I shall hold it. No one else! Not my son, not Presbyter Sylvester and certainly not Lord Charon. You have your task. Make sure you complete it faithfully! You," she snapped her fingers at Burrus, "will follow me!" Trailed by a doleful-looking Burrus, she swept out of the chamber.

Presbyter Sylvester kept staring down at his feet. Claudia went to the door, closed it and came back.

"Is this chamber secure?" she whispered.

Sylvester half smiled.

"Is it?"

"It must be," he replied, "otherwise Helena would not have met you here."

"If the Empress wishes words with Burrus, I certainly wish words with you, Presbyter Sylvester. One thing I did not report to Helena was that Attius was actually preparing a letter to you offering to reveal the secret of the Galilean's tomb. I suspect he was asking for security, patronage, reward, advancement; I don't know. He was murdered before the letter was written. Only a draft on a scrap remained." Claudia took the message from her wallet and handed it over for Sylvester to study. "Now, Presbyter," Claudia continued, "why should Attius be writing to you? Please," Claudia's voice turned impatient, "we are all comrades; Murranus here is your protector. We need the truth."

"The truth?" Sylvester grimaced. "From what you reported to us earlier, Valentinian apparently did survive and is now working with Lord Charon. He knows the whereabouts of Peter's tomb and is using Charon to blackmail and threaten Helena. It also means," Sylvester tapped his foot, "that Valentinian was responsible for the destruction of the Christian community in and around the Vatican Hill. He is a very dangerous character. The description Decius provided is interesting, but is it relevant today?"

"What will Valentinian do if the Augusta does not agree to his terms?"

"One of two things," Sylvester replied quickly, "or three. First he might sell the secret to someone else. Some powerful Christians in Rome would love to buy the relics of our founder. Second, out of spite, he might destroy the tomb or just leave it abandoned, let its memory be forgotten, a constant reproach to us, the Church of Rome."

"Third?"

"Loot the tomb and take whatever is there to Licinius in the East. Yes!" Sylvester rubbed his chin. "Licinius would love to bait us with that."

"And the death of Attius?"

"Ah." Sylvester leaned forward. "One thing Helena does not know is that many years ago Attius was a Christian but turned apostate. He was baptised into the Christian Church to be an informer for the imperial authorities, this was discovered and he was ejected. He too belonged to the community of the Vatican Hill. If Constantine had known that, Attius might not have been pardoned but suffered rigorous punishment. He may have learnt the whereabouts of Peter's tomb when he was pretending to be a member of the Christian community, or as a *scrutor*." Sylvester chose his words carefully. "I suspect that Attius was going to beg for my intervention and protection. If he fell at my feet and revealed the secret of the tomb, that might have been possible. I often prayed he would be forced to go down that path. He knew I kept silent about his past because I realised that one day he would be forced to divulge his

191

secret. He nearly did," Sylvester added wistfully. "Ah well," Sylvester handed the scrap of parchment back. "According to that, Caesar's old friend holds the secret." He pulled a face and shook his head. "I know nothing of that. I doubt if Attius was referring to Constantine."

"So who?"

"Perhaps Maxentius or some other emperor . . ."

Sylvester paused as Helena, accompanied by a sheepish-looking Burrus, swept back into the chamber. She plumped herself down on the cushioned seat, flailing her fingers at Claudia to sit rather than kneel.

"Your report earlier," Helena demanded, "you mentioned the Nefandus and a possible trap?" She stretched out her hand as if examining her fingernails. "Now that Attius has been killed, the Nefandus should not be your concern, but I have reflected: those poor women!" She paused and smiled girlishly, as if recalling some secret from her own past. Claudia remembered some of the stories about Helena's rather adventurous youth. "I feel sorry for them," Helena hurried on. She turned and gestured at Burrus. "I've given that brute the warrant. Go down to the Tullianum. Select six women condemned to death or the mines. They can choose life or death. Tell the Domina at the House of Isis to bathe, clothe and beautify them all in a day. They can wander the streets armed with a dagger and a centurion's whistle." She pulled a face. "The women might try to escape, but they'd be recaptured. They have nowhere else to go."

"And whom should we use as soldiers?"

Helena gestured at Murranus. "You have gladiator friends? They'd be ideal for such a venture, fast and swift. They'll receive soldier's pay for a week. Tell the Domina to send all the bills to Chrysis; the same for you, Murranus. All reasonable expenses shall be met by the imperial treasury. Oh, by the way, no one is to be told about it, especially not that uncle of yours. Murranus, you do the same! Swear your men to secrecy, deploy them after sunset. Claudia, I leave the other details to you . . ."

The Tullianum prison, reflected Claudia, truly was the gateway to hell, a place of horror. Narrow steps led down past slime-covered walls into huge black pens, horrid cells where prisoners were nothing more than dark clustered objects. Faces devoid of all hope glimmered out at them. A hideous gloomy pit, its darkness broken by flaring torches and the glow of braziers. Soldiers in leather kilts, their faces and chests smeared with dirty sweat, moved to the jingle of keys and chains. Foul odours swirled like a fog whilst the eerie silence was broken by shrill screams and despairing groans.

"The shambles of humanity," the chief jailer called the inmates, men and women held there for torture or questioning before being dispatched to the mines, the stake or the arena. He proudly led Claudia and Murranus to what he referred to as the heart of his kingdom of the underworld, a cavern-like chamber where prisoners could be inspected. The women had been gathered there, a huddle of wretched humanity dressed in ragged filthy clothes, bodies covered in prison slime, faces almost unrecognisable, hair all tangled and matted. They stared miserably at Claudia and Murranus. Some squatted down; others just stood looking slightly crazed, blinking in the light pouring through the grille above them. Claudia whispered to Murranus, who moved quickly amongst that crowd of unfortunates. He spoke in the lingua franca, searching for those who could understand him, who showed a flicker of interest, some life and energy remaining. A few responded; many seemed to be dead already, their pathetic, empty eyes waiting for what further terrors life held for them. At last six prisoners were selected. Murranus paid the jailer, giving strict instructions that the women were to be transported secretly and safely to the House of Isis. At the mention of that place, the jailer's greasy face broke into a grin. They were to be manacled, Murranus insisted, and brought to the house in a covered wagon. The jailer himself was to ensure this and wait with them.

Claudia and Murranus fled the Tullianum into the fierce sunlight of the old forum. The white marble buildings seemed even more dazzlingly bright after the stygian darkness of the prison. Claudia felt hot and rather queasy, the crowds milling about noisy and bothersome. Faces peered at her. Fingers plucked at her cloak as traders offered cups of fresh water or platters of sliced, juicy fruit. Lawyers touted for business. Scribes shouted out their skill in copying letters or drawing up documents. Imperial police swaggered by, clubs at the ready. Self-important senators and *equites* processed solemnly up steps to some council chamber whilst priests, shrouded in incense smoke, prepared to do sacrifice in the temples. The sacred carts waited nearby, carrying the intended victims for the noonday sacrifice; lambs, goats and birds of every kind squealed and cried plaintively whilst farmyard odours billowed across to catch the nose and throat. Soldiers diced at the foot of a statue whilst being entertained by an acrobat who swirled in her coloured rags, long black hair swinging, to the beat of a tambourine. The gilded youth of the city paraded and posed, their heads protected by broad-brimmed straw hats or elegant parasols carried by slaves. Sedan chairs and brilliantly caparisoned litters forced their way through, carried by sweaty retainers who gasped and shouted: "Make way, make way!" Very few did. Claudia clutched Murranus' hand as he steered her out across the busy squares, along the broad thoroughfares and on to the streets stretching into the Caelian quarter.

They went straight to the House of Isis, where the Domina received them in her private chamber, an austere room with stools, chairs and polished acacia-wood tables. The walls were a restful green with black borders at the top and bottom along which rich golden fruit had been painted. In the far corner stood two heavy reinforced chests as well as reed baskets full of documents. The Domina herself arranged the stools, gestured at her visitors to sit, then noisily rang the hand bell, ordering a servant to bring a platter of poppy-seed biscuits, sweet wine-cakes, honey biscuits and long glasses brimming with the delicious-tasting juice of crushed pears. For a while they just ate and drank. Claudia half listened as the Domina gave instructions to servants at the door that they were not to be disturbed. She returned, handing Claudia and Murranus napkins, then sat back in her chair.

"Very few people come here." She smiled. "This is my treasury."

"You keep your wealth here?" Claudia asked.

"Some of it," the Domina replied, leaning back in the chair. "Ulpius the banker looks after the rest."

Claudia immediately thought of Attius and wondered what progress Sallust was making.

"Well," the Domina forced a smile, "there's been no more deaths, so how can I help you?"

Claudia put her glass down and in terse sentences described the trap she envisaged. How she had visited the Augusta and the Tullianum. Six girls were to arrive shortly. She wanted them bathed, cleaned and dressed, decked out finely, their nails and faces painted. The Domina's first question was to be expected.

"Who is to pay?"

Claudia retorted that all reasonable bills would be met by the imperial treasury. The Domina nodded.

"And secrecy?" she asked.

Claudia insisted that as few people as possible should know what was happening. She described how each girl, possibly tonight, but certainly on the morrow, would wander the streets after dark, armed with a centurion's whistle and a dagger. They would act, Claudia added, once Murranus' men were deployed.

196

"It's only a matter of time," she concluded, "before we catch him."

The Domina, eyes half closed, seemed to be assessing the situation. Claudia realised the woman had little choice; this was the Empress' order, whilst any expense would be passed on.

"The other girls might envy them."

"The other girls won't know and still might be murdered," Claudia retorted, "and then what?"

The Domina nodded. "I agree. What happens to these women afterwards?"

"They'll receive pardons from the imperial writing office, perhaps a few coins, and be sent on their way."

"And if they want to stay here?" the Domina asked archly.

"They are free to go wherever they wish," Claudia declared. "But first the Nefandus must be caught."

The Domina nodded again and excused herself. Claudia and Murranus were taken out into the small garden. Claudia insisted that Murranus leave immediately.

"I will take charge of these unfortunates," she whispered. "You must go down to the gladiator school. Recruit good men, about seven or eight, and swear them to secrecy; they'll be given soldier's pay for a week. They should be ready by tomorrow night at the latest. Now go."

Murranus kissed her gently on the lips and brow and made his farewells. A short while later the Domina came into the garden, sitting close to Claudia as if they were old friends.

"This will be dangerous," she said. "Those girls could be killed."

"Somebody is going to be killed anyway," replied Claudia, edging away.

"Do I make you feel uncomfortable, Claudia?"

"No, I'm just tired."

"I heard from Narcissus about the attack on the She-Asses. Your uncle Polybius has virtually marshalled the entire quarter to clear the place and have it ready again. He's already describing himself as the new Horatius in Rome."

Claudia just smiled.

"Life is hard," the Domina continued, peering across the garden. "I did not ask for this life and, I suppose, neither did you. Your Murranus, you love him?"

"Yes I do, and he loves me."

"Then hold fast to that moonbeam," the Domina murmured. "The world of men, Claudia," she shook her head, "is not a pleasant one. We women have to live by our wits, and they have to be sharp as knives."

"Talking of keen wits . . ." Claudia turned her face squarely. "The plan I'm preparing? Tribune Macrinus is a skilled soldier, a policeman, a man of great cunning; surely he tried the same?"

"No, no!" The Domina blinked, then looked away. Claudia sensed she was lying.

"Whilst I wait for these girls to arrive," Claudia continued, "do you have a list of the dead, the girls killed by the Nefandus? You do have a funeral club? A statement of expenses?"

The Domina looked as if she was going to refuse.

"I would like to look at that list," Claudia insisted. She stretched out her hand and brushed that of the Domina. "I am not your enemy; I simply wish to end all this."

The Domina hurried away. A short while later she returned carrying a scroll tied with a red ribbon. She unrolled this, opening it at the place Claudia wanted. Claudia moved to catch the light better. She studied that sorry litany of deaths. Sometimes the murders were clustered together. Other times a week, maybe even two, passed before the next one occurred. She realised the Domina was watching her closely and wondered what she and Macrinus wanted to hide. The girls' names were listed. Claudia quickly counted twenty-five, one more than she had thought. Each corpse had been laid out and prepared before being taken in a funeral procession to some cemetery for cremation. The ashes were sealed in an urn then buried in a plot specially bought by the Domina.

Claudia had hardly finished reading when a servant burst breathlessly into the garden declaring how a hideous-smelling cart had appeared driven by some nightmare figure from Hades. Claudia swiftly thrust the scroll back at the Domina and followed the girl out. The cart was drawn up in an alleyway running alongside the house. Claudia told the jailer to unlock the cage, and the girls clambered out. Despite the dirt and squalor, most of them had realised there was fresh hope of life. Claudia caught the occasional gleam of an eye or a smile, whilst some of them had even made pathetic attempts to prettify themselves.

The rest of the afternoon was spent preparing the girls. They were stripped of their rags, which were burnt, then taken to the bathhouse, where they were washed and washed again before, at Claudia's insistence, they were given something to eat and drink. After that the beauticians applied their arts. Claudia insisted that the Domina swear all in the House of Isis to strict secrecy under pain of being dispatched to the Tullianum. Once she'd received solemn assurances that this would be so, she sat and dozed in the garden. Murranus returned. He'd faced no problem hiring the men. He'd also called in at the She-Asses. Uncle Polybius, Murranus raised his eyes heavenwards, with a legion of helpers had cleaned up all traces of the previous night's attack. He was now preparing a victory banquet at which he would tell everyone, for a price, about "The Great Battle at the She-Asses", where he, like Horatius on the bridge, single-handedly drove back legions of *inferni*. Murranus was still laughing at Polybius' antics when a servant arrived to inform them that the women were ready.

The Domina had assembled them in her chamber, where Claudia was sure there'd be no peepholes or eyelets. Claudia was truly surprised at the transformation of the prisoners. They were now pretty young women, dressed in the colours of the House of Isis, broad scarlet bands tied tightly around their chests. Their hair was curled, faces and nails painted, and gleaming trinkets jingled on their wrists and fingers. Murranus put down the sack of sheathed knives and centurion whistles which he'd borrowed from the gladiator school, and Claudia moved around the girls asking their names and a little of their lives. Most were from the slums of Rome, found guilty of theft or acts of violence. However, they were resolute, strong women, Claudia concluded, who'd not be taken easily. She then stood on a small stool and told them exactly what had happened and what she planned. When she finished there were no objections. The women muttered and gossiped amongst themselves, then a redhead, who introduced herself as Livia, stepped forward.

"Mistress Claudia, we thank you. We are free from that hellhole, but what you propose is dangerous."

"So was the Tullianum," Claudia retorted.

"We accept that. We will be armed with a knife and a whistle. There will be men hidden close who will come to our rescue. I for one — and indeed all of us — am prepared to take this risk, but we have questions. What happens to us if the plan fails?"

"You will still be freed, pardoned, given a coin and sent on your way."

"And if we are successful?"

"You'll be freed, pardoned," Claudia smiled, "and given a few more coins, then sent on your way. No one will hurt you. You'll carry the Empress' personal warrant." This provoked a murmur of approval from the others.

"And if we die?"

"If you die, I will ensure that you are given honourable burial. However, unless you go out into the streets tonight and other nights, I assure you, some woman is going to be killed by this barbaric assassin."

"And what happens," Livia asked cheekily, "if we meet someone we rather like?"

"You are free," Claudia replied. "What you do is a matter for you to decide, but I ask you to keep yourselves safe."

"Who are we looking for?" a woman shouted. "Do you have any description?"

Claudia shook her head. "I tell you this, however. Be careful. Be wary of the unexpected. Someone wandering the Caelian quarter garbed in fine clothes who perhaps shouldn't be there by himself. Above all, anyone dressed in the uniform of an imperial officer; be most wary of him."

"I always am!" someone shouted from the back.

"And if this Nefandus is caught," Livia glanced at the Domina, "could we stay here?"

"If you are acceptable!" she snapped. "If you promise to abide by the rules of the house, why not?"

"One more thing," Livia declared. "Before I go out into the streets tonight, I would like a deep-bowled cup of your best wine."

Claudia agreed. She informed them that once they'd left this chamber, they must act as new members of the House of Isis. They must tell no one. Once the sun had set, they were to wander the streets.

"All night?" one asked.

"You may come back for a rest," the Domina retorted, "but you now know your task. The sooner this man is caught and killed, the better."

202

CHAPTER
TEN

Some evil spirit, as it seems probable . . . impelled these men to atrocious deeds.

Claudia and Murranus returned to the She-Asses. The day was drawing on. They passed the great sycamore where Torquatus was still plying his trade; he shouted her name and wandered over.

"I still haven't discovered a solution." He tapped the side of his head. "I promise you I am thinking. You don't mind if I ask my customers?"

"I don't mind if you ask the Emperor himself," Claudia retorted. "Torquatus, I'm tired. I wish you well with your riddle. As I wish myself!" she added in a whisper, grasping Murranus' hand. "I still haven't found the solution either."

Back inside the She-Asses, Claudia realised she would get no rest. Polybius was full of the previous night's exploits. He had quickly repaired all the damage: the shutters, the kitchen door, the scuff marks on the grass and the trampled flower beds. Any sign of the hideous life-and-death struggle waged in the garden had been swiftly removed. The tavern was full of the usual rogues as well as those who'd drifted in eager to hear the news. For a while Claudia sat next to Murranus at a table. She was about to leave when

Oceanus unrolled the great leather cover he'd placed in front of the main door of the tavern. Apparently this had become wet with either wine or blood, Claudia couldn't see which. The leather had stuck to the lock and Oceanus had to prise it loose with his dagger. Claudia went and crouched by the lock. The substance was sticky: probably honey or unwatered wine. She stood up, opened the door and peered through the keyhole; the slit was not clear, as if something was still stuck on the other side.

"I wonder?" she exclaimed going back into the tavern.

"You wonder what?" Murranus asked.

"Nothing." She smiled. "I just wonder if the Nefandus will strike tonight."

In the end nothing happened. Claudia retired late. She woke up during the night but all was quiet. She went back to sleep. After all Murranus had promised her he'd rouse her if anything did occur. The following morning, as she broke her fast in the garden, Murranus sat down beside her to share the diced chicken Celades had prepared.

"Nothing," he said, cocking his head as if half listening to the birds singing at the far end of the orchard. "Nothing at all. I deployed my men; they reported they'd never been so bored in their lives. Apart from the occasional lady from the House of Isis, nothing exciting."

"And the young women?"

"Oh," Murranus chewed on a piece of chicken, "they enjoyed themselves; they were free."

204

"They all reported back?"

"Of course," Murranus declared. "If they fled, where could they go? For some of them this is not just freedom, it's a miracle. I wager if they pray, your name will be mentioned." He kissed Claudia on the side of her face. "Now I will take some rest myself, and you?"

Claudia just shrugged. "Sit and think?"

"About me?"

Claudia fluttered her eyelids. "Of course, my darling, what else?"

In the end Claudia drifted back to the notes she had made, but still she could discover no loose thread, so she busied herself tidying her chamber and helping downstairs. In the late afternoon she had a visitor. Sallust the Searcher, grey as ever, slid like a ghost into the She-Asses. Claudia immediately whisked him away from the other customers to share a small jug of wine, some bread, cheese and dried ham. The sun was still strong; noises floated from the tavern. Sallust sipped at his wine.

"I have done what you asked," he began.

"Were you successful?"

Sallust moved his head from side to side. "Yes and no, but for you, Claudia, I asked everyone in my tribe to help. Now . . ." He took a scroll out of his leather wallet and unrolled it using the cups as weights. "First, Attius Enobarbus . . . well, rumour has it that he was once a Christian. You know that?"

Claudia nodded.

"He became an apostate, a spy under Maxentius, a zealous searcher, a destroyer of all things Christian. He had no love for any of his companions. Attius was never a popular man. He could be violent with women; his concubine Drusilla could bear witness to that, but I understand that she too is dead. The only interesting fact I found about our mutual friend was when I visited the banker Ulpius. Now he is not really supposed to reveal his records, but as he said, he had no love for Attius, the man is dead, and, of course, he wanted the gold piece I offered. To put it bluntly, mistress," Sallust pursed his lips, "Attius Enobarbus, according to Ulpius, had very little money indeed. In fact, no more than a hundred solidi lodged with him."

"Impossible!" Claudia breathed. "I have seen the records. Attius stole money from the Christians, he plundered their sacred objects; he amassed quite a fortune."

"That is what Ulpius thought."

"Could there be another banker?" Claudia asked. "Someone else holding money for him? Of course," she whispered.

"Yes, Claudia, I can guess what you are thinking. Attius Enobarbus wasn't exactly a favourite amongst the powerful. He was well known as a supporter of Maxentius, only tolerated by Constantine. He wouldn't entrust his money to anyone." Sallust scratched his face. "Ulpius thinks that Attius may have hidden his money away; only the gods know where it is now."

"And Deacon Valentinian?"

"Oh, now there is a sinister and mysterious character. He was very well educated, personable and charming. He was promoted very quickly in the persecuted Church and became leader of the community around the Vatican Hill. Then he disappeared, and Christians in that particular community were rounded up and herded off. Very few survived; indeed, according to my searchers, none at all."

"And Lord Charon?"

Sallust smiled. "Claudia, I'll be honest: total failure. In Rome, the likes of me do not interfere with the likes of Lord Charon. I left that well alone. I cannot help you there."

Claudia nodded in agreement. "And the Nefandus?"

"Not much more than you knew, except for one thing. There were rumours along the alleyways that the Nefandus was killed."

"I know that," Claudia replied. "In the civil war."

"No, that he may have been murdered."

"And Tribune Macrinus?"

"Now there is a strange one: a regular army officer with a good reputation. A man of integrity as an administrator. He loved his wife then she fell ill. One new thing I did discover about him: Tribune Macrinus was very friendly with the Domina who runs the House of Isis."

"She claimed he hardly visited there."

"Well, that might be true, as it is that he loved his wife, but he became deeply enamoured of one of the Daughters of Isis, a young woman called Briseis."

Claudia closed her eyes and tried to recall the list of the dead she'd inspected at the House of Isis. "You are sure of this?" She opened her eyes. "Tribune Macrinus?"

"It was a brief romance." Sallust leaned across the table all wide-eyed. "You know how it happens, mistress? Macrinus was a faithful husband, but Briseis was very, very beautiful. True, he may hardly have visited the House of Isis or wandered the alleyways of the Caelian quarter, but from what I heard, he and Briseis used to meet in the imperial parks on the other side of Rome. He was deeply smitten by her."

"And what happened?"

"I don't know." Sallust tapped the parchment in front of him. "We can only search out what we know. Briseis disappeared. She may have left or died. In the chaos which broke out in Rome after Constantine's victory, anything could have happened." He spread his hands. "Look at me: unfortunate enough to back the wrong side. If it hadn't been for you . . ."

"Yes, yes." Claudia held her hand up. "I'm aware of all that. So . . ." She stared up at the branches of the tree; the apples were ripening well, Polybius would be pleased.

"What, mistress?"

"Briseis disappeared, the Nefandus disappeared. I am sure Macrinus said someone else disappeared."

"His wife died?"

"Yes, yes, but someone else . . ." Claudia paused as the door of the kitchen was thrown open. Titus Labienus, a goblet in one hand, a piece of parchment in the other, strode out declaiming the lines of a play.

"Who on earth is that?" Sallust asked.

208

Claudia looked over her shoulder. "Oh, ignore him. He is one of the victors in the Great Battle of the She-Asses."

"Yes, I've heard about that. Lord Charon lost many men. He will not forget that."

"And neither will I," Claudia added grimly. "That's Titus Labienus."

"Titus Labienus?" Sallust repeated. "Are you sure that's his real name?"

"Why?" Claudia asked.

"Just a coincidence," Sallust declared. "Don't you know your history, Claudia? Caesar had a very faithful lieutenant of that name, but in the civil war Titus Labienus deserted his old friend and joined Pompey. I believe he was killed in the subsequent fighting."

Claudia closed her eyes and recalled that fragment of parchment: Attius' words about the secret of Peter's tomb being held by "Caesar's old friend".

"Do you know where Labienus is buried?"

"Caesar was generous. He allowed the corpses of his enemies to be brought home for honourable burial."

"I suspect he's buried on the Vatican Hill," Claudia murmured. "Sallust, there is not a document in Rome you cannot prise open for me. Can you find it for me then draw a map showing the exact location of Titus Labienus' tomb on the Vatican Hill? I am sure you will find he is buried there." She leaned across the table and grasped his hand. "Please? Now, if there is anything else . . ."

Sallust shook his head.

"In which case," Claudia rose, "finish your bread and wine and just ignore Caesar's old friend." She gestured at the actor still walking up and down reciting to himself. "I have someone to visit . . ."

The Domina saw Claudia immediately, leading her out into the small garden.

"Are you concerned about the girls? They are still here; they are behaving themselves. In fact," she smiled, "they are proving very popular. I must remember that, perhaps petition the Empress that such women be released into my service." She forced a smile. "Why have you returned?"

"I would like to look at the list again, the one from your funeral club giving the names of the victims of the Nefandus."

The Domina made to object. "I have shown you —"

"I would like to see it, Domina. I need to see it now."

The woman hurried off and returned with the scroll. Claudia sat down in the shade and searched its entries carefully.

"What is the matter?" The Domina had lost her poise; she looked nervous and kept licking her lips, fingers playing with the silver necklace around her throat.

"Briseis?"

The Domina blinked.

"What is the matter?" Claudia rose to her feet. "I asked you a name. Briseis, the young girl whom Tribune Macrinus was so enamoured of. What happened to her? Was she killed by the Nefandus?"

210

"Of course not! Otherwise her name would be there!"

"So what happened to her?" Claudia insisted.

"She left!" The Domina became all prim and proper. "She just left."

"And you have proof of this? I mean, wouldn't she have to buy herself out of here? Give you a present? Wouldn't she need expenses to travel? Where did she come from?"

"Some village in Sicily . . . I don't know. The family moved to the mainland, Briseis ran away and came here."

"Then if she ran back," Claudia declared, "there must be some record? Are there girls still here who worked with her?"

The Domina sat down.

"Are there?" Claudia repeated.

The Domina put her face in her hands. "Of course there are! I will tell you the reason for my embarrassment. Briseis just disappeared. We never knew if the Nefandus killed her or whether she became frightened and ran away. I have no record of her leaving, nothing at all."

"Of course!" Claudia snapped. "I thank you. Now perhaps I could have a word with my six ladies . . ."

Claudia returned to the She-Asses very satisfied. She believed the murk and gloom which confronted her was beginning to dissipate. For a while she sat in the garden and prayed soundly that tonight the Nefandus might strike and be captured. The young women seemed in good heart, exhilarated, relieved to be away from the Tullianum. They were confident they could confront and escape any danger in the filthy alleyways and runnels of the Caelian quarter. Murranus returned and informed her that the men were ready and deployed. Perhaps tonight the Nefandus would appear? Claudia fought to control her own excitement. She wanted to interview Tribune Macrinus but she realised that must wait. Instead, she returned to the front door of the tavern, where a doleful Torquatus appeared to announce that so far he was unable to solve the riddle. Claudia shook her head understandingly.

"Can you solve it for me?" he asked.

"Not yet," Claudia smiled, "but why not come in? I am sure Polybius might have a few ideas."

Much to Claudia's relief, Torquatus refused and wandered off. Once he was out of sight, she opened the door again and studied the lock. The tavern door was very similar in strength and build to that of Attius' secret chamber; the wood was thick, the lock obviously the work of some craftsman. Claudia pulled the key in and out, then, going to the kitchen, returned with another key, but the lock could only hold one at a time.

"It must be," she breathed.

Sorry came wandering over, asking if he could help. Claudia absentmindedly shook her head, ruffled his hair and wandered off to her own room. She found it difficult to relax, especially as Polybius and his assembled horde were intent on a good night's feasting. She heard the toast being offered in reply to Polybius' boastful speech, in which he and Labienus emerged as

212

true warriors. The party spilled out into the gardens, where coloured lights had been displayed. Labienus' troupe, the Satyricons, cavorted wildly in their grotesque masks and costumes as Polybius escorted everyone round his famous battlefield. Standing by the window watching them, Claudia smiled. Polybius and Labienus were really no more than children living for the moment. They had totally forgotten their wager with Torquatus. Polybius, tapping the side of his fleshy nose, had assured Labienus that his niece would resolve all problems. Claudia sat on the edge of the bed and wondered about doing just that.

The evening was quiet, not even a breeze, so the piercing whistle shrilled clearly. Claudia jumped to her feet, hastily put on her sandals, donned her cloak, grabbed a walking stick and fled down the stairs. The dining hall was empty except for Petronius the Pimp and Simon the Stoic fast asleep in each other's arms. They remained so despite the crashing and pounding at the door. Claudia opened it. Murranus stood there with two of his burly escorts. One of them carried a torch. Murranus pushed back the hood from his head, face gleaming with sweat.

"Come, Claudia!"

Again the whistle blast shrilled.

"At the far side of the fountain," one of the men whispered hoarsely.

Shouts and yells echoed further up the street and across the square. Claudia hurried with the rest. Dark shapes flittered across her path as beggars and other night walkers disturbed by the commotion sought sanctuary elsewhere. Claudia kept her eye on the trackway covered with muck. They reached the square, and went round the fountain and down a side street, where two of Murranus' gladiators clustered at the mouth of a runnel. In the flare of the torch Claudia caught the glint of red hair. One of the men was holding Livia by the arm. When she saw Claudia, Livia broke free and ran to her, hair ruffled, face grimy, a cut on her left arm staunched with a rag.

"They're down there!" She pointed. "They are definitely down there!"

"Where is your dagger?" Claudia asked.

"I stabbed one of them."

"They? One of them?" Claudia repeated. "What do you mean? What is happening? There is more than one?"

"They are trapped." One of the gladiators had been speaking to a boy who'd come hurtling naked out of a doorway, roused by the screams and whistles. "The alleyway is blind on either side, the same at the bottom."

Murranus grabbed a torch and, dagger in one hand, walked down the runnel. "You are trapped!" he shouted. "Come out, one of you is wounded. We know that from the woman you attacked."

Claudia joined him. At first she could see nothing but blackness; then she glimpsed something move and glint.

"They have to come out," Murranus declared. He shouted over his shoulders for his companions to join him. More gladiators arrived and, led by Murranus, began to edge their way down the runnel. Claudia went back to where Livia now crouched, her back to the wall. The naked boy standing beside her was patting her gently on the head. Claudia fished into her wallet and gave the lad a coin. He disappeared into the house whilst she sat next to Livia. She inspected the wound but it was only superficial, a dagger cut just above the wrist.

"Tell me what happened," Claudia demanded. She paused as more of Livia's companions, alarmed by the noise and whistles, came running, bangles jingling, their loose robes flapping about them. Claudia told them all was well, that they should stay together, collect the other girls, adjourn to the She-Asses and ask for Polybius, who would look after them. The women didn't need a second bidding but hastened away laughing and joking, relieved to be away from the lonely streets and the danger now brewing. Claudia stared down the runnel. Murranus and his gladiators were moving slowly, torches glowing in the stinking blackness.

"Where are they?" Livia asked.

"Where are who?" Claudia demanded, coming back and crouching beside her.

"The *vigiles*. I passed them earlier in the evening. They shouldn't be far."

A cold prickle of sweat ran across Claudia's neck. She peered down the runnel. Murranus was now shouting warnings.

"Tell me what happened," Claudia insisted.

"Just like last night," Livia replied, wiping the dirt from her face, "I chose streets near the She-Asses. I felt more comfortable. At first I was frightened, but most of those who approach are fairly timid. A young boy who wanted a fumble, an old man trying to relive his youth and, of course, the usual drunken louts. Tonight I chose the same streets and went round and round. That little boy who came out? I talked to him earlier. He reminded me of the son I once had. Eventually the streets became lonelier except for beggars, raptors, thieves, but they tend to leave you alone."

"Of course they would," Claudia agreed. "The Domina is well known. She has her own ruffians and bodyguards to take care of any nuisance. Go on."

"Tonight was no different," Livia continued. "I came down to the square and bathed my hands in the water. I trailed my fingers along a dirty wall. The two *vigiles* passed me. I walked on."

"What were they like?" Claudia asked. "The *vigiles*?"

"Arrogant. One of them has a nasty face which hides a nasty soul, but I've met the same in the Tullianum and elsewhere. I am Livia from the Tullianum!" She laughed at her own joke. "Anyway, tonight there was little custom. I thought of walking down to the She-Asses to beg a drink and just sit for a while; then I heard a sound, my name being called. I came down this street; a man stood at the entrance to the runnel. He was dressed like an imperial officer in helmet and cloak. He certainly knew my name, said he'd seen me before. I asked him what he wanted. He opened his hand. I glimpsed more silver coins than I'd ever been offered. I could see why those other girls were trapped! I forgot about the danger. He led me further down. He told me what he wanted, then pushed me up against the wall, telling me to kneel down in front of him. He seemed to be fumbling at his kilt to free himself. Now, Claudia, I've been in prison where there are no lights, no flames, no candles, no lantern horns, no oil lamps. Your eyes grow accustomed to the dark. I was not nervous or frightened. What the officer had asked me to do . . . well, the jailors at the Tullianum had demanded the same. Then I heard a sound to my right further down the runnel. I turned quickly and glimpsed another shape hastening towards me. I realised what was going to happen. There wasn't one but two, and the other meant danger. I had my dagger in the sash hidden by the folds of my tunic. I got up. I said I felt sick, I didn't want to do it. The officer tried to grab me. I pulled away. He dragged me back. By then my dagger was free. I drove it here, deep into his side, and then I fled blowing that whistle. They would have escaped but the wound I dealt was serious."

Claudia patted her on the head and got up. She walked to the mouth of the runnel. Murranus' group were now deeper down. She could hear shouting, the clash of steel, dark shapes moving, then Murranus and his companions were shifting back. Claudia suspected whom they were bringing. Achilleos, wounded deep in his side, was spitting curses; Nereos, bruised, with a bloody scrape to his left arm from his attempted flight, was all shamefaced. Murranus pushed both of them out of the street and into the square. The other gladiators formed a ring around the prisoners. Murranus forced both men to their knees in the pool of fluttering torchlight. Achilleos was so weak he had to lie down grasping his side, moaning quietly to himself. Now and again he lifted his head and cursed. Claudia crouched before the prisoners.

"You are the Nefandus," she declared, "aren't you? Both of you. You wander these streets. Your first victim, Marina, objected, didn't she? Her nails were encursted with the hair and blood of both of you, but the second, Fausta, you were prepared for her, it was easier."

Nereos just blinked.

"You have evil souls," Claudia continued. "Former soldiers; I wager when some enemy town was taken, no woman was safe from you. Then you were demobbed from the army. You secured the posts of *vigiles* in the Caelian quarter, the bottom of the heap. You swaggered around and took a liking to the Daughters of Isis, but, of course, they demanded payment. The Domina can be resolute and enforce her demands. What happened, Nereos? Did one of the girls insult you and your companion, so you plotted your revenge?"

"It didn't begin like that," Nereos stammered. "At first we thought it would be a little fun, but the girls objected. Achilleos had heard all the stories about the Nefandus and said it might be time he returned. The first girl we took down an alleyway. We were clumsy; after we had taken her, she began to scream and threaten us, and before I knew it, Achilleos had his sword out and cut her from crotch to throat."

"After you'd taken her?" Claudia demanded. "You raped her, both of you? Narcissus the embalmer found so much semen he thought the poor girl had been attacked by some bull. Don't excuse yourself, Nereos, you're just as evil and as nasty as this one here. You took a liking to it, didn't you? It was easy for you, a former soldier, to borrow a helmet, a cloak and act the part. One of you would be the officer, the other the lookout ready to spring the trap. As for the second girl, Fausta. By then you knew exactly what to do. The same as you tried on Livia tonight. Down a dark alleyway, some sordid runnel. You now know this quarter better than anyone: the short cuts, the side turnings, the recesses in which to hide, where the light is good or bad, who goes where and when. You'd pass someone like Fausta. You'd know what route she'd take and you'd be waiting; that's why it was so hard to capture you. There were two of you, *vigiles*, responsible for enforcing the Emperor's peace." She stood up and kicked Nereos' leg. "For the evil you've done, you'll die on the cross."

Nereos moaned. Achilleos blathered some curse between blood-splattered lips.

"Mistress Claudia . . ." Nereos lifted his hands beseechingly.

"No mercy," Claudia declared. "Not for Marina or Fausta or Drusilla."

"A quick death," Nereos pleaded, "for both of us, and I will tell you something you don't know."

Claudia looked at Murranus standing grim-faced in the torchlight. Livia, who'd crept up, now burst into the circle in an attempt to claw Nereos' face. One of the gladiators dragged her off.

"Tell me what you know and I'll be the judge."

"You mentioned Drusilla, Attius' concubine. True, we passed her the night she was going to the tavern, but we did not kill her."

Claudia stared down. "Are you sure, Nereos? You are going to die anyway."

"It was the Daughters of Isis . . . I . . ." His voice trailed away. "It is as you say: two old soldiers wandering these filthy streets, and those girls, all perfumed and painted, demanding silver. If I had my way we would have just forced them, but one of them mocked Achilleos, taunted his manhood, said it wasn't much. We met Marina. We both took her, promising her silver afterwards, then Achilleos killed her. Once that was done, we went back to the barracks and called up the records. We discovered how the Nefandus worked, details such as the removal of the victim's eye." He shrugged. "We knew that already, but we searched for other information. Later we attacked Fausta. I tried to plead with Achilleos to stop, especially when you began to snoop." His voice turned bitter. "But life goes on, one step after another. I swear by anything beyond the veil, we did not hurt Drusilla; we met her and let her go. She was too powerful. When we heard about her death, we wondered if somebody was imitating us as we had the real Nefandus. It was not us."

Claudia stared down at Achilleos, blood spilling out of his nose. He'd never live long enough for crucifixion.

"Is there anything else, Nereos?"

220

"May the gods have mercy on us," Nereos muttered.

Claudia nodded at Murranus. He came up behind Nereos, grabbed him by the hair and, as Claudia turned away, slit the man's throat from ear to ear. Then he crouched down and delivered the same mercy cut to Achilleos.

"Their corpses?" he asked, straightening up.

Claudia pointed to a corner of the alleyway. "Have them gibbeted there with a placard round their necks. Let the people of the Caelian quarter know the murderers have been trapped and killed." Then, spinning on her heel, Claudia walked as fast as she could, hand over her mouth, back to the She-Asses, with Livia hastening beside her thanking her profusely.

CHAPTER
ELEVEN

I was anxious to allay the virulence
of this disorder.

Once back at the She-Asses, Claudia grew more settled. She told Livia to join the other girls now enjoying a bowl of wine in the far corner, laughing and talking with Petronius the Pimp and Simon the Stoic who'd both woken revived and refreshed. Others were drifting in from the garden, aware that something had happened. Murranus returned, saying that the gladiators he'd hired were already gibbeting the corpses. Claudia just shook her head and went up to her own chamber, followed by Murranus. Once inside, she crouched down against the wall and put her face in her hands. The icy determination which had held fast when she'd questioned Livia, Nereos and Achilleos was fading. She felt slightly sick, her mind confused with images of that dark alleyway, the torchlight, Livia, Nereos trying to protest, Achilleos spitting out blood and curses. Murranus left her alone, walked over to the window and stared down at the revellers in the garden.

"The news will soon be all over the quarter," he murmured. "Once Polybius knows, he will be taking his fellow conspirators up to show them the corpses and

222

describe the exploits of his keen-witted niece Claudia. Did you suspect the *vigiles*?"

"No, not until tonight. I thought the killer might be some powerful officer from the city garrison or a dissolute senator who enjoyed watching young women die. Ah well! As for those two . . . Of course, they covered for each other, they knew this quarter like the palms of their hands and they had access to the records. The rest was easy."

"But they were only copying the Nefandus."

"Oh yes, I know that. Tomorrow morning Murranus, I assure you, we shall get up early and start at dawn. I wish to visit Tribune Macrinus." Claudia sighed, got up and shook herself. "Those men brought their deaths on themselves." She walked across and stood by Murranus, stroking his arm. "Aren't we strange creatures?" She gestured at the garden. "There people rejoice, eat and drink, laugh and tease, and yet only a walk away, we have just executed two hideous beings who inflicted gruesome deaths on innocent young women. I suppose that is why I always find it hard to accept Sylvester's arguments about a loving God."

"Perhaps it was the loving God who brought them to justice," Murranus replied. "Are you coming down?"

"No." Claudia stood on tiptoe and kissed him gently on the lips. "Find out where Macrinus' house is and wake me just before daybreak. We owe him a visit. Ask Sorry to bring me up some watered wine and anything Celades has cooked, something soft on the stomach."

Murranus promised he would, and left. A short while later Sorry brought her a platter and a goblet of wine.

He was full of questions about what had happened, explaining how rumours were already rife in the dining hall and garden. Claudia just laughed, kissed him on the head and ushered him out of the door. She ate and drank slowly before returning to her writing desk. She took a sheet of vellum and wrote down the names: Tribune Macrinus, his wife, the Domina, Briseis. Who else? She sat and stared, trying to recall every detail she'd learnt about that enigmatic tribune, and at last she found it. "I wonder," she murmured. She rose and closed the shutters, then lit another oil lamp and brought it closer. Taking another sheet of parchment, she wrote down the name Attius Enobarbus and the questions that still vexed her.

Primo. Why had Attius and the rest been sent to Byzantium? What was the real reason? Why the secrecy? Was there some other reason Attius was pardoned apart from knowing the whereabouts of the Galilean's tomb? Claudia shook her head; she could not answer that.

Secundo. Attius was a brute of a man. He had very few friends. He liked hurting women, he was a violent bully. He'd been pardoned by Constantine yet he seemed to live in fear of what he called "a greater demon". Who was he referring to, Lord Charon or Valentinian?

Tertio. The Icthus casket. Claudia nibbled the end of her pen. Why would Attius keep the secret of the Galilean's tomb in a casket? Once there it could be stolen, surely? A man as cunning as Attius would commit it to memory and destroy any evidence. The enigmatic reference to "Caesar's old friend" proved that. Yet if the whereabouts of the Galilean's tomb was not kept in the Icthus casket, why was that casket taken?

Quarto. Attius' money. He'd undoubtedly amassed a small fortune hunting Christians, seizing their wealth and smashing their shrines. He must have invested some of that ill-gotten plunder. However, according to Ulpius, Attius was a relatively poor man. But that did not explain that fine villa, the opulent furnishings, Attius' high style of living. So where did he keep his money?

Quinto. The afternoon Attius died, he met his colleagues out in the garden then returned to his chamber. Macrinus and Narses later followed him down but left him alive. Someone else apparently persuaded Attius to open the door to that chamber, murdered him, removed the Icthus casket, then fled, but not before locking the door from the inside, in itself a total contradiction.

Sexto. Drusilla, probably the only person who had loved Attius, his concubine. She had received a letter and left the villa to come to the She-Asses. Why? According to Nereos, he and Achilleos had not assaulted and killed her. So who had?

Septimo. Attius was an apostate, a bully, a hunter of all things Christian, yet he had begun to draft a letter to Sylvester, possibly asking for his protection and patronage. Why Sylvester and not the Emperor?

Octavo. Lord Charon had undoubtedly played a part in all this. He liked the idea of bullying the Empress, of demanding money and displaying his power. Behind him lurked that enigmatic figure, the sinister former deacon Valentinian.

Claudia put her pen down and stared at the lamp, the moths dancing furiously above the flame. She picked up another piece of parchment. Was there any connection between Macrinus and Attius apart from the obvious ones? She sat and reflected, her eyes closed. Slowly but surely she was edging her way down this dark passage of mystery towards a solution, and she believed she was nearly there.

Lord Charon sat and watched Hecate and her assistant prepare the rite. The night sky was clear; only a light breeze ruffled the gorse and trees of the desolate cemetery along the great Appian Way. A warm, close night. All around them rose the crumbling remains of the dead. Lord Charon peered up at the sky. A few clouds had appeared; this was a night, Hecate had assured him, when the *lemures*, the ghosts of the dead, haunted this, their last resting place. Elsewhere Lamia, that terrifying woman from Hades, with her donkey legs and ragged stomach, prowled hungrily for the living, whilst the *versipelles*, the werewolves, hunted the lonely trackways and crossroads across the city. Lord Charon hardly believed in such creatures, yet many of his followers were constantly vigilant against any sign of ill-luck, be it a snake on a roof, a rat picking a hole in a sack of flour or a crow chipping away at a statue. They'd pray at the first rumble of thunder, whistle when lightning flashed and carry live fleas in a white cloth against curses.

Lord Charon stared into the fire the witches had prepared. He certainly needed a change of luck. The attack on the She-Asses had been a disaster, a hideous defeat. Cerebus had warned him that many of his followers had lost comrades and were openly bitter and resentful. Should they, Cerebus asked, trust Valentinian? After all, who was that man? Had he not betrayed his own sect, the Christians, in their catacombs? What proof did they have that he held the secret of the Galilean's tomb? Lord Charon had listened quietly and nodded. Secretly he seethed with rage at his losses, but who was to blame? Claudia, that little snooping mouse of a woman? Hecate had sent her a curse. Should he have taken more robust action? Yet the attack on the She-Asses had failed. Perhaps an assault along some lonely street? He lifted a wineskin and took a generous mouthful to calm a stab of fear. He had to be careful, prudent. Claudia was a favourite of the August bitch; if she died, only the gods knew what Helena might do! The attack on the She-Asses was bad enough; already rumours were rife that the Emperor might send cohorts to make a thorough sweep of the cemetery.

Lord Charon had grown very wary. He had deployed spies around the city to see what could be discovered, but he also intended to sacrifice. He stared at the two ugly women with their bare feet and dishevelled hair, faces deathly pale, all garbed in black, as they chanted their mournful spell. They had raided tombs for bones which they'd ground to dust, and now they invoked the shades of the dead. They tore the earth with their nails and poured into the trench they'd dug the blood of a black lamb which they'd cut to pieces. Charon watched intently, trying to ignore the squeaking of bats as they flew from one tomb to another. Hecate had brought two wax dolls with her: one represented himself, arms raised in an imperious, threatening manner; the smaller one was carved in a position of supplication. Both dolls were thrown into the fire before a rough statue of Priapus, the god of gardens, carved out of fig wood. The wax spluttered and melted. The witches watched intently as the fire died, then Hecate busied herself amongst the red-hot embers, sifting, searching. She crept towards him, face all bloodied, eyes staring.

"Be careful," she hissed. "If a choice is to be made, do not cast your dice with Valentinian. Twice cursed, he'll remain cursed. Remember that!"

She scurried away to finish the sacrifice. Lord Charon stared into the night. Perhaps it was time he changed sides. Valentinian had brought him nothing but ill-luck; an impudent, treacherous man who had dared to use his name. Yet who *was* Valentinian? And when would he show himself? He had demanded no more meetings since the defeat at the She-Asses. Charon smiled to himself. Valentinian was no fool. The advice he had given had proved disastrous. If he did show himself again, Charon clicked his tongue, perhaps there might be a different outcome . . .

Valentinian squatted in the garden of the house of Attius Enobarbus, keeping to the shadow of the orchard trees. Usually the garden would have been illuminated with scintillating lamps and translucent alabaster jars, their perfume mixing with the aromas of the fallen fruit, the last flowers of summer and the clear tang from the herb gardens. Now all was dark. Only the occasional light glowed from the villa. Death had doused everything. Drusilla's corpse lay within. Already servants and slaves were fleeing; they'd seized goods, valued possessions, and stolen away. Ah well. Valentinian stared at the stars. He too must be gone. He had no intention of seeking a fresh meeting with Lord Charon. The attack on the She-Asses tavern had been a most humiliating setback. Lord Charon would demand compensation and guarantees. No, it was time he disappeared again. Valentinian peered down at the man lying bound and unconscious beside him. He would have to make sure that no one else knew what he did. It would be good to say farewell to Frontinus, the villa, Attius Enobarbus, the Appian Way, but where to next?

Valentinian closed his eyes. It was ironic that Attius' villa lay on the Appian Way, the very road along which, two hundred and fifty years ago, the Galilean Peter had fled, trying to escape Nero's persecution. According to legend, Peter had met Christ walking towards Rome: "*Quo vadis, Domine?*" he had asked — "Where are you going, Lord?" Jesus had replied, "I am going back to Rome to be crucified again." Peter had come to his senses and returned to the city, where he was arrested, tried and condemned. He'd been executed in Nero's circus, telling his executioners to crucify him upside down as he was not worthy to follow the example of his master. Afterwards his corpse had been secretly taken away and buried. Only Valentinian knew the truth about that tomb. So what should he do now? Perhaps hide away, take the Galilean's remains and flee to Licinius in Nicomedea?

The man lying next to him on the ground gained consciousness and strained against his bonds, groaning through the gag around his mouth.

"Ah, Narses!" Valentinian whispered. "Well . . ." He leaned over and removed the gag. "Where were you going?" He kept his own mask secure; it disguised both his face and his voice.

"I was to see Frontinus," Narses gasped. "He asked me to come here."

"Why?" Valentinian asked.

"I . . . I don't know. He said it was very important. I am desperate . . ."

"Desperate for what, Narses. What do you know?"

"I don't know anything."

"The Galilean's tomb: do you know where that is?"

"I tell you, I don't know." Narses' voice rose to a scream.

Valentinian forced back the gag. "Are you sure you don't know, Narses? I mean, you were Attius' companion."

The man just stared back, shaking his head.

"Ah well," murmured Valentinian, "the night is passing. I have asked you enough. What you know, or what you don't know, doesn't really matter any more." Picking up a hammer, he shattered Narses' skull with two or three brutal blows, then got to his feet and dragged the corpse towards the villa. He opened a side door and went along a passageway, thrusting Narses' corpse into a chamber. The villa lay in darkness; no servants were about. Valentinian moved from chamber to chamber, slashing the oilskins he'd prepared. Then he took a torch and threw it into one room, watching the oil erupt in a sheet of flame.

Satisfied, Valentinian left the villa. For a while he just stood in the shadows watching the fire spread, the flames bursting greedily out of windows. Those servants who had stayed now fled. Valentinian grinned. At least he had paid his respects to Drusilla: her body would be cremated, her ashes mingled with those of the house she had loved. For him, though, there was nothing left. He turned, hurrying away from the conflagration he had caused.

Claudia did not need to be woken early the next morning. She was up well before dawn. She washed, changed and went down to the kitchen to find something to eat, and was ready to leave once a heavy-eyed Murranus stumbled down the stairs to greet her. Claudia nudged him awake and eventually he was ready, armed with a sword and club, his cloak about him. They made their way out of the tavern and up towards the square. The corpses of Nereos and Achilleos hung gruesomely, nailed to pieces of wood on the corner; a placard placed at the foot of the scaffold proclaimed their crimes and punishment. Claudia averted her eyes.

"Why Macrinus?" Murranus asked. "Why now?"

"We have to finish the mystery," Claudia murmured. "There is still something to be done. Macrinus knows more than he's told us."

They hurried on through the Caelian quarter up toward the Claudian aqueduct. A dull grey morning, yet even at that early hour, the poor were eager to escape their rat-infested garrets with their host of fleas, dim lights and rickety furniture. Pedlars were already walking around with trays full of trinkets. Cookshop boys hastened about trying to entice customers with spiced sausages, salted ham, bowls of pease pudding and craters of warm watered wine. A snake charmer had crawled out from beneath the bridge where he'd slept to play to the crowds, whilst an enterprising monkey-trainer, whip in hand, was coaxing an ape, dressed in a helmet with a shield on its arm, to hurl a javelin at a target. Claudia and Murranus hurried past along Glassmaker Street, across the fleshers' market, where poulterers were already hanging up slaughtered pheasants, partridges, storks and cranes, making special show of flamingos, the tongues of which were regarded as a great delicacy. Butchers displayed joints dripping blood. Porters, bowed under bundles, pushed handcarts or wheel-barrows to serve other stallholders eager to start the day's business. Hungry clients were hurrying down to their patrons' villas. Murranus caught Claudia by the arm.

"I've told you where Macrinus' house is; we are going in the right direction, but —"

"We have someone to visit first," Claudia teased back, "and before the day gets busy. Now, where is Goldsmith Street?"

They found this and hurried halfway up. Ulpius the banker was busy; he was already setting up his stall, above which securely tagged gold chains, silver bracelets and jewelled cups swung winking in the morning sun. His apprentices were breaking fast nearby, buying hot sausages and strips of bacon from an itinerant cookshop. Ulpius watched them patronisingly, standing in his dark blue tunic, fat legs apart. He turned as Claudia called his name, his heavy, rubicund face beaming with pleasure. He scratched his mat of snowy white hair, small black eyes studying her carefully.

"I wondered if you'd come and see me, Claudia. How is Uncle Polybius? Is the She-Asses still making a profit? I heard about the great battle there. I must visit the place myself."

"Inside," Claudia whispered. "I need to talk to you, Ulpius."

"Then come, my dearest," Ulpius teased. "I shall take you into my holy of holies."

They went through the shop, down a dim, narrow passageway into quite a grand chamber with a mural on one wall showing a cat killing a partridge, whilst on the other, behind the imposing desk, a skeleton stood holding a huge set of weighing scales. Ulpius waved to the bench before the desk; he caught Claudia's glance and grinned over his shoulder.

"Macabre images," he declared. "They are quite a favourite with my customers. When people do business, it's good to know how all things end. I have this." He went across, opened the *arca*, a metal-bound cupboard where he kept his valuables, and drew out a large silver skeleton articulated so it could bow and dance. "I've thought of offering this to Polybius. I am sure it would be popular at the She-Asses." He caught Claudia's hard glance. "But," he sighed, "you're not here because of the She-Asses, are you? Sallust must have told you about Attius' wealth." He placed his fat hands on the desk and stared stolidly at Claudia. "There is only so much I can say."

"Ulpius," Claudia leaned forward, grasping the edge of the desk, "you know and I know that you can tell me what you want, either here or at the Palatine Palace. My uncle does good business with you. I have the ear of the Empress; you could become even more prosperous . . ."

Ulpius' eyes smiled; lips parted, he ran his tongue along even white teeth. "Now that's a message to warm the heart of any banker. So," he leaned forward, "what shall I tell you?"

"Attius lodged little wealth with you, true?"

"Yes."

"So where would he keep the rest? Another banker?"

"I told Sallust that I doubted that. If I was Attius, a man disliked by Constantine, a supporter of the old regime, I would always have my assets constantly liquidated."

"In other words, be ready to flee at a moment's notice."

"Precisely. I suspect that Attius kept his wealth at home," Ulpius gestured at the metal-bound cupboard, "either in something like that, or in a chest or coffer which he'd hide away. Claudia, whenever there is unrest or agitation, people start burying their wealth, usually in their gardens. I am sure a vast treasure trove exists throughout Rome, most of it buried and forgotten." He spread his hands. "Well, those who buried it never survived to dig it up again. I suspect Attius did that. I'll also tell you something I didn't tell Sallust, since I only learnt it recently. You recall the recent chariot race, how Scorpus was the favourite, and many wagered that he would win?"

Claudia nodded. "We were there."

"As was I. Now you know Scorpus' chariot had a very nasty accident, something to do with a pin fastened to the inside wheel. The wheel struck the *metae* and broke, Scorpus lost the lead and Pausanias won. Rumours abound how the race was fixed." Ulpius shrugged. "It's quite easily done. A horse lamed, a wheel tampered with, reins frayed. Scorpus could have been a victim. Now, bets are placed as close as possible to the starting time. On that particular day, so I've learnt, Lord Charon — oh yes, the self-styled king of Rome's underworld, wagered a tremendous amount of money that Pausanias would win. He'd first bet on Scorpus, following everybody else, then he abruptly moved his money."

"Do you think Lord Charon interfered with the chariot?"

"No, no, I don't, that's too dangerous for him; people chatter. If you are going to interfere with a race, it has to be one man paying another. The more people in a conspiracy, the more dangerous it becomes. Lord Charon keeps his hands well hidden. To arrange such an accident he would have to bribe people, send messages, well, you know . . ."

"But the chariot race *was* fixed." Murranus smiled. "I've seen the same done in the arena."

"Ah yes, but something else happened. Another wager was placed." Ulpius winked conspiratorially, "Oh yes, Lord Charon moved his money, but on the morning of the race, about an hour before the start, a mysterious gambler appeared."

"Who?"

"Well if I knew, he wouldn't be mysterious, would he?" Ulpius quipped. "Anyway, this mysterious gambler put up gold but not the solidi of Constantine; all the coins passed to the various brokers were gold and silver coins of Galerius and Maxentius."

"In other words," Claudia said, "someone who'd held office under those emperors. Someone who'd amassed gold and silver coins then fell from power, but kept his hoard hidden away and never traded it for new coinage."

"Precisely."

"Attius Enobarbus," Murranus declared. "He had grown wealthy under Maxentius by persecuting Christians. Maxentius was killed at the Milvian Bridge. Attius hoarded his wealth away against the evil day; he couldn't reveal it lest it was seized."

236

"You'd make a good banker, Murranus. Ah, by the way, if you ever re-enter the arena —"

"Not now!" Claudia intervened. "There is only one problem, isn't there?"

Ulpius nodded, spreading his hands. "It cannot be Attius; he'd been murdered. I knew that, as did the whole of Rome, so who was that mysterious gambler?"

"One of the other *scrutores*?" Murranus asked. "Someone like Narses?"

"I doubt it," Ulpius replied, pushing back his chair and getting to his feet. "They were not wealthy men like Attius. Oh, by the way, have you heard?" He stopped halfway round the desk, fingers drumming on the top. "There was a fire at Attius' villa last night . . ."

Claudia thanked him for the news and stood up. "A fire," she murmured, "and I think I know who started that, but first . . ."

"Who?" Murranus asked. "Valentinian?"

"Now there's a name." Ulpius waggled a fat finger.

"What do you know about him?" Claudia demanded, following the banker to the door.

"What I know about him reeks of evil, but to be truthful, it's very little."

"What?" Claudia insisted.

"Attius once came here to draw some money. He talked of 'the good old days'. I asked him if he knew what had happened to Valentinian, the deacon in charge of the Christian community around the Vatican Hill. You see, Claudia, sometimes I stay in the shadows —"

"In other words you hide from the law?"

"Yes, well, a number Christians used to lodge their money with me; they tended to trust me. Some of these were from the Vatican community, yet they all disappeared; their money is still in my care. I made enquiries. I heard stories about Valentinian being a possible traitor in that community. Anyway, I asked Attius Enobarbus about this. He replied, almost in a whisper, that if there was ever a demon behind the mask of a human face, it was Valentinian." He shrugged. "That is all I can tell you." He ushered them through the shop and out into the street.

Once outside, Claudia glanced around. A hawker stood ostensibly buying a piece of spiced pork. Claudia was sure she had passed him on the street coming up. She walked on, slipping her hand into Murranus', but then glanced quickly back. Yes, although he'd turned away, the hawker had been watching them, and she wondered who he was.

"You're very quiet, Murranus," she teased.

He paused and stared around. "Do you think we are being followed?"

"I know we are being followed, but it doesn't really matter." Claudia squeezed his hand. "The mystery is clearing; the truth is beginning to emerge, but first, Macrinus."

The tribune's house stood in its own grounds on the corner of Scythe-Makers' Street, a comfortable two-storey dwelling behind a gate leading into a small courtyard in front of the main double doors. Murranus hammered on the polished black wood; there was the sound of sandals slapping on the floor, followed by the rattle of locks being turned and bolts being drawn. Tribune Macrinus, dressed in a knee-length white tunic, pulled the doors back and greeted them with a smile.

"Claudia!" he exclaimed. "I was certainly expecting you."

"Of course you were. The Domina must have warned you. I thought you might flee, but there again, what point would there be in that? I am also sure you have no slaves or servants, not even a freedman like Crastinus to spy on you. You do remember Crastinus?"

Macrinus ignored the pointed questions and waved them in. "Come," he said softly. "I have not finished eating; you must join me." He led them through the imposing doorway into the atrium, where a magpie, chained to its stand, wished them "good luck and good morrow". Macrinus stopped to feed it a morsel. "Something I collected on my travels," he explained, leading them along a small peristyle with a roofed colonnade, ornamental shrubs and flowers. In the centre a sunken cistern, its clear water decorated with floating lotus petals, housed small, darting golden fish. Claudia also noted the barred and padlocked door at the end of the peristyle just before Macrinus took them into the exquisitely furnished *triclinium* with its couches and small tables. He offered them something to eat and drink; Claudia and Murranus declined, so they adjourned to the small library, a square chamber furnished with stools and a broad-backed chair, desk, coffers, reed baskets and an open cupboard with pigeonholed shelves. The walls were limewashed and decorated with painted panels depicting Aristotle tutoring a young Alexander. Busts of philosophers stood on plinths. Macrinus ushered them to stools and sat facing them on a leather-backed camp stool.

"I thought you wished to eat?" Claudia asked.

"It will wait. More importantly, you are to be congratulated. The Domina informed me how you trapped the Nefandus."

"Did she also tell you about Briseis?"

Macrinus glanced away.

"Briseis?" Claudia insisted. "She was a Daughter of Isis. You knew her, yet you told me you had little to do with that guild."

"I didn't, except for Briseis."

"Tribune Macrinus, who was she?"

"I loved her," Macrinus replied flatly. "I was married. My wife was dying. My career was finished. All I had left was patrolling the filthy streets of the Caelian quarter. Then I met Briseis, hair like gold, fair of face, lovely in aspect. She was witty, generous and kind. She transformed my life; she brought light into the dark." Macrinus spoke as if to himself. "Everything about her was fresh and joyful. I felt guilty, yet," he smiled faintly, "what could I do? I loved her. May the gods have mercy on me! My wife soon knew, yet she bore me no ill-will. She even insisted that when she died I should do what was most honourable: take Briseis from the House of Isis and marry her. If all Christians were like my wife, I would accept their baptism tomorrow."

"Tribune Macrinus," Claudia broke in, "where is Briseis?"

240

"Fled."

"I don't believe you. Your freedman Crastinus, you mentioned him once but never again."

"He fled too."

"The two of them together?"

"Yes, yes."

"You never mentioned that before."

"It was a personal matter."

"So Briseis and Crastinus were secretly having an affair. You discovered it and they fled. Did they take any of your wealth?"

"No."

"Did the Domina search for Briseis?"

"I cannot say."

"Did you search for her?"

"I tried to, but the chaos in Rome . . ."

"Where did Briseis come from?"

"Sicily."

"Did you search for her there?"

Silence.

"Did you go there?"

Again a silent, hard stare.

"Your wife was Christian?"

"You know that."

"Did you shelter Christians during the persecution?"

"Of course, quite successfully."

"So you hated the likes of Attius Enobarbus?"

"I despised him and all his kind."

"Did you start the rumours that he was the Nefandus?"

"Yes, and I enjoyed doing that."

"So you really hated him, a matter which caught the attention of the Augusta. You were just the person she needed to watch Attius and the rest when they were sent to Byzantium. Why?"

"I had my orders. I'm a soldier; I followed them."

"Did you argue with Attius and his followers when you were away?"

"I went with them. I watched them where possible. I avoided talking to them."

"Strange." Claudia rose and went over to examine one of the busts. "Here we have a Tribune of Vigiles in charge of the Caelian quarter; during a period of violent murder he falls in love with a young woman. She disappears, as does the freedman Crastinus, around the same time, just before Constantine marches into Rome. You apparently hated the Nefandus, yet now, when his name is mentioned, you dismiss it as a matter of little relevance. You live in an empty house by yourself. No slave girls, no servants, no freedmen, not even a porter. A magpie, trained to speak but no dog, no pet, no companion. I find that strange, Tribune Macrinus." She turned and stood over him. "What I find even stranger is that you are a very experienced officer, which is why you were appointed to the Caelian quarter, but you never captured the Nefandus. The Augusta has a high regard for your qualities, hence your trip to Byzantium: someone who could be trusted, who hated Attius and would keep an eye on him, not because he was the Nefandus but because of something else, a matter we shall come to in a while. Now as you know, Macrinus, the Caelian quarter is a rat warren of alleyways; you could deploy a legion there and not catch a malefactor. Yet it must have occurred to you to set a trap, a lure, and what better than a beautiful woman? After all, you'd tried everything else, hadn't you? You yourself admitted how the Nefandus seemed to read your mind. He was baiting you and still you couldn't make any progress. Now let me tell you what I suspect happened." Claudia went and sat down. "And if I give an explanation which is not the truth, and you can prove that it's so, then I shall get up, leave your house and never trouble you again."

CHAPTER
TWELVE

*The very light of day itself was darkened,
as it were, in grief and wonder at these
scenes of horror.*

Macrinus blinked, rose, went across to a small silver-topped table and poured himself a generous cup of wine. He offered one to Claudia and Murranus; they shook their heads.

"I'm listening," he declared, sitting down.

"You were in charge of the *vigiles* in the Caelian quarter. They amounted to very little; they never do, do they? Former soldiers, usually drunks, bully-boys. You, however, took your job seriously. Your wife was Christian so you were eager to concentrate on maintaining law and order and leave the likes of Attius Enobarbus and Severus to hunt poor Christians. It was a humdrum existence until the Nefandus appeared to begin his bloody work. You, in the course of your duties, visited the Domina at the House of Isis; you met Briseis and your life was transformed. You loved that young woman, but your real work was to catch the Nefandus. Of course, he eluded you, he baited you; you were at your wits' end. Then the woman you loved, Briseis, offered to act as a decoy, and tragically, she was murdered. I suspect her death led you to identify the Nefandus as your freedman, Crastinus, the trusted

244

body-servant who'd read your reports, debated the matter with you and listened at doorways when you discussed the matter with your wife. Briseis' corpse wasn't handed over to the funeral club at the House of Isis; her name is not listed amongst the victims. The Domina agreed. You took special care of her corpse, didn't you? You also took care of Crastinus. You probably tortured him, then secretly executed him. The killings stopped. To all intents and purposes, Briseis and Crastinus had simply disappeared. People's curiosity might have been aroused, but there again, Constantine was marching on Rome. The world was about to be turned upside down, and who really cared about poor whores killed in the Caelian quarter or an old tribune who'd finished his task and resigned? Who'd be bothered about a freedman and a young prostitute who had vanished? Armies were clashing, empires toppling, and even at the best of times, life in Rome can be very, very cheap."

Macrinus drank greedily from his goblet. Claudia caught the smile in his eyes.

"And what proof do you have of this?" he asked, cradling the cup. "What evidence can you offer?"

"Oh, I suppose," Claudia replied, "that could be found, but there again," she rose, walked to the door and turned, "I could ask why a man like you lives in a house like this all alone, empty, unless you wish to hide something. When the persecution raged, your poor wife helped the Christians. You are a soft-hearted man, Macrinus. You have a gentleness in you; you too helped that persecuted sect. Where did the Christians hide when they came here? After all, not even the likes of Attius Enobarbus would dare raid the house of a tribune, the officer in charge of the Caelian quarter, respected by the authorities, whoever was Emperor." She walked back. "Please, show me where the Christians hid."

Macrinus eased himself up and walked across to a coffer; he opened this and took out a bunch of keys. "What does it matter now?" he said quietly. "What does it really matter? My wife is dead. Briseis is dead. What is there left? You'd best follow me."

He led them out of the library, back to the corner of the peristyle and the heavy fortified door Claudia had noticed on arriving. He took off the bar, inserted the keys in the main lock and the one above. Then he pushed open the door and beckoned them forward. Claudia shook her head.

"Tribune Macrinus, I would prefer it if you went down first and lit whatever torches and lamps are necessary."

The tribune shrugged and went down the steps. They heard tinder rasp and saw the glow of light. Claudia, followed by Murranus, went carefully down the steps, small, narrow and steep, the walls on either side freshly plastered. At the bottom stretched a large chamber; it reminded Claudia of Attius Enobarbus' secure room.

"By the lords of light!" Murranus breathed.

Claudia's eyes became accustomed to the gloom. She was aware of a great chest or coffer to her left, some drawings on the whitewashed walls, but it was the horror at the far end which drew her gaze. She walked slowly towards it. The hideous scene was etched more firmly by the lamps Macrinus lit on either side: a skeleton crucified to the wooden beams embedded in the redbrick cellar wall. Claudia stared at the gruesome tableau: the sagging skull, the nails hammered expertly through the wrist bones as well as the wooden rest to support the feet, crossed over each other with a huge spike thrust through them. She did not know which was more chilling, that macabre sight or the small table and comfortable chair set before it, as if this was some favourite sculpture the tribune loved to sit and relish while he savoured a goblet of wine. She stared at the possessions piled beneath the nailed feet: combs of boxwood, ivory and tortoiseshell, necklaces, white and purple bands for the hair, a beautifully carved hand mirror, silver earrings and a bracelet fashioned out of cornelian. She crouched down, touched these lightly, then crossed the cellar to that long casket of polished cedarwood. She ran her hand along the side and felt the etchings carved there; on its lid were beautifully sculptured lotuses and lilies. She turned and glanced at Macrinus, who seemed unperturbed by what was happening.

"Please lift the casket lid. It is Briseis, isn't it?"

He nodded and obeyed, gently raising the lid, tilting it back then pulling down the golden linen sheets to reveal the mummified corpse of a beautiful young woman, her eyelids resting gently against skin which looked as if it had been brushed with gold. Claudia didn't feel chilled or troubled, but rather awed. This cellar held, and mingled together, both deep hate and profound love. She walked back to the cellar steps, sat down and stared at Murranus, who was examining the crucified skeleton more closely.

"It's been lacquered," Murranus declared over his shoulder. "Hasn't it? It's been painted to keep the bones from crumbling. Who did that?"

"I did."

Macrinus walked over, picked up the chair and brought it across so he sat in front of Claudia.

"I did." His gaze never left hers. "I made careful enquiries with the Egyptian embalmers, those who dressed Briseis' body so beautifully for burial. I swore them to secrecy and rewarded them richly. They were only too willing to do what I wanted. Stranger things happen in Rome."

"And Briseis' corpse was brought here?"

"Oh yes."

"Long before you crucified Crastinus?"

"Yes." He made a face. "Some time before I crucified Crastinus. That reprobate knew she was entombed here."

"Tell me what happened," Claudia demanded. "The truth."

"You know most of it," Macrinus declared. He leaned back in the chair. "When I crucified Crastinus, I called myself the Iudex, the Judge. I was correct. There was no one in Rome to carry out proper judgement. What could I do?"

"From the beginning," Claudia murmured. "Please, tell me from the beginning."

248

"From the beginning it was as you said. I was a veteran officer, discharged with honour and given responsibility for the Caelian quarter. I bought this house, but my wife fell gravely ill shortly afterwards. She was a good woman, Claudia, beautiful in character as she was in everything else. I truly did love her. Anyway," he took a deep breath, "there was nothing the physicians could do for her. They said it was a matter of time, of feeding her drugged wine as whatever rottenness lurked inside her would kill her eventually. I would have done anything to help."

"And Crastinus?"

"A young slave. I bought him. He was educated. He came from somewhere in Greece; his father had been caught up in a revolt, but not before he had educated Crastinus, who was skilled as any scribe. He became the son we never had. I indulged him, I spoiled him, I freed him. I gave him a position of honour and security in my family. He became my confidential scribe; he knew everything I did. When I was appointed to the Caelian quarter, he proved to be a most skilled administrator. I should worry about nothing, he said, but look after my wife. He would do everything he could to assist me."

"And he never betrayed the demons inside him?"

"Oh, on reflection, occasionally. He would rant particularly about the stupidity of his feckless father at being drawn into the revolt, but he truly hated his mother. She used to scorn and mock him."

"Why?"

"Crastinus had a good mind and sharp wits, but he was ugly, with close-set eyes and a rather protuberant lower lip. He looked slightly deformed. He also had a stammer when he became nervous; apparently his mother used to ridicule this. I always thought such demons had been exorcised; I trusted Crastinus implicitly. Then the Nefandus appeared. I hunted him, Claudia, as skilfully as I've hunted anyone in my life. I did everything I could to capture him, but he always seemed to elude me. Then the baiting began, the mockery. I grew more concerned about the Nefandus than I did about my wife or my other duties. I left more and more of these to Crastinus. Then I met Briseis."

"Did Crastinus know about her?"

"Of course! He said he adored her, loved her deeply and would do anything to help."

"And your wife's attitude to Crastinus?"

"My wife always had the deepest suspicions about him. She claimed he had a dark heart; a man of the deepest night. I asked her why." He smiled thinly. "Like all women she said it was not a matter of logic but something deeper. She said she would sometimes catch Crastinus watching her and she'd glimpse the hate raging in his eyes, but, of course, I didn't believe her. I felt guilty about Briseis, and Crastinus was such a help. True," he breathed out noisily, "I grew concerned at how the Nefandus seemed to know every move I plotted to capture him. I suspected the *vigiles*, but I had little proof. I became obsessed with capturing the Nefandus, as was Briseis. She was courageous, full of fury at this brutal killer of so many of her sisters.

"Now after I had met Briseis, she stopped consorting with other men, an arrangement I made with the Domina. I gave her money and looked after Briseis." He paused, fighting back the tears. "One night I had to stay at home; my wife was vomiting, unable to rest. The servants were of little assistance. Crastinus told me to remain and look after her; he would go into the barracks and take care of matters. On that night Briseis took it into her head, may the gods bless her, to trap the Nefandus. She thought if she was armed with a knife and a cudgel, she'd be able to protect herself." He paused to swallow hard. "They found her corpse the next morning just like the rest, ripped from crotch to throat, her right eye missing. I was beside myself with grief. I told the Domina that Briseis was my concern. I would look after her. Crastinus helped me. He knew an embalmer, an Egyptian skilled in such matters. I took her corpse there." He waved to the casket. "I told my wife. She too agreed that Briseis' corpse should be brought back here. I would not forsake her in death.

"Briseis' murder deeply affected my wife. She sank into a stupor, a sleep from which she never recovered, and so she died." He breathed in deeply. "I was distraught. I drank and I brooded. The killings continued, then one day the Domina sent me a letter. She'd come across a small casket containing Briseis' possessions; would I like to have it? I didn't go to the House of Isis; the casket was delivered here. It contained," he gestured at the grisly scene behind him, "small trinkets, rings, necklaces, but there was also a letter from Briseis. Most of the Domina's girls are

251

educated. Briseis had written me a note the afternoon before she was killed telling me what she'd planned, saying that she loved me, and that the only person she had confided in was —"

"Crastinus," Claudia offered.

"Precisely. She had told Crastinus that she was going to act as a decoy, then explained to him that no one, especially me, knew what she had planned."

"Did Briseis trust Crastinus?"

"No, she didn't. Like my wife, she was deeply suspicious, very wary of him, and, on reflection, for the same reason: that he wore a mask which sometimes slipped to show the darkness within. When I read that note, Claudia, I believed Briseis was offering herself as living proof to show who the Nefandus really was."

"But she must have known it was dangerous?"

"I could see the logic of her actions," Macrinus replied. "She may have had suspicions about Crastinus, but I did not. If she had voiced them, I would not have believed her. I'd have called in Crastinus and confronted him; he was so glib he'd have refuted and denied the charge. Claudia, I regarded him as a son. The Nefandus would have ceased his depredations, at least for a while, until Crastinus' cunning mind devised a way of protecting himself." Macrinus cleared his throat. "I now speak with the wisdom of hindsight, but Crastinus had already marked Briseis down for death, whatever happened. Once I'd captured him, I made him confess. He truly hated her."

"Briseis must have thought she could be successful?"

"Yes, she was full of confidence that she could succeed without hurting herself. She always said the Nefandus was an arrant coward. When they found her corpse, it was clear she had put up a struggle, whilst the knife she carried was missing. I then remembered how Crastinus, after Briseis' death, had pretended to be distraught. He'd kept to himself but he'd also changed his style of clothing; usually it was a sleeveless tunic, but for days after her death he wore one with sleeves, as if he wanted to hide something. At first I couldn't accept the truth until I reflected on Briseis' letter and how the Nefandus always seemed to evade me, the personal insults, the baiting. I decided that if that was the path to be followed, then so be it.

I acted as if I trusted Crastinus more than ever. One night I told him I felt ill, unable to attend my normal duties. He left and I followed him. Nothing happened that night, but a few nights later was different. Instead of going to the barracks, Crastinus went along an alleyway not very far from the She-Asses, a dark, narrow slit of a place. He used it to disappear into the night. I stood and watched. A Daughter of Isis passed. I saw this dark shape emerge. Strange, when Crastinus left the house he'd gone empty-handed; somewhere along his route he had hidden away a leather sack, containing a helmet and a cloak which he must have stolen or bought. He was now wearing these." Macrinus sucked on his teeth. "Even from where I stood I could hear the clink of coins, the girl laughing as she followed him into the darkness. I ran across, but," he shook his head, "I was too late. I heard a scream abruptly cut off, nothing else. For a while I just blundered about in the dark, and by the time I'd reached the spot, Crastinus had disappeared, leaving his bloody work behind him!"

Macrinus wiped his mouth on the back of his hand. "That night I came back to my house. I guzzled wine until I was sick and slept all the next day. Crastinus came down, so solicitous and caring. It was all I could do to keep my mask on and stare at his, but even then I was planning my revenge. In Rome there was growing chaos. Maxentius and his Praetorian guards were forming up ready to leave and confront Constantine. I took Crastinus out into the garden. We sat there for a while as I reminisced. All the time my heart seethed with a murderous hatred. I felt like stabbing him on the spot, but already I was secretly calling myself the Iudex, the Judge. I was determined to make him confess. We came down to the cellar here. I prepared wine, heavily laced with opium. Crastinus was soon in a deeply drugged sleep. I had everything prepared." He shrugged. "I am a soldier, Claudia, I have served on every frontier of our empire. I have attended more crucifixions than any man would in several lifetimes: deserters, murderers, criminals. I propped Crastinus' body up against the wall, keeping it in place with poles. Once you've nailed the hands, it's easy. You hammer the spike through a hole between the bones on the wrists. If you put it through the hand, the nail simply rips through skin and flesh and drops away."

"The pain must have roused Crastinus?" Murranus asked.

"Of course it did, but I fed him more opium. The right hand, the left hand then the feet: a wooden prop nailed to the beam, the feet are crossed, and a spike through the gap in the ankle bones, first the left, then the right. People think that a crucified man dies of blood loss; he doesn't. He dies of asphyxiation; his ribcage closes over his lungs, and he literally chokes to death. So to keep himself alive, Crastinus had to lift himself up on his feet, gasping for air. At first there was begging and pleading. He hoped to probe for some gap, a doubt in my mind. I just brought that chair, a wine jug and a goblet and listened to him. For the first few hours I let him chatter away. By then the pain was becoming excruciating. I offered him more drugged wine, on one condition: he confessed the truth."

"The other servants?" Claudia asked. "They must have heard the screams?"

"First, this cellar is deep," Macrinus replied. "Second, because of the chaos in Rome, I'd freed all my servants. I'd given each a few coins and said I did not know what the future held. They were all free, free to go. What did I need with servants after Crastinus? I vowed I would never allow anyone in here again. Anyway, Crastinus tried to bluster, but the pain was too much and he confessed. I made sure he told me the truth: the various victims, times and places. How he used to check my papers and listen at doors, how it was ever so easy. I fed him some wine as a reward. He came round and begged for more. I returned with my questions about Briseis. He confessed how she may have suspected him and that he'd made a mistake in killing her. In the end he accepted he was going to die and so returned to the insults. I asked him why he hated me so much. He replied: 'Why not? What had I done to be sold as a slave, to be patronised?' I asked him about the cruelty to his victims. Do you know what he said? 'The cut in their bodies was revenge for my mother.'"

"And the eye?" Murranus asked.

"Apparently his mother used to turn away and grin at him out of the corner of her eye, relishing his humiliation. He never forgot that look; he'd take his victim's eye and burn it. In the end he took days to die. I watched him. I savoured every single moment. Do I have a demon in me, Claudia? All I could think of was those poor girls, of Briseis, of the trust Crastinus betrayed. I didn't know what was happening in Rome. The tramp of legions, the crash of empire, people fleeing for their lives or hiding their treasures. It all passed over me. As for Crastinus' corpse . . ." He smiled thinly. "At first I thought I'd burn his bones, but why? I left the body to rot here until the chamber smelt like a charnel house, but I didn't care. To me it was a perfume. I have slept on battlefields. I've seen corpses piled higher than the long grass. I had caught the Nefandus! I, the Iudex, had carried out judgement! Crastinus' body would be a shrine to that. The months passed. I cleaned up the mess and fumigated the chamber. Once Crastinus was nothing but a skeleton, I returned to my embalmer. I asked him how human bones could be preserved. He gave me some liquid. I painted each one carefully. I wanted to preserve it; I still do."

"You also removed certain documents at the barracks, hence the gaps in the records?"

"True, Claudia. I felt deeply ashamed that the Nefandus had been a member of my household."

"And Attius Enobarbus?"

"Oh, him! I knew about Attius and the *scrutores*, Maxentius' bully-boys. The Domina often complained about Attius' violent ways, but she couldn't do much. He was still powerful, with a financial interest in the House of Isis. What could she do? I spread the rumour that he was the Nefandus; perhaps it might frighten him away from the Caelian quarter, but it didn't, at least not until Constantine's victory. After Crastinus' death I remained in a stupor. At last I broke free from it; I realised the world had moved on. Power had changed hands. Constantine and Helena were now masters of the world, with Licinius lording it in the East. I returned to my books and then Helena sent for me. Would I be *custos* — keeper — on a surveying expedition to Byzantium? I didn't care where she was sending me. Of course Helena knew about my wife and the way I'd helped Christians; Presbyter Sylvester also recognised that. They thought I would be the ideal choice. They knew about my dislike, even hatred for Attius Enobarbus. I accepted the post. It would be good to be away from this house, to think for a while, to reflect."

"Weren't you concerned that someone might come in here and discover this?"

"What did I care?" Macrinus spread his hands. "Anyway, just in case, I asked Helena that my house be locked, sealed and guarded by imperial troops whilst I was absent. I explained it was full of fond memories of my wife. I didn't want violators or robbers to pollute it. She, of course, agreed; it was easily done. The door to this cellar was barred and locked; imperial guards patrolled outside. Who would dare to break in? I also told her that when I died, as an act of thanks, I wanted my corpse to be burnt here in my house, the entire place consumed by flames. The Augusta was surprised. I explained how this house was my life, it was full of memories. I had no servants, no children, no heir. Again the Augusta agreed. I doubt if she ever gave it a second thought. She and her son were absorbed in greater plans than a tribune's simple house standing in its own grounds near the Caelian quarter."

"And so you went to Byzantium?"

"Of course. It was good to travel. I rather liked being in charge of Attius Enobarbus, keeping a close eye on a former bully."

"Even though you knew he wasn't the Nefandus?"

"He was still a bully."

"Then the new Nefandus appeared in the alleyways?"

"Claudia, I've seen cruelty and savagery second to none. I realised what had happened. Somebody else had studied those gruesome murders and was simply imitating them for his own amusement. When I met you," he smiled, "I had a feeling you'd be swifter than me, quick to the kill. I told the Domina that."

258

"You never thought of warning us," Murranus asked, "about the original Nefandus?"

"How could I? What use would that serve?" Macrinus rose. "The real Nefandus lasted so long because he was Crastinus, my aide, my lieutenant, my helper, my son! I made a terrible mistake, and Briseis and others paid for it."

"Did you have any suspicions?" Claudia asked.

"I wondered if the new Nefandus was a member of the *vigiles*, but, remember, I suspected the same about my own troop. Ah well." He sighed. "What are you going to do now, Claudia? Ask Murranus to detain me, take me to the prisons on the Palatine?"

Claudia picked up her cloak and swung it about her shoulders.

"On what charge, Tribune Macrinus? You're a good officer. You did your best. You carried out judgement against Crastinus; you call yourself the Iudex and that was your right. Last night Murranus here executed Nereos and Achilleos for their crimes. You did the same to Crastinus and obtained the truth. He would have been crucified anyway. As for Briseis, you loved her in life, so why not in death? Oh no, Tribune Macrinus, I only ask you one thing."

"What?"

"I ask you, for the love you bore your wife and for the love you bore Briseis." She pointed at the grisly remains crucified against the far wall. "Burn that, burn it now. Purify this chamber. Briseis deserves better. Judgement has been carried out. Sentence passed and executed. Leave it alone."

259

Macrinus nodded.

"One more thing." Claudia fastened the clasp on her cloak. "Does the name Valentinian mean anything to you?"

"I've heard of it, but only in passing."

"And the location of the Galilean's tomb?"

"Oh, I am sure that Attius Enobarbus and some of the *scrutores* may have known: just a few words I overheard when they were in Byzantium, but not enough evidence to challenge them."

"And Frontinus, Attius' freedman?"

Macrinus pulled a face. "Nothing but an empty cask, a man who kept in the shadows, but there again," he smiled, "what do I know?"

Claudia nodded. She turned to go up the steps, Murranus following her.

"Claudia?"

She paused.

"I have something else to tell you." Macrinus waved her back. "You have been just and compassionate; it's the least I can do."

Claudia came back down the steps.

"I was sent to Byzantium. Helena chose Attius Enobarbus and his colleagues for a very good reason. You may not believe this, but the Emperor Constantine . . ." Macrinus paused and took a deep breath. "The Emperor Constantine and his mother Helena have plans for a new Rome."

"Of course," Claudia agreed. "There's building work going on here already."

"No, no. Constantine intends to move the centre of empire from Rome to Byzantium; that city will be renamed after him." Macrinus smiled at Claudia's gasp of astonishment. "Think about it," he continued. "The Empire is now divided between East and West. Sooner or later Constantine will march against Licinius. I would wager Constantine will win. There will be no more division of the Empire. Second, as you know, Constantine has no great love for Rome; it declared for Maxentius. It's now a sprawling city, hard to defend."

"So he moves the centre of empire," Claudia whispered, "from Italy to the Hellespont, the very place where East and West meet?"

"Precisely. From this new city he will be able to exercise complete authority over his new empire; that's why Attius Enobarbus and the others were chosen. They were sworn to silence. They went there to map out the land, to assess water supplies, local quarries, harbours, roads, everything the Emperor is going to need to build his new city, and it will happen, Claudia."

"Of course." Claudia smiled. "That's why Lord Charon made a reference in his last letter to "a new Rome". He, too, knows this news and was threatening the August Ones with revealing it to everybody else. There would be turmoil in the streets, riots."

"It's supposed to be a secret," Macrinus continued. "It won't happen immediately, only when Constantine is ready. Nevertheless, preparations have begun. He and his mother intend to move their seat of power to Byzantium, rename it and build a new empire with a new faith. It follows logically."

"How did you find this out?"

"I listened at doors. I studied what they were doing. After a while I could reach only one conclusion. When I returned to Rome, Helena interrogated me, asking what I knew. I was honest and told her the truth. I also told her it did not matter to me where she ruled the Empire from; I was more concerned about my next jug of Falernian. She just laughed. I said that whatever I was involved in, I was sworn to secrecy. I would reveal it to no one outside my household." He smiled. "You are now part of my household, at least for a while."

"And does Presbyter Sylvester know this?"

"I don't know." Macrinus pulled a face. "What does that matter to me? Look, Claudia, I can tell you no more . . ."

Once they'd left Macrinus' house, Claudia turned and stared back at the black polished wood of the front door.

"So many places," she murmured, "so full of secrets." She pointed in the direction of the Palatine. "There are even more over there. Little wonder Presbyter Sylvester isn't happy. The Church of Rome is exercising its muscle over the bishops of other cities. He certainly wouldn't like a new rival in Byzantium."

"And the tomb of the Galilean?" Murranus asked. "That's why Helena is searching for it, isn't it?"

"I wonder," Claudia stared up at the sky; she reckoned it must be an hour off midday, "if Helena wishes to take the saintly remains and move them to her new city. Can you image that, Murranus? A new

Rome on the Bosphorus and Hellespont, the meeting place between Europe and Asia, a holy city crammed full of churches, all holding the great relics of the Christian religion; a centre of government and the focus of faith. Helena is determined to follow that path, which is why Presbyter Sylvester is so unhappy."

"Should we question him?"

"No, no. A more important meeting awaits. Come, my beloved."

CHAPTER
THIRTEEN

*For it had been in times past the endeavour of
impious men (or rather let me say of the entire
race of evil spirits through their means),
to consign to the darkness of oblivion
that divine monument.*

They could smell the smoke from Attius Enobarbus'
villa as soon as they passed through the busy
Aurelian Gate. The house itself had been devastated,
reduced to nothing more than smouldering timbers
and blackened walls. Looters had moved in, and a
few soldiers stood around wondering what to do.
Claudia showed her warrant, demanding to speak to
an officer, and hid her surprise when the giant,
shaggy-headed Burrus, together with a cohort of his
Germans, came striding round the corner of the
blackened, stinking building. Burrus was not in a
good humour. He stopped before her, drew himself
up, bowed, then curtly declared that the Augusta was
furious. Claudia asked why. Burrus explained how
Narses, the last of the *scrutores*, had escaped from
the Palatine and could not be found. The German
pointed a finger at the pile of flame-ravaged timber
and stone.

"Arson, deliberately started, and everything is gone.
If the fire didn't take care of something, the servants

264

certainly have. Drusilla and Frontinus are nothing more than charred ash."

"Frontinus!"

"Recognised by the ring on his hand, the chain round his neck and whatever is left of his sandals. I must go." Burrus' watery blue eyes stared down at her. "The Augusta will not be pleased. She is already asking about you."

"Tell her I work and strive to please," Claudia answered sweetly. She stood on tiptoe and kissed Burrus on the cheek.

The Germans gave a collective moan of pleasure. Burrus grinned, patted Claudia on the head, ordered his companions to follow and swept on. Claudia watched them go.

"I always think of them," she murmured, "as big and bristling, highly amusing, yet in truth they are so dangerous, so fickle." She turned back to Murranus. "Once they've drunk deeply, if Helena didn't restrain them with the lash of her tongue or the cane, Burrus and his ruffians would march into Rome and take the head of everyone who didn't like her. Ah well, let's view the devastation."

They walked round the smoking ruins. Sparks still rose, black smoke curled, the hideous, rancid smell of burnt oil made them gag. An eerie sight. On Claudia's right the gardens of the villa stretched serene and beautiful; on her left lay a trail of destruction from the vestibule of the villa to its rear chambers. A few servants and slaves still wandered about like children tragically bereft of their parents. A cohort of *vigiles* from the barracks along the Appian Way looked businesslike but seemed unable to stop the petty pilfering as a servant found some item, undamaged by the flames, picked it up and wandered off. Claudia and Murranus gingerly crossed the tangled, still hot ruins and found the steps leading to Attius' secure room. They went carefully down and along the passageway reeking of smoke, only to find that the chamber too had been looted: the great oaken desk had been taken apart and removed, along with the bed, stools and small tables. Of Attius' records and manuscripts nothing remained. They returned outside, where an old servant, the head gardener Arminius, was trying to make some sense of the chaos. His unshaven cheeks were wet with tears; all he could do was moan at what had happened.

"It was just before midnight." He gestured around. "The villa was settling down, Drusilla's corpse was laid out in the atrium, Frontinus was busy about his duties. The candles and lamps were doused." He blew his cheeks out. "And then the fire started. It was as if Jupiter had loosed some fiery thunderbolt, the whole villa consumed in flames from one end to the other."

"So it was deliberate?"

"Oh yes," the old man declared, "it had to be. It started in so many places at the same time. Even before I was aroused from sleep, smoke was billowing everywhere; there was nothing we could do. The wells are far away, Frontinus was dead, there was no one to organise anything. The servants soon realised it was nothing but chaos, so they saved what they could and kept it for themselves. Attius' chamber, you've seen it, because it lay beneath ground was saved, but it was cleared out this morning. Nobody knows what will happen next. I mean, Attius' heir is in Massilia; it will take him weeks to get here. By then there will be nothing left, not even the gardens!"

"Frontinus' corpse?"

Arminius led them around the ruins. They went deep into the gardens, into a small enclosure where those corpses rescued from the ruins had been laid out under shrouds of coarse sacking. Arminius, muttering to himself, picked up a flap, looked at the corpse beneath and shook his head. There must have been at least about a dozen bodies. At last Arminius found Drusilla's; it was nothing more than scorched bone. Beside it lay Frontinus, his face and body completely burnt; only the charred feet, in thick scraps of heavy sandals, remained. Claudia crouched down, running her hand over these.

"What's the matter?" Murranus asked.

"Never mind." Claudia got up, wiping her hands on the sacking before drawing it over the grisly remains. "Arminius, you're in charge of the garden, yes?"

He nodded.

"In the last few days have you noticed anything untoward, irregular, out of place?"

Arminus stood, fingers to his lips, muttering to himself.

"What was that?" Claudia asked.

"Holes!" Arminus declared. "I found holes where there shouldn't be."

"What holes?"

Arminius led them deeper into the garden, to a small, elegant paradise; water splashed and sparkled in fountains before coursing along artificial channels which fed small ponds and fish pools. A place of shady porticoes, with avenues of trees, cypress, plane and elm, the latter being used as an aid for climbing vines. The air was rich with the scent of shrubs such as myrtle, box, oleander, laurel and bay, their fragrances mingling with the heavier perfume of roses and violets. Arminius stopped beneath a great elm and pointed at a hole dug into the earth, more of a gash really; the ground had been hacked and torn to the depth of at least a sword's length.

"There's others," he declared mournfully.

"I am sure there are," Claudia replied, "but come. Attius is dead, his house will give up no more secrets."

Murranus questioned Claudia about her parting remark as they left the villa and walked up towards the soaring fortified gateway through the Aurelian wall. Claudia, however, just shook her head, her mind teeming with jarring images: the blackened dead, the charred remains, the horrid smell of burnt oil, the curling wisps of smoke, the stench of death and decay mingling with the fragrances of the garden. They passed under the gateway, dodging carts and wheelbarrows, the surge of people all busy on their own affairs. Peasant farmers, assisted by their families, pushed or carried produce into the city. Fishmongers, with their smelly slats full of freshly caught produce, bawled out prices. Women bearing baskets crammed with vegetables jostled hunters carrying bloodied hares slung on poles, whilst sweaty, red-faced cooks offered strips of roasted suckling pig. A group of priests from Macedonia, resplendent in their multi-coloured robes and tawdry jewellery, paraded drunkenly before the image on their portable shrine. Iberian dancers, swarthy-faced and festooned with glittering trinkets, stamped and whirled to the music of the tambour, flute and castanets. The streets beyond the gate were equally busy with hawkers, vendors, pimps and prostitutes. An aged hag had attracted a crowd of wealthy young women and was teaching them how to invoke the macabre rites in honour of Tacita, the Silent One. Claudia wondered idly about the curse sent to her. In the end, what did it really matter? These mysteries would not be settled with curses, chants or magic but with careful scrutiny, hard facts and not a little danger.

They entered the Caelian quarter and crossed the square leading down to the She-Asses tavern. Torquatus was busy; he lifted his hand and shouted that he had made no progress; had Claudia? Should they settle the matter now? Claudia, averting her eyes from the gibbeted corpses, just shook her head, eager to be away. The She-Asses was relatively silent; the excitement of the previous days was now making itself felt. Celades was singing to Caligula in the kitchen. Poppaoe, full of resentment at the way Polybius' generosity made her work, was busy with Januaria cleaning tables and sweeping the floor. Murranus excused himself and went into the kitchen. Poppaoe came hurrying over, her pretty face all sweat-laced, and informed Claudia that Sallust was waiting for her in the garden.

Claudia found the Searcher sitting on the bench, staring sadly around.

"It's beautiful," he murmured as she joined him. "If I hadn't been so foolish and thrown the dice for the wrong side, I could have had a garden like this."

"Oh come," Claudia teased, "you have enough wealth for five such gardens. Why are you here?"

"Titus Labienus, Caesar's old friend," Sallust replied. "His ancient tomb is in the Vatican cemetery." He handed across a small scroll. "I've drawn a map, or rather I have had one drawn for you. Whatever you are seeking you'll find there."

"And you are sure it's the Titus Labienus I'm searching for?"

"Claudia, when have I ever been proved wrong? True, others have that name, but only one was the old friend of Caesar. I think you'll find I am right." He got up, drained his goblet and stared down at Claudia, his face much harder, eyes all questioning. Claudia realised this man was as consummate an actor as anyone else. He played the role of the tired old man, but that was only an image; behind the mask, Sallust had a sharp mind and a resolute will.

"What's the matter, Sallust?"

He crouched down, putting his hand on her knee.

"You're going out there, aren't you? At least take Murranus."

"Why do you ask?"

"Claudia, the Vatican cemetery is like the one along the Appian Way. On the outskirts you are safe; the deeper you go, the more dangerous it becomes. Now, as you know, I buy information from individuals others ignore: beggars, pimps and prostitutes. To put it bluntly, Lord Charon's men have been seen there; not just the occasional spy, but groups of them. For the time being it's a place to be avoided."

"What do you think," Claudia whispered, "the tomb of Titus Labienus holds?"

"I doubt if it is treasure." Sallust peered across the garden. "I suspect it will provide a secret entrance to the old catacombs. You're going there, aren't you?"

"The sooner the better," Claudia replied. "I have to; what I am pursuing is probably trapped there."

"You should take others with you."

"I daren't take too many people; that might attract the attention of Lord Charon. It would be safer if only Murranus and I went."

Sallust rose to his feet. "Then promise me one thing, Claudia. Do not leave for the Vatican until I send you help; whether you accept it or not is neither here nor there, but at least you will have a choice."

Claudia agreed, and once Sallust had left, busied herself with humdrum tasks, cleaning her chamber and helping Poppaoe in the small outbuilding which served as the bathhouse. She joined in the chatter and gossip of the tavern even though in her own mind she was trying to sift the truth from the lies, the facts from the fable. She wanted to leave immediately to pursue the hunt, but she decided to wait until the help Sallust had promised arrived.

The sun was beginning to dip, the trees rippling under cool breezes, when Oceanus announced that a strange visitor was waiting for her by the front door. Claudia went out. A small man, almost a dwarf, stood there. He was dressed in a belted dark green tunic with a dagger in a sheath, sandals on his feet, a grey cloak clasped about his shoulders. In one hand he carried a walking cane, in the other a leash attached to a large, mournful-faced dog. Claudia bit her lip. Never had owner and dog had so much in common, at least in facial expressions.

"I am Bellato. Sallust sent me. You may have use of me." Bellato patted the dog on the head. "This is Pugna; it means battle. Do you need us?"

For someone so small, Bellato's voice was surprisingly deep.

"I don't know!" Claudia recovered from her surprise. "You'd best come in."

The new arrival caused consternation. Caligula marched in, tail up, from the garden, hissed with disgust, and fled, as did Januaria and Sorry, who claimed they were "mortally frightened" of dogs. The others clustered round, commenting on the dog's long, lugubrious face, questioning black eyes, protuberant, powerful jaws and long snout, which kept sniffing the air. Celades wandered in from the kitchen with a piece of chicken, but Pugna turned his nose up at it. Celades inspected the hound carefully, its large head, powerful legs, long sleek body and strange ochre colouring; he then grandly declared how auxiliaries serving along the great wall in northern Britain used such animals for hunting. Murranus agreed, claiming he had seen imperial troops use similar dogs around the marshes

272

and treacherous trackways of his native Frisia. A general discussion then ensued, prompted by Petronius the Pimp's assertion that the dog was from Iberia; this diverted attention, so Claudia took her guest out into the garden to the orchard table. She served Bellato what he wanted: a bowl of hot lentil soup, soft bread, cheese and a bowl of cherries, along with a cup of watered wine. All the time Pugna sat on its haunches like a soldier come to attention, head unmoving, eyes watching not its master but Claudia, large pink tongue licking its lips in a slaver of froth.

"Why didn't he want the chicken?" Claudia asked.

"He doesn't like chicken," Bellato answered. "If you really want to have a friend, Mistress Claudia, give him some meatballs crushed with pepper and cumin and moistened with a little berry juice."

Claudia walked back to the kitchen and had a word with Celades, who shrugged.

"I'll do what I can," he muttered.

Claudia went into the dining hall, where Petronius the Pimp had now declared himself an expert on all things canine. After a while she went back to the kitchen door and stared out. Bellato was eating hungrily; Pugna hadn't moved at all. She wandered over, sat down and stared at the little man. His face was extraordinarily similar to the hound's: long, with a turned-down mouth and furrowed cheeks, the eyes wide-spaced and mournful, almost as if he was about to burst into a funeral dirge.

"Who are you?" Claudia asked. Almost immediately she regretted asking the question, as Bellato put his spoon down and launched into a detailed description of Sallust's family and how he, Bellato, was the son of Sallust's cousin twice removed. The little man chattered on.

"And Pugna?" Claudia intervened eagerly. "You've always had him with you?"

"Ever since he was a pup."

"And what do you do?"

"Mistress, we are as close as any charioteer with his favourite horse. I grew up with Pugna. If you want anything found, trapped, quarried or searched out, Pugna will do it! His sense of smell is a gift from the gods, and although he doesn't look it, he can be as ferocious as a lion. Sallust often hires me to search for corpses along the river bank or among entangled undergrowth." Bellato's face broke into a surprisingly genial grin. "Even down catacombs; that's where you're going, isn't it?" He paused as Celades came through the kitchen door and shouted at Claudia. She went over, took the platter of meatballs and brought them back to Pugna. The hound didn't even sniff them. Claudia had never seen food disappear so quickly; head down, Pugna munched away, ears flapping, that great pink tongue rolling from one end of its jaws to the other. When it had finished, it looked up, the expression in its eyes was one of pure adoration. Without being ordered by its master, the hound ambled over, put its two great paws on Claudia's lap and ceremoniously licked her face. Claudia laughed and tried to hide. The dog continued until it was satisfied, then sat back on its haunches, rigid as a sentinel, eyes fixed on Claudia as if she was the source of all good things.

"You are kind, mistress," Bellato declared. "I can tell that from your eyes. Most people mock or ignore me. You served me, then you served Pugna. We will do whatever you want."

Claudia stared up at the sky. The sun was setting. She had to go now; it was essential. She asked Bellato to wait, hurried back into the tavern and dragged Murranus from a dicing game with Simon the Stoic.

"We must go now," she murmured. "Be well armed: your sword, a club, a dagger, and stout boots against the briars. Bring a sack with a lantern, pitch torches and a tinder."

Murranus pulled a face. "Why now, Claudia? Can't it wait until the morning?"

"We must go now," she insisted.

"Why not wait for help from Burrus?"

"No, it's best if we enter the Vatican cemetery by ourselves. Now come!"

Murranus hurried away. Claudia searched out Oceanus and made him repeat the message he was to take immediately to the Palatine Palace. "You must seek an audience with either Helena or Chrysis the chamberlain," she urged. "Tell them that I am going to the Vatican cemetery."

Oceanus made to dissuade her.

"No, I must go." Claudia shook her head. "Tell Helena to act as swiftly as possible."

"What are you going to do there?"

"Don't let Polybius or Poppaoe know," Claudia warned. "Tell the Augusta that we are searching for the tomb of Titus Labienus." She made Oceanus repeat that. "Titus Labienus," she insisted. "She will have maps for the cemetery. She will find it. Burrus must be disapatched there as soon as possible. Yes," she murmured. "I suspect the real danger will only emerge once we've found the tomb." Claudia made Oceanus repeat the details one more time, then hurried back into the garden.

A short while later, Claudia and Murranus, with Bellato running in front, Pugna tugging on the leash, entered the warren of streets of the Caelian quarter going down towards the Tiber. Of course, Pugna provoked a great deal of interest; people then recognised Murranus and wished to hail him or draw him into discussion about previous fights, but the former gladiator just shook his head. Claudia also noticed that if anyone approached her, Pugna immediately stopped and growled, a deep, threatening noise which persuaded everyone to keep their distance. They quickly passed through the crowds: the usual pimps and prostitutes touting for business, hawkers and traders, the weird and wonderful of Rome wandering out in their garish rags, selling all sorts of produce or trying to tout for custom for this or that, a wine shop, a gambling game or a new girl from Cappodocia. Auxiliaries and *vigiles* wandered about in their leather armour, their unshaven faces flushed with drink, eyes bleary, hands clutching cudgels, eager for a fight. The

276

air was rich with the smell of slops, kitchens and cookshops, the fishy tang of garum sauce mingling with the aromas of roast meat and freshly baked bread, the last of the day.

They reached the streets running along the Tiber down to the Pons Aemilius and hastened across into the tangled forest of decaying masonry, gorse, heather and trees that covered the Vatican Hill. Here and there lights shone from villas or towers. The journey was uneventful, though Claudia was certain they were being followed; just before they crossed the bridge, she turned and glimpsed the same hawker she had seen on the edge of the Caelian quarter. Yet there was nothing she could do except hope that Oceanus delivered her message as swiftly as possible. She remained preoc-cupied with her own thoughts, muttering bland replies to Murranus' questions. Now and again she smiled reassuringly at Bellato. Occasionally Pugna would wander back to sniff at her ankles or try to lick her face before being urged on.

Claudia had often visited the great cemetery along the Appian Way; the Vatican was no different. Once off the trackways, they entered a terrain of marshes, brackish streams, tangled undergrowth, decaying monuments, battered table-tombs, and crumbling headstones, pillars and statues. The noise of the city abruptly faded away, to be replaced by eerie, nerve-tingling sounds: the cry of a hunting bird or the slither and crackle of animals through the undergrowth. Claudia had brought Sallust's map, though she had already committed its simple instructions to memory.

She searched for the clump of terebinth trees, a rather rare occurrence in that sea of gorse and briar. They took a wrong turning, but at last they found the terebinth grove just as the sun dipped to bathe the cemetery in a strange reddish glow.

The table-tomb of Titus Labienus stood by itself. Murranus put his bag down, took out a lantern, struck a tinder and lit it. Bellato crouched on the ground, Pugna beside him, whilst Claudia carefully inspected the inscriptions on the side of the tomb. She made out the name, followed by other abbreviations extolling Labienus' rank in the army and what he had achieved. She felt the ground around; it was hard and undisturbed. She turned her attention to the covering slab on the table-tomb; she pushed it and it moved slightly.

"We need light."

After some difficulty they fired two more lanterns and a cresset torch. Claudia held the latter whilst Murranus pushed away the slab. Then she leaned over, lowered the torch and inspected the inside. She noted the smell, the scorch marks on the stone as well as the bracken heaped in piles, proof that the tomb had been recently opened. She clambered in, felt around and soon found the ring to the trap door which she pulled up. Murranus helped Bellato and Pugna in. The dog remained eerily silent but Claudia could sense its tension, its nose close to the ground as they carefully made their way down the steep, narrow steps into the darkness below. At first there was more confusion and chaos. Pugna, however, remained silently rigid, staring into the darkness, ears pricking up, nose busy sniffing the air. Bellato crouched beside the hound, hands on its collar. Murranus lifted a small lantern and they peered around. Claudia glimpsed crude cresset torches wedged in wall crevices. Murranus lit some of these. The dog growled deep in its throat. Bellato soothed it and pointed at the five tunnels running off the chamber.

"Someone is here," he whispered.

"How do you know?" Murranus asked.

"I don't; Pugna does."

Claudia strained her ears but could not hear anything. She took a deep breath and caught the smell of acrid smoke and something else, bittersweet, the tang of corruption. She stared around. A cold, stark cavern, the rocky walls and the graffiti carved there obscured by shadows dancing in the light of the lantern horns and torches. Was this the path to the tomb of Peter the Galilean, or was it a trap? She stared at Pugna. The dog remained straining, staring as if it could see something no one else could.

"Which tunnel?" Murranus asked.

"Let Pugna decide," Bellato replied. He whispered into the dog's ear, scratched its head and rose to a half crouch, the leash tied securely around his wrist. Pugna walked forward, at first stiff-legged, then going down, belly almost touching the ground, edging towards the second tunnel on the left. The smell of oil, smoke and that bittersweet tang grew stronger.

"Are you sure?" Claudia whispered.

Bellato smiled at her through the darkness. "There is something in that tunnel," he said, "and it's not pleasant and it's not far. Do not go in front of Pugna."

They edged into the darkness, the dog crawling forward, Murranus and Claudia desperately trying to ensure a pool of light was shed before them. The dog growled deep in its throat and stopped. By now Claudia could almost taste the sickening smell. Bellato pointed in front of him.

"Down there," he whispered, "not far, on the ground." He stepped aside and, pulling the dog, allowed Claudia and Murranus forward. "Take care," he added, his voice sounding sepulchral in that hollow, shadow-filled place.

Murranus and Claudia went forward. Claudia put the lantern down. Murranus crept a little further. A hiss from behind them made them stop. Bellato came up at a half-crouch, Pugna moving like a shadow beside him.

"Let me go forward," he urged. "Be careful. Pugna is very wary, there might be traps."

Claudia watched Bellato and Pugna, two shapes disappearing into the darkness. She heard a slight cry. Pugna growled and Bellato called urgently to them. He was already retching as he backed away. Claudia, covering her mouth and nose with her hand, peered down at the hideous remains. One corpse was blackened beyond any recognition; the other had had its head severed, and was nothing more than a bloated, slimy mess of flesh. Claudia lowered the lantern.

"Gavinus and Philippus?" she whispered. "It must be! Valentinian must have taken Gavinus' head, but

280

what could cause such hideous wounds, such a gruesome death?"

Bellato had now recovered. Pugna still sniffed the mangled remains. Murranus crouched down. "Philippus was burnt alive," he said. "Gavinus?" He glanced up. "Doesn't the Vatican Hill swarm with vipers? I think that's what killed him. Look." He moved the lantern and pointed to the mottled legs, the purple marks just above the ankles.

Bellato was now studying the ground. Pugna seemed uninterested, backing off. "They weren't killed here. Look," Bellato remarked, pointing to marks on the floor.

They returned to the cavern, and Murranus investigated the mouths of the other tunnels. It was an eerie atmosphere, Bellato muttering to himself, Murranus whispering questions, yet there was also that ominous silence, as if some malignant presence lurked in the shadows.

"Do you think Valentinian is here?" Murranus asked, coming back into the cavern. Bellato and Pugna were also examining the tunnel mouths.

"Oh yes," Claudia replied. "Murranus, this will be more dangerous than anything you've met in the arena. Valentinian will fight. He'll try to escape, he'll want to kill us. He never expected us to make this discovery. He is a desperate, vengeful man, but the question is, which tunnel and where will it lead?"

"This one." Bellato returned, Pugna straining on the leash, and pointed at the middle tunnel. "That is where the two men were killed. There is a sheet of oil on the floor. I suspect rock adders and vipers nestle in the crevices on either side. We have to be careful."

Murranus said that he would lead the way, but Bellato pulled at his arm and smiled.

"You may be champion of the games," he whispered, "but here, Murranus, in the tunnels beneath the earth, Pugna is the champion. He will keep us safe."

They entered the tunnel, pausing at the place where Gavinus and Philippus had been killed. The signs were obvious: the place still reeked of charred flesh and, glancing to the left and right, they could glimpse the scales of the vipers nestling in the crevices.

"They are not dangerous," Bellato declared. "The fire, started probably by a torch dropped on this oil, would have roused them. Vipers always slither towards the warmth. They'll also be wary of Pugna." He paused and told Murranus to lift up the lantern as far as he could. He did so, illuminating the large puddle of oil.

"It stretches for about a yard," Murranus whispered. "How do we get round it?"

"We don't," Bellato replied. He stretched out his cane and put it in the puddle. "It's only a few inches deep. It is safest to walk through the centre, away from the walls. Extinguish the torches." Claudia did so. Bellato whispered something to Pugna, who went forward, seemingly impervious to the oil. Bellato followed, then Murranus and finally Claudia. She could feel the oil wet her feet, and the harsh smell caught her nose and throat, but at least she was safe. On either side, in the light of the lantern, she glimpsed the silvery skins of the snakes, but they posed no real danger.

282

Claudia had experienced the same when playing as a child: snakes were only dangerous when they were startled, trodden upon or deliberately provoked.

At last they were through. They turned a corner and the rest of the tunnel stretched before them, a hollow blackness beckoning them on. There was no more oil and Murranus could detect no evidence of any viper or adder. Pugna, however, remained cautious, slinking forward slowly despite Bellato's urging, then stopping and growling quietly. Bellato asked Murranus to hold the lantern out. He did so, crouching and stretching his arm as far as he could. Again Bellato made to move forward. Pugna refused. Bellato pointed to the bracken and branches strewn on the ground.

"A trap," he whispered, "there!"

Murranus moved forward, using Bellato's walking cane to prod the ground. Suddenly, without warning, the cane slipped through the bracken.

"A pit," Murranus observed with his back to the wall. He edged forward, testing the ground in front of him. At first it seemed solid, then the bracken gave way again, revealing a pit about a yard deep. In the dim light of the lantern, Claudia glimpsed the short, sharp stakes embedded below. She also caught the smell of dung and faeces.

"An old trick." Murranus gestured them forward. "Those stakes are daubed with human dung. If they didn't kill you outright, they would certainly poison the blood."

They passed safely, turned another corner and paused. The tunnel stretched before them, and at the far end, lantern light glowed eerily.

"Valentinian!" Claudia whispered. "He must be there."

"Why didn't he try to flee?" Murranus asked.

"He cannot," Claudia murmured. "I suspect there is only one way in and one way out. He will fight."

Pugna now seemed more eager, straining on the leash, ready to dart forward. Bellato followed, almost at a run. In the beacon light at the end of the tunnel, a figure appeared. A torch was thrown, followed by another, illumining the darkness. Murranus screamed at Bellato, who stopped and crouched just as the first arrow came whirring through the air. Murranus and Claudia immediately threw themselves down. Again that shadowy figure in the dancing light; another arrow loosed through the darkness. Like the first, it smacked into the wall of the tunnel and clattered to the ground.

"It's a Scythian bow," Murranus murmured, "powerful and deadly. Valentinian seems very skilled."

CHAPTER
FOURTEEN

So that it might well be said of him,
as it was of the Egyptian tyrant of old,
that God had hardened his heart.

More arrows followed. Claudia hastily reflected on what they should do. If they went forward, they would come within easy range of the archer. If they retreated, he would follow and there were those other traps to go through again. She stared at Pugna and Bellato, almost one shape, now crouched together both staring into the darkness. Bellato was whispering something, and without any warning, he released the leash, smacking the dog on the flank, screaming at it, pointing forward. The hound moved swiftly, a long, dark shape racing silently down the tunnel towards the lantern light. Bellato jumped to his feet and followed. Claudia and Murranus hastened after him, still fearful of other traps. Ahead of them screams, yells and growls showed that the dog had found its quarry.

They reached the lantern light. Claudia blinked as they stumbled into a circular cavern. She glimpsed a table, a stool, some chests and coffers with a bed in the far corner. The smell of cooking was strong. On the far side was a small recess, and near this, pinned to the wall, was Frontinus, Pugna growling at him, teeth bared. Claudia had never witnessed such a transformation: no longer the serene, docile dog but a savage war hound growling menacingly at every move Frontinus made. On the floor nearby lay a quiver full of arrows. Murranus hastened up, kicked these away and plucked the dagger from its sheath on Frontinus' belt. Bellato whistled and Pugna reluctantly backed away. Now and again the dog would turn and growl menacingly. Frontinus, his unshaven face gleaming with sweat, slipped down the wall and stared hatefully at Claudia. He made to move, but immediately Pugna growled, walking stiff-legged towards him. The hair behind the dog's head and along its spine was thickly ruffed and erect.

"You should not move," Bellato advised. "Pugna is close, he is very swift. He could take your throat in the blink of an eye."

Frontinus swallowed. "I will not move," he murmured. "Call him off."

Bellato chattered in a tongue Claudia couldn't understand; the hound reluctantly withdrew and crouched beside its master. Murranus picked up the bow and threw it away even as Claudia passed Frontinus and walked into the small recess. She lifted the lantern and stared at the wall. The tomb was simple: the ledge variety, very common in the catacombs. The rock must have been gouged out, the corpse placed inside and the front replastered. In the light of the lantern she could distinguish the signs of the Icthus, the chi and rho as well as the words "Here lies Peter". Other Christian symbols decorated the plaster and the walls around it. The ground beneath was smooth from the knees and feet of those many pilgrims who'd come to venerate this sacred Christian shrine over the centuries. Claudia walked back into the cavern and, taking a stool, sat before Frontinus.

"My companion Murranus," she began softly, "is probably a little confused. He thought we were hunting Valentinian, former deacon of the Roman Church; instead we have found Frontinus the freedman. However, you are not going to deny you are Valentinian? The Emperor's torturers would certainly establish the truth, and, of course, a diligent search will be made." She leaned over and tapped the man's cheek gently. "Oh, you have changed, grown fatter. You have shaved your head and face. After all, you are no longer a presbyter but a freedman, Attius' steward. Very clever! I suppose no one would recognise you, Valentinian, but there again," she smiled thinly, "I suppose there are very few who could. They are all dead, thanks to you."

"Say whatever you have to. I have not denied I'm Valentinian, but for all that, what proof do you have that I am?"

"You are here." Claudia stared around the darkened cavern.

Bellato crouched next to Pugna, the dog's eyes fixed on this dangerous man. Murranus stood by the entrance to the tunnel, his sword drawn lest Valentinian try and escape.

"So are you." Valentinian peered at Claudia. "And the game is not over yet. You have to leave." He gestured at the recess. "So much over so little! A collection of dried bones belonging to a Jewish fisherman who was crucified upside down on the hill above us." He blinked and wiped the sweat from his brow.

Claudia studied him carefully. She was certain that Valentinian believed there was still hope, but from whom, and how?

"Have you no faith at all?"

"Only in myself." Valentinian pointed at her. "You have sharp wits, I could see that. My original question: how do you know I am Valentinian?"

Claudia moved to ease the cramp in her leg, then rolled her head to release the tension in her neck. "I want you to listen carefully," she began. "Many years ago you were a deacon, a member of the Christian community of Rome, a leading figure in the Church, responsible for the area around the Vatican Hill, that sprawling, derelict part of Rome beyond the Tiber. The persecutions broke out. You were given swift promotion in the hierarchy. For a while you acted the part of scholar, priest and holy man. You dressed as a presbyter and grew your beard and hair long, which, I understand, was the custom of the Christians. You enjoyed status and power as the persecutions under Diocletian and Maxentius increased in fury. All of Rome was turned upside down in a relentless search for Christians and their holy places. To make it brief, I suspect you were captured and may have been tortured; you apostatised and turned traitor. You came and went, providing your captors with the names of every single one of your congregation. Little wonder the Christian

288

community around the Vatican was wiped out to a man. Presbyter Sylvester told me about that. Of course eventually you had to disappear completely. Your captor was no less a person than Maxentius' bully-boy Attius Enobarbus." Claudia paused. "Is that how you were caught? Attius Enobarbus had been a member of the Christian community around the Vatican?"

"Our paths had crossed," Valentinian sneered.

"Oh, I am sure they had. You may have been tortured, but Attius saved you from that. A deal was struck."

"And my part of the bargain?"

"You supplied him with names and places and he took you into his household as his freedman. He used his authority to change your identity and history in the records and elsewhere so that you emerged as an educated slave from Iberia. You waxed fat. You changed your appearance. You're a highly intelligent man, Valentinian; with your head and face shaved, you could act any part you wanted. You told me you had served Attius Enobarbus for years, leaving the details as vague as possible. Attius would regard you as a great find, a source of boundless information, but one piece of information," Claudia held her hand up, "you kept to yourself, at least for a while: the location of Peter the Galilean's tomb. That was one jewel you would not freely hand over.

"Attius, of course, was renowned for his exploits, and Maxentius used him for this task or that, always hunting Christians, until the world was stunningly turned upside down. Constantine declared himself

Emperor and marched on Rome; worse, he proclaimed that he would tolerate, even actively support, the Christian faith, and Attius Enobarbus' days came to an end. You were both trapped, caught in a net of lies and intrigue. Attius might betray you, but there again, you could betray him. He might depict you as an apostate, but you could describe him as the same as well as being a great destroyer of all things Christian, a criminal who had amassed tremendous wealth from his depredations. Like two gladiators in the arena, neither of you could secure the advantage. So you continued the pretence. You must have wondered if Attius would survive Constantine's purge; I am sure if he hadn't, you would have devised other plans for a safe escape."

"Attius could have written to Constantine and Helena and offered them my head."

"Oh no," Claudia disagreed. "As I've said, once he'd done that, you'd be free to confess all you knew about his destruction; not only that, but where he had hidden his great wealth, the plunder he'd stolen from Christians and hidden away in his own garden. I cannot provide precise details of time and place, but I am sure that the two of you negotiated and reached an amicable agreement. Attius would continue to protect you; you would continue to protect him. As a guarantee, you eventually gave him most of the details about the location of Peter the Galilean's tomb, here beneath the sepulchre of Titus Labienus. You also warned him that it would not be easy to enter; it was full of traps, not to be risked. You are a persuasive man, Valentinian. You also argued that it would be best to wait, to let time pass. In fact, I suspect you'd already made your decision. You were going to kill Attius and sell the location of this tomb not to the Emperor, who would certainly question you on how you knew it, but to Lord Charon. You needed the king of Rome's underworld to carry out your blackmail and make himself as well as you rich.

"However, what Lord Charon did not know was that you'd also decided to make a handsome profit from what you'd stolen from Attius. You made your decision, I strongly suspect, soon after Constantine marched into Rome, but circumstances held you hostage. Attius went into hiding, and was then offered an amnesty by the Emperor and later dispatched to Byzantium on that secret mission. Oh yes, I know all about that: Constantine's dream of a new Rome! You'd find that interesting, something else you could use. Attius returned. By now he was beginning to think more clearly, plot his own course. He regained his courage. He'd survived Maxentius' fall; perhaps he could win favour, go back to his old faith, strike a deal, make a bargain? Presbyter Sylvester would intercede for him. Naturally you knew that, didn't you? You sensed that Attius was about to make his move, hand over Valentinian the apostate and deliver the secret whereabouts of this tomb. He'd weave a tale that he was held hostage by you, that he was terrified of you but had now realised the error of his ways. So you struck first."

"How did I know that he was going to do that?"

"Because he sensed you were about to move against him. Two villains bound by the past! Two murderers circling, looking for an opening! Two apostates ready to swear each other's life away. Little wonder Attius kept to himself, hiding away in his secure chamber. He was protecting himself from you without provoking your suspicion or anyone else's. He was getting ready, as you were. He daren't even tell Drusilla; that would be too dangerous, though as I shall show, you had already marked her down for death." Claudia shook her head. "I wonder what Attius plotted? Your murder, or betrayal to the authorities? Perhaps he was confused; he delayed, you did not!"

"Attius was a coward," Valentinian sneered. "When did he regain his courage? A rat of a man, a weakling. He would never —"

"Oh, but he did, in Byzantium," Claudia cut in. "He and the rest realised why they had been dispatched there, that they must enjoy some confidence and favour with the Emperor. Attius probably promised the others that when he returned to favour he'd take them all with him. He overlooked how intelligent and secretive you are. How easy it is to move from being Valentinian to Frontinus the freedman, prying at doors and keyholes, studying manuscripts, listening to this and that. You certainly realised it was time to be gone. On your return to Rome, you persuaded Lord Charon to form an alliance with you. It would be easy for you to contact him. After all, you had once been a member of the Christian sect, hunted through the catacombs, sewers and alleyways of the city. You would know a great deal about Lord Charon, whilst your years working with Attius Enobarbus would only enhance such knowledge." Claudia paused. "I shall come to that later." She moved sweaty tendrils of hair from her face. "You enticed Lord Charon by using Attius' wealth to bribe someone in the stables of the charioteer Scorpus to weaken a wheel on the champion's chariot. You've lived in the underworld, Valentinian; you'd know how to do that. The price would have been very high. However, you also used Attius' wealth to lay a wager that Pausanias would win. You told Lord Charon to do the same and he obeyed. A gamble, but well worth it."

"To do that I would have to reveal myself." Valentinian ignored Murranus' mocking laugh. "And Attius' wealth? How —"

"Come." Claudia leaned forward. "Murranus here was a gladiator. Games are fixed, wagers are laid in shadowy, lonely places where those who meddle go masked and hooded. As for Attius' wealth? Well, wait a while. You certainly used it to fix that race and so attract Lord Charon's attention."

"And if Scorpus had won?"

"Nonsense!" Claudia smiled. "You're Valentinian! No money, or at least only a small part of it, would be paid until you were sure of the deed; that's the custom." She spread her hands. "In truth, what did it really matter? Attius was dead; it was his wealth. You still had the tomb."

Valentinian shrugged. "What proof do you have for this?" he scoffed.

"In time," Claudia murmured, "in time the truth always bubbles out, as it will now. You are trapped, Valentinian! How do you know Lord Charon will not turn on you? He lost many men in his attack on the She-Asses; that was probably at your behest, wasn't it? You wanted me dead. You also wanted the same for Narses and Severus. They may have suspected where this tomb was, so they too had to be silenced. At the time such an attack would appeal to Lord Charon, an opportunity to show his strength and display his power in Rome. However, it proved to be a costly mistake, and I wager Lord Charon has not forgotten that."

Valentinian licked his lips nervously, then blinked and wiped the sweat from his brow. Claudia noticed his breathing was sharper and more rapid.

"It was a risk," she conceded, "a dangerous one, but, only for a while, you had decided to disappear. You'd take what was left of Attius' wealth, not to mention what you had down here."

"What wealth? You keep —"

"Attius' wealth," Claudia insisted, "and, if your blackmail was successful, whatever Lord Charon divided with you. Then you'd go where? To Licinius' court in the East? But this could only happen after the real business was done. Attius had to be removed. You did it so simply. On the afternoon he was murdered, Attius held a meeting with the other *scrutores* in his garden; perhaps they wished to discuss an approach to the Empress. Attius retired to his secure chamber below ground. He was visited there by Macrinus and Narses. They left. You went down. Attius may have drunk deeply or you may have put something in the wine. He lay sprawled on his bed, half asleep. You took the dagger and stabbed him."

"And the locked door?"

"That was easy to arrange. People see what they want to see. You had positioned something over the keyhole on the inside of the door. If anyone peered through, it would look as if the key was still there. Once Attius was dead, you moved quickly. Only a small amount of blood dripped from your hand before you cleaned yourself. You seized the Icthus casket, which," Claudia shrugged, "must be somewhere here. You left Attius' chamber, removed the key and locked the door from the outside."

"I might have been seen. Drusilla —"

"Oh, I am sure you made certain she was busy elsewhere. The passageway leading to Attius' secure chamber was long and vaulted; you'd have heard any approach. Attius' death, and your theft of the Icthus casket, would be very swift. Outside in that shadow-filled passageway, with the day dying, you'd face very little risk indeed."

Valentinian wiped the sweat from his cheeks and peered at Claudia. She was sure he was only half listening to her; his mind, agile and teeming, would be searching for a way out.

"You wanted time," Claudia explained. "The Icthus casket contains nothing about the whereabouts of Peter the Galilean's tomb — Attius had memorised that — only a list of Attius' wealth and where he'd hidden it on his property. Once you had that, you knew precisely where to go both in the villa and, above all, in that large and splendid garden outside. Attius, naturally, had secretly buried his treasure as any man disliked by the authorities would, just in case Constantine changed his mind and he had to flee." Claudia gestured round. "I am sure that amongst these coffers lies the Icthus casket, containing a full list of Attius' wealth and a map of the garden showing precisely where it was hidden.

"Now, on that fateful afternoon, life in the Villa Hortensis continued quietly. You, pretending to be busy in the garden, searched out these treasure troves, whilst Drusilla, as she was meant to, tried to gain access to Attius. She hammered on the door, peered through the keyhole and reached the conclusion that the door was locked from the inside and therefore something hideous must have happened to her master. She was correct. You came hastening down. You'd now had time to study the maps, charts and lists, perhaps even retrieve some of the treasure. However, you now acted the faithful steward. The door was eventually broken down. In the confusion you stepped quickly through, removed the blockage over the inside keyhole and inserted the key into the smashed lock. It would be easily done; the room was ill-lit, Drusilla fearful for her master, the other servants confused and frightened. If the lock had been too damaged to take the key, you'd have dropped it on the floor and later claimed the battering had knocked it out. What did it matter? Such details were minor; haste was the order of the day. True?"

Valentinian glared back.

"Drusilla —"

"Drusilla examined the room," Claudia continued, "but you had nothing to fear. Everything was going according to plan, even though chaos and mystery clouded the truth. You then moved swiftly. Attius' wealth was all in coin or precious stones, ready for use; even though that coin carried the heads of other emperors, it was still gold and silver. A very heavy bribe was paid to someone in Scorpus' stable to fix that chariot race. You then used such information to inveigle Lord Charon, urging him to move his wager from the favourite to Pausanias. You yourself did likewise and immediately sent that blackmail letter, in Lord Charon's name, to the Emperor and his mother." Claudia paused as Bellato sprang to his feet, Pugna also stood up rather reluctantly, eyes still on Valentinian.

"What is the matter?" Claudia asked.

"I don't know," Bellato murmured. "Pugna seems a little restless."

Murranus walked a short way down the tunnel, straining his ears. "There's nothing," he came back, "nothing at all."

Bellato, followed by Pugna, squatted directly in front of Valentinian. The little man sat plucking at his lower lip, staring at the tunnel entrance then back at Claudia.

"Other problems remained," she continued. "Attius must have shared the secrets of the Galilean's tomb with the *scrutores*, or at least some of them." She nodded. "Yes, that would be logical. They would want some guarantee that he was speaking the truth, precise details about its location."

"Why should he share such knowledge?"

297

"The same reason that you shared it with him. After Constantine's victory, you all needed each other — at least for a while. Attius had to keep his colleagues with him; he certainly didn't want any of them to reveal the full extent of his work for Constantine's rival Maxentius. To take care of possible trespassers, you'd already prepared traps. Gavinus and Philippus were your victims. They hastened down here like children running along an alleyway. One was consumed by fire, the other attacked by those vipers. You later dragged their corpses into the other tunnels and used Gavinus' head for your own grisly purposes and those of Lord Charon. As regards Narses and Severus, you and Charon must have learnt they were going to visit the She-Asses and decided that it would be an appropriate occasion not only to kill me and stop my probing but also to silence those two *scrutores* for good."

"But I was there that night," Valentinian remarked. "I was in the She-Asses. I was as vulnerable as anyone else."

"Nonsense!" Murranus called out. "You bolted from the tavern at the first sign of attack. You lurked in an alleyway to see what would happen. One of Lord Charon's men, Decius, knew a little about you. You watched him leave safe and unscathed. You realised he must have talked, so you killed him. You are an actor," Murranus continued. "You take off one mask, Valentinian, and put on another, Frontinus. You are ready to change roles whenever it suits you."

"Murranus is correct." Claudia looked at this cunning man who had caused so much destruction.

298

"One person you were fearful of was Drusilla. You didn't really know what she'd seen, learnt, heard or reflected upon. How many times, when we met in Attius' chamber, did you say 'Drusilla might know', or 'ask Drusilla when she returns'?" Claudia shook her head. "You could say that, push probing questions away. You knew Drusilla could never answer them because you had murdered her. You'd silenced her for ever and could attribute anything to her. She could never contradict you or provide fresh information. You made it seem as if she was Attius' life-time companion, someone who could vouch for you. A lie. I am sure Drusilla only joined Attius' household after you. You even claimed that she had confided to you how the Nefandus had threatened Attius. A farrago of nonsense, a way of implying that the Nefandus might also have been responsible for Attius' death. He certainly wasn't!"

"Drusilla was not my enemy."

"She still had to die! However, another mysterious death at the Villa Hortensis would only provoke suspicion. You'd heard about the Nefandus' reappearance. I would wager that Drusilla was the only person who liked Attius, indeed loved him deeply, and you exploited that. You left the villa and sent a message to her saying that someone wished to meet her at the She-Asses, probably offering information about her master's death as a lure. Drusilla was still grieving; her wits were dulled, her mind confused. She would do what many people would in such a situation: hasten away unaware that she was running to meet her murderer. There is only one path down to the She-Asses tavern, and you were waiting for her. You pretended to be the Nefandus; you attacked and killed Drusilla, taking the letter and leaving her corpse as if she too was a victim of that gruesome assassin. You then hastened back here, the mournful, distracted steward. Of course one real problem still remained. You did not wish to stay much longer in Rome. You wanted to collect your wealth and flee." Claudia paused. "From the very start you realised your plot had to proceed swiftly: the return from Byzantium, Scorpus' race, Attius' secret plans, the whereabouts of his wealth . . ."

"I could have acted before —"

"No!" Claudia retorted. "Like now, Valentinian, you are calculating the hours; you're waiting for something or someone, aren't you?"

Valentinian glanced away.

"So it was with your murderous plot. Time was of the essence; it might only be a matter of days before suspicions were raised and fingers pointed. The attack on the She-Asses was a disaster, so you decided not to wait for Lord Charon. You were also determined that your alter ego Frontinus would die. Acting as Attius' steward, you invited Narses down to the Villa Hortensis on some pretext and murdered him, probably in the garden. The household was already depleted, servants and slaves had fled. You dragged Narses' corpse inside and doused it in oil, but before you flung in the lantern or lit the fire which ravaged that villa, you put your ring on his finger, the chain from round your neck around his and your sandals on his feet. You did it in haste," she smiled, "and made one small error, putting the sandals on the wrong feet, then tying the thongs. We've all made that mistake but always change them before fastening tight.

"Now, to all intents and purposes, Narses had disappeared and Frontinus had been killed in a terrible blaze at his master's villa. You hastened here. Protected by secrets and the traps in the tunnel, you could wait. Eventually you would leave, taking with you what remained of Attius' wealth and the relics of Peter the Galilean to sell somewhere else." Claudia eased herself up. "But, of course, you didn't know about Sallust the Searcher or Pugna the hound. You thought you'd be safe. If Murranus or I had come blundering down here, we'd have met the same fate as the others. You felt fairly confident until Pugna, like some hound of God, trapped you. Now," she beckoned at him, "you'll face the Empress' justice. Murranus, gather what wealth is here, empty the coffers into the bags, then we'll leave."

Murranus bound Valentinian's hands, though loosely so he could move his wrists. He then beckoned Bellato and Pugna close. Man and dog took up position on guard. Valentinian simply slid down the wall. Claudia noticed he kept swallowing quickly whilst peering down the tunnel. She wondered what assistance he expected. Lord Charon? She suppressed a shiver of fear. They still had to leave this catacomb and make their way through that desolate, derelict cemetery in the dead of night. She only hoped Oceanus had delivered her message and Burrus would arrive in time. She felt a pang of regret. Perhaps Burrus and his cohort should have accompanied them, but she'd been frightened that Valentinian might flee. She went and stood over Murranus as he searched through the various coffers and chests.

"I think it's this one." He picked up an exquisite black silver-embossed casket, on the top the shape of a fish and underneath the word "Icthus".

"This probably belonged to some poor Christian Attius plundered," Claudia murmured. She opened it, took out the yellowing scrolls within and, going over to a lantern, went through them quickly. They were as she had expected. No reference to the Galilean's tomb. However, from the drawings on one scroll, Valentinian had apparently laid traps not only in the tunnel they'd come down but along the others as well; mostly pits, though in one place the ceiling had been loosened. There were a number of official passes, cleverly forged, and the all-important list of Attius' wealth, in coin and precious jewels, as well as the plan of the garden in the Villa Hortensis, showing exactly the locations where Attius had buried it. The map was most precise and clear; it would not have taken long for Valentinian to plunder these treasure troves.

Claudia rose, went back into the small recess and stared at the Galilean's tomb. Such a simple monument, yet it had caused so much intrigue. A man who had dedicated himself to Christ and endured gruesome martyrdom would never have expected his last resting place to cause such deep dissension. She examined it carefully, running her fingers over the graffiti, examining the soft polished stone beneath. Then she returned and confronted Valentinian.

"The Empress' justice," she declared, "can be swift, but your death may be long. I want to ask you one question: that is the tomb of Peter, isn't it?"

He forced a smile. "What do you think?"

She crouched down to face him. "What I think, Valentinian, is that along those different tunnels are other tombs. I suspect you have done your very best to falsify and mislead, misrepresenting other graves as that of Peter the Galilean. True?"

He nodded imperceptibly. "From the very start," he spoke softly, "just after the Galilean was executed, the emperors began searching for his tomb, yet it remained a mystery. True, there are decoys, false tombs, but that was to protect the real one. Many have searched and paid with their lives, not just Philippus and Gavinus. If you go through the other tunnels, you'll find the skeletons of those who tried and failed, as you might yet." He grinned.

"Trusting to your luck, are you?" Murranus called out. "I have fought in the arena, and I assure you, luck never lasts for ever!"

Once ready, they started back along the tunnel, Bellato and Pugna going first, followed by Valentinian with Murranus right behind him, dagger drawn. Claudia brought up the rear. They edged round what Murranus called the pit of stakes, and negotiated the pool of oil until they were safely back in the antechamber. They climbed the steps, Murranus shoving Valentinian before him. It was good to be out in the night air. The sky above was starlit, and a soft breeze wafted the various smells of the vegetation, but even as they were preparing to leave, torchlight appeared, and figures slipped out of the night, faces hidden behind grotesque masks. More torches were lit and Claudia realised that the tomb of Titus Labienus had been ringed by those waiting for them. A man swaggered out of the darkness. He was dressed like some *lanista* from a gladiator school in a leather kilt with a belt across his shoulder, in one hand an axe, in the other a club. He reminded Claudia of a vulture, with his lean face, shaven head, sunken cheeks, pointed ears and those black eyes, even in the dancing light they provoked a chill of fear.

"Ah." He made a mocking bow. "Domina Claudia, may I introduce myself?"

"You are Lord Charon."

The man gestured elegantly with his hand. "Well done. Of course I am. And you," he pointed at Murranus, "must be the famous gladiator." He turned to Bellato, now gripping Pugna by the leash; the hound was straining, growling deep in its throat. "Keep that under control. In the darkness around stand swordsmen and archers. I have only to issue the order and all of you are dead." He gestured at the sacks Murranus had placed on the ground beside him, the jingle of coins and jewellery echoing invitingly. "I suspect that is Attius' wealth. I will take it. No, no," he warned. Three men came out of the darkness, arrows notched to their bows. "I have heard of your reputation, Murranus.

Please, for your own safety, drop your dagger and leave the sacks. I assure you I mean no harm."

Murranus obeyed. Claudia licked her lips and stared round.

"My Lord Charon." Valentinian spoke up.

Immediately the outlaw chief strode forward. He punched Valentinian in the face and, when he fell to the ground, started kicking him. The faint night breeze carried the sound of hunting horns. Burrus' men had reached the fringes of the cemetery. Lord Charon held up a hand.

"Listen." He turned back to Claudia. "The wealth is mine, and so is Valentinian; because of him I lost good men."

"I helped you!" Valentinian pleaded. "I gave you the race."

"Either way I would have won!" Charon smiled. "Listen now, Claudia. Tell your Empress this. I respect the tomb, I take the wealth, I will punish Valentinian and she will not hear from me again."

Claudia, Murranus, Bellato and Pugna could do nothing. The area around the tomb became alive with men. Dark figures scurried forward, the sacks were plucked up, Valentinian was seized and pushed into the blackness. Once again the war horns brayed, but by the time Burrus reached them, Charon and his legions had melted away.

Two days later, Claudia and Presbyter Sylvester sat in the shade of Uncle Polybius' orchard sharing a jug of his best wine. Murranus stood on guard at the kitchen door, allowing no one out until Presbyter Sylvester was finished. The priest sipped at his goblet, stared up at the branches then glanced at Claudia.

"I bring the Empress' thanks."

"I am grateful for that."

"She has now secured the tomb. It has been declared an imperial reserve. No one can go near it without her written permission."

"And the other matter?" Claudia asked. "Constantine's plans for Byzantium?"

"The Emperor still keeps that a secret, as must you and Murranus."

Claudia held up a hand. "There's no need for that," she declared. "What Constantine and Helena plan for this world, or the next, is no business of mine."

Sylvester cocked his head and listened to the sounds of revelry from the tavern.

"Your uncle Polybius is preparing a great feast?"

Claudia laughed. "It's all at the expense of Torquatus the Tonsor. He and I had a wager; he lost." She then told Sylvester exactly what had happened. How Attius Enobarbus had been killed and how Torquatus the Tonsor had been unable to solve the mystery.

"So easy," she whispered, "so very, very easy. We all think what we see is real; only later do we realise that most of what we perceive is an illusion." She glanced directly at the priest. "And you, Presbyter Sylvester, are you not frightened by the Emperor's plans to move the centre of the Empire from Rome, the city of your Apostles Peter and Paul?"

"Militiades is getting old and weakening," Sylvester replied slowly. "Soon there'll be another election to the bishopric of Rome. Someone new will sit in the Chair of Peter. Whoever it is," he smiled thinly, "must be able to establish that he is the owner, the proud guardian of the remains of Christ's First Apostle."

"Are you talking about yourself, Presbyter?"

"Perhaps; the Holy Spirit will decide."

"With a little help from yourself?"

Sylvester just smiled and shook his head.

"Who will guard the tomb?" Claudia asked. "Why is the Empress so keen to possess a relic which rightfully belongs to you?"

"I have my suspicions."

"Does she intend to move such a sacred relic to her new city at Byzantium?"

"No, Claudia, Helena hopes to blackmail us whilst we hope to negotiate with her. Go to the great gates of Rome and the highways leading out; beneath these lie the catacombs, the cemeteries of our Christian dead. A city beneath the earth with chapels, shrines, monuments and memorials; these are in our possession. In Rome itself, palaces like the Lateran have been handed over to us. Helena is shrewd. She knows that in a decade, maybe even less, Rome won't be so much the city of the Caesars as the heart of the Universal Church. I doubt if she intends to move the tomb; that would be sacrilege. What she wants is for us to hand over secrets from elsewhere."

"What secrets?"

Sylvester sighed and stared down the garden, scratching his chin.

"The persecutions are over. Throughout the Empire the Emperor's writ runs; Christians are to be tolerated, even favoured. Helena has her eye on much more precious jewels than the remains of a fisherman, even though that fisherman was Christ's right-hand man. In Palestine, the country of Christ's birth, where he lived, died and rose again, are Bethlehem, Jerusalem, Calvary and the Holy Sepulchre; these are the places Helena really wants. Over the centuries various emperors violated and polluted our sacred sites; as with the tomb of Peter the Galilean, we know precisely where such places are located. I suspect that Helena will hand over the tomb of Peter when we hand over our knowledge about Bethlehem, Bethany, Emmaus and Jerusalem, all those places associated with Christ."

Sylvester got to his feet, turned to ensure no eavesdroppers lurked and retook his seat. "You've been to the Vatican Hill, Claudia? It lies beyond the city walls, a godforsaken area, but Helena knows, and I know, that in years to come, the Vatican will belong to us, the Church of Rome; it will become our centre, our heart. Constantine will build a church over the shrine. We, in time, will occupy that church and own it. The Bishops of Rome will build their palaces and curial offices around it." Sylvester spoke with such conviction, Claudia realised that this was already planned, plotted and devised; this cunning priest was just waiting for the opportunity to advance his cause with Helena and her son.

"And in the end," she said, "the Emperor and his mother will do exactly what you ask?"

Sylvester shrugged. He swirled the wine around his goblet and glanced across at Claudia. "Our Church," he declared slowly, "must, like a fish, swim with the course of the river. That river is directed by God. Think, Claudia! Perhaps it might be for the best. We Christians have emerged from the catacombs and now we hold power. Our influence is felt at every level of government, the Emperor is in our grasp, the Empress Helena is our firm supporter, and yet that poses danger. Perhaps," he mused, "it might be best if the two divided: the secular power in Byzantium, the spiritual power in Rome." He caught Claudia's glance and laughed softly. "I know what you're thinking."

"Yes, Presbyter Sylvester?"

"That is what we want."

"Perhaps it is. Perhaps you do intend to take over this city which persecuted you, which was once dominated by the likes of Attius Enobarbus and Valentinian."

"You've heard the news?" Sylvester asked.

Claudia shook her head.

"Valentinian's corpse was found crucified to a tree deep in the cemetery along the Appian Way. It must have taken him hours to die. They'd nailed his hands and feet and sliced his body. Lord Charon sent a most submissive letter to the Empress, apologising for his insubordination and assuring her of his good will."

"And Helena?"

Sylvester narrowed his eyes. "What does she care for Lord Charon?" he murmured. "She dreams of empire."

Claudia got to her feet.

"And you, Claudia?"

"Such a price," she whispered. "Think, Presbyter, of all those hideous deaths: the victims of the Nefandus, Attius, Drusilla and all the others." She paused. "I once told Murranus that life was about the light and the dark. On reflection," she breathed, "it is, but there's a deeper problem: which is the light, which the dark?"

"Our Church will decide that!"

"Really, Presbyter?" Claudia leaned closer. "Helena is not the only one who dreams of empire. You dream even greater visions and see things in the dead of night, but me? I'm Claudia! I dream of Celades' good cooking, a goblet of wine and Murranus sitting next to me. To me, Presbyter Sylvester, that is all the empire I want."

Author's Note

The main themes of this novel are based on fact. Rome was a sprawling city with a vast population which had to be fed and housed. The slums were notorious breeding grounds for gangs of ruffians, and Juvenal's *Satires* clearly describe the dangers of going out after dark or wandering in places no self-respecting citizen should. The recent excellent television series *Rome* accurately depicts the rivalry between the various criminal gangs and their control over the Suburra. Life was very cheap. Assassins could be hired and entire crowds bought, a fact not lost on successive emperors, who adopted the policy of "Bread and Circuses" to keep the city's population happy. Policing was equally dangerous. Many of the gamekeepers were ex-poachers, and the *vigiles* won a reputation for being corrupt and venal, though occasionally individuals would emerge as outstanding public figures intent on enforcing the law rather than seeking personal profit.

Life, like the poet said, was very, very cheap in Rome. Slaves could be bought and sold, ill-treated at will, being virtually bereft of any rights. The amphitheatre and the arena, the bloody spectacle of men fighting each other or prisoners being thrown to wild animals, were popular. Execution was commonplace. Prisons such as the Tullianum were simply a holding pen before prisoners were dispatched to the stake, the mines in Sicily, or the cross. Crucifixion was regarded as the most effective punishment. Horace described it as *"horribile"*; the most accurate translation of that is "disgusting"! Macrinus' account of the death of Crastinus is correct; a crucified person died of asphyxiation. The cross was seen as something to be despised and regarded with horror. Even the Christians did not develop it as their principal symbol until much later on. Instead they used the word "Icthus", the letters of which, in Greek, stand for "Jesus Christ, Son of God and Saviour". The chi-rho symbols were also popular.

The novel also refers to a serial killer in Rome. I think it is a mistake to regard the serial killer as a phenomenon of the twentieth and twenty-first centuries. In fourth-century Rome, where a donkey was more valuable than a slave, prostitutes were regarded as a legitimate target for any deviant. I agree there is no evidence for serial killers being on the loose, apart from one reference to a poisoner in second-century Rome who passed through crowds scratching people with a poisoned needle. Nevertheless, men like the Nefandus must have existed and carried out their bloody work until they were either killed themselves or caught red-handed.

From the very start Christianity had secured a foothold in Rome. Peter the Galilean definitely went there, whilst Paul was imprisoned in the city. According to history and tradition, both were executed in Rome sometime around AD 66 during Nero's persecution after that emperor decided to blame the great fire of Rome on this new, dangerous sect. Before this, Christianity had tended to be associated with the Jewish community. However, as the gap widened between the two faiths, the Christians in particular became despised, hated and feared. Roman authors make reference to Christians assembling at night "to eat their God", a possible reference to the Eucharist. Of course, the new faith made a powerful impact on Rome's society, particularly amongst the slaves. Christianity preached that all men and women were equal before God, each individual destined for eternal life. This revolutionary concept was quickly embraced and fervently adhered to. Nero's persecution was merely the start. During the pogrom, Paul was executed, according to tradition, by decapitation as he was a Roman citizen. Peter, however, decided to flee Rome. He left the city and was going along the Appian Way when he experienced his vision. If you ever walk there, as I have, you can visit the church built on the spot where he decided to turn back to face the consequences of both his status and his preaching.

The Vatican area was, as described in the novel, rather desolate and wild, notorious for its vipers and poor soil. Successive emperors tried to cultivate and develop it, but met with only moderate success. Apparently Peter's tomb was hidden from the Roman authorities and not revealed until Constantine's reign, when that emperor built a church as a shrine over it.

The secrecy surrounding the tomb is understandable. Various emperors had attacked the great Christian sites in both Italy and Palestine. A good example of this is the pagan temples built by the Emperor Hadrian on the site of the Holy Sepulchre and elsewhere. Constantine, and particularly his mother Helena, spent a great deal of time and wealth searching out and defining these holy places and the relics they might hold. Helena's finding of the True Cross is, of course, famous. She worked zealously in both Rome and Palestine to record and bring into prominence the principal Christian shrines at Bethlehem, Jerusalem and other places in Palestine.

Militiades and Sylvester are historical figures; Sylvester later became Pope. Both men were committed to the strengthening of their religion and the closest co-operation with the Emperor and his mother. The Bishops of Rome laid great emphasis on Peter's tomb. They used it to argue their own spiritual authority over other bishops. The management of Peter's shrine has always been supervised by the Papacy. At the beginning of the Second World War, Pope Pius XII decided on in-depth excavations beneath St Peter's Cathedral to establish where the fisherman's tomb actually lay and what it contained. An excellent book on this topic is that by John E. Walsh, *The Bones of St Peter; the fascinating account of the search for the Apostle's body* (Victor Gollancz, 1983). I do recommend it as a most enjoyable and yet erudite study of the topic.

The great persecutions of the Christian faith described in this novel also took place. Some emperors did tolerate the new religion, but others, like Diocletian, decided to destroy it root and branch. One of the reasons for this harassment was the incredible increase in the number of Christians between AD 260 and 300, and with it a vast extension of the network of catacombs along the roads leading out of Rome. According to one source, no fewer than 11,000 Christian graves have been identified dating from this period in the catacombs. (If one visits Rome, a walk along the Via Appia to the catacombs of St Sebastian is well worthwhile.) Diocletian's persecution was particularly fierce and relentless; it was sustained by Maxentius and was only brought to an end by Constantine's victory at the Milvian Bridge in AD 312. However, once the persecutions ended and the Christian Church was tolerated, even supported, fresh problems emerged. Fierce debates took place about what should happen to those who had lapsed during the persecution or apostatised, becoming government informants, not to mention the clashes over important matters of doctrine. Constantine, to his credit, managed to maintain excellent relationships with the bishops and the Christian faith, though he himself was not baptised until shortly before his death.

The emergence of Byzantium as Constantinople is a fact of history. Constantine was determined that there would be only one Emperor and one Empire. It wasn't until AD 324 that he managed to defeat his rival Licinius, and after that, work on the new city increased in pace. It did provoke problems for the Christian Church. The Bishop of Rome's claim of supremacy over other bishops, particularly Constantinople, lay at the root of further disputes which would last down the centuries. Once the emperors had left, Rome became increasingly a Papal city, with the Pope supporting the interests of the "Romans of Rome". In fact, the Popes took over the administration and government of the city. A hundred years after Constantine, Pope Sixtus sponsored an architectural revival, whilst Leo the Great successfully intervened to prevent Attila the Hun from seizing and attacking Rome. Indeed, by the reign of Pope Gelasius in 492, the Papacy was desperately trying to establish what it could and could not do in the city as well as define the legitimate sphere for temporal as opposed to spiritual authority, a matter which would take centuries to resolve. Not until the nineteenth century and the unification of Italy was the Papacy restricted to the Vatican, and only after the advent of Mussolini, during the 1920s and 1930s, was a successful rapprochement reached between Church and state.

Paul Doherty, 2007
www.paulcdoherty.com

Also available in ISIS Large Print:

The House Of Death

Paul Doherty

Spring 334 BC and the young Alexander is poised with his troops at the Hellespont, waiting to launch an invasion into the empire of the Persian King, Darius III.

Knowing he must win the approval of the gods, Alexander makes sacrifice after sacrifice but the smoke does not rise — the sacrifices are tainted. Worse, the guides hired to lead him through Persian territory are being brutally murdered, Persian spies are active in the camp and Alexander's own generals harbour secret ambitions.

Into this whirlpool of mistrust comes Telamon, a great friend from Alexander's boyhood. He sets about revealing the secret enemies within the camp while Alexander displays his true heroic stature, throwing off fears and panics and leading a bloody attack on the Persian King.

ISBN 978–0–7531–6795–3 (hb)
ISBN 978–0–7531–6796–0 (pb)

The Waxman Murders

Paul Doherty

October, 1300. War cog "The Waxman" is bound for Orwell. Its Master, Adam Blackstock, is taking an ancient manuscript, "The Cloister Map", to be deciphered by his brother. But Blackstock is slaughtered when ships flying the colours of the Hanseatic League overrun the cog.

Three years later, Wilhelm Von Paulents, a representative of the League, arrives in Canterbury, in possession of "The Cloister Map". Sir Hugh Corbett is sent by the king to negotiate for ownership. But less than 24 hours after their arrival, Von Paulents and his travelling companions have been barbarously assassinated.

How could this have happened when their lodgings were under guard? Even more puzzling is the fact that "The Cloister Map" has not been stolen. So why were the murders committed? It falls to Corbett to investigate and as he once again enters the world of shadows, he soon finds his own life under threat . . .

ISBN 978-0-7531-8034-1 (hb)
ISBN 978-0-7531-8035-8 (pb)